"You're s... me, Rosie.

"Saturday night I couldn't find you. Kansas scouted you out when I was about to call the police," Everett continues.

Rose is intrigued. Images come to mind—of strange men with flashlights and barking dogs on leashes, all wanting to find her. She tiptoes to the door, opening it a crack, half expecting some leather-jacketed, grim-faced sheriff. It's Everett there, with the pleading look in his eyes. How is she supposed to stay mad at him anyway, especially when he's carrying the biggest box of chocolates she's ever seen?

He holds the candy out to her. A pang stabs at her conscience. Everett is such a good man. He doesn't deserve what she did.

Rose's vision has blurred. His scent fills her whole head. His damp skin against hers is all she wants.

If this could last forever, their closeness, maybe what happened years back wouldn't really matter.

Nancy Pinard

Nancy Pinard was raised in an arts-oriented family who attended a Methodist church in Dayton, Ohio. She danced with the Dayton Ballet Company, but gave up her dream of a career in dance when she suffered an injury that required surgery. Her other love, literature, led her to teach high school and junior high English. She began writing while she was raising two sons, and while her husband served as senior pastor to a large congregation. In 2005 she completed an MFA in creative writing. She now teaches at Sinclair Community College. Her short stories have appeared in literary magazines and an anthology. *Butterfly Soup* is her second published novel.

nancy pinard
butterfly soup

BUTTERFLY SOUP

copyright © 2006 by Nancy Pinard

isbn-13:9780373881062

isbn-10: 0373881061

Chapters two and five of *Butterfly Soup* first appeared in an altered form
in *The Vincent Brothers Review*, Issue 17: Vol. VII, No. 1. as the short
story "Returning to Kansas."

This edition published by arrangement with Harlequin Books S.A.

® and TM are trademarks of the publisher. Trademarks indicated with
® are registered in the United States Patent and Trademark Office, the
Canadian Trade Marks Office and in other countries.

TheNextNovel.com

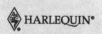 HARLEQUIN®

PRINTED IN U.S.A.

For Ron, Joshua and John

Acknowledgments:

It is no small task to nurture a writer's progress through a manuscript. Many fellow writers invested their attention in multiple drafts. The guidance and insight of the following writers was invaluable: Ed Davis, Katrina Kittle, Nancy Jones, Suzanne Kelly-Garrison, Diane Chiddister, Hallie Kranos and Sharon Shaver. The Byliners— Lynn Campbell, Peggy Barnes, Diane Bengson, Caroline Cooper, Celia Elliott, Lynn Dille, Vincenzina Krymon, Doris LaPorte and Sarah Rickman.

I am thankful to Clint McCown for his attention to my work at the Antioch Writers' Workshop. The reference librarians of the Wright Memorial Public Library researched fine points of verisimilitude for me. My cousins, Karin and Dr. Andrew Bailey, and friend Dr. Pat Ronald supplied me with medical opinions during revision.

My best friend, Louise Greene, shared memories of her Catholic childhood.

My agent, Elizabeth Trupin-Pulli, believed and stood firm, listened when I lost heart, refused to give up. I am honored to call her my friend.

My editor, Ann Leslie Tuttle, likewise persevered until she found the work's perfect home. Her determination and enthusiasm have brought my dream to the readership. Thanks also to Adam Wilson, editorial assistant, who ably guided me through the process.

My husband, Ron, and sons, Josh and John, gave me the freedom to find my voice. They have loved me and honored my needs. That's an inestimable gift. May every woman have such an extraordinary family.

CHAPTER 1

The phone rings so early on Saturday morning, Rose Forrester tears herself from sleep and runs to the kitchen, the dread of dire illness or accidents propelling her down the stairs to the rhythm of the Hail Mary repeating in her head. "Yes?" she pants into the receiver.

"Rosie? You'll never guess what!" Helen Slezac's voice is squeaky with excitement. Rose hears the swoosh of washing machines in the background.

"Helen? It's only six-fifty. We're sleeping in," Rose whispers. She hopes her descent didn't waken the household. Everett has been looking tired. And Valley came in late from her date.

"I know. I know. But this one can't wait. I had to tell you."

Rose tries to chase the edge from her voice. Poor Helen has been divorced so long, she's forgotten the pleasure of drowsing in bed. "Tell me what?"

"I got in early and was waiting for the dryer to quit tumbling to yank Jed Peterson's stuff before it wrinkled—you know how picky he is—when I looked up to see an old friend walking into Millie's."

Rose's heart has slowed to match the *glub-dub* of the washers. She pictures Helen at her usual post—at the pay phone by the Laundromat's front window, spying on the donut shop. "Who, Helen? Tell me."

"*Rob MacIntyre.*"

Rose mouths the syllables. Her third finger finds her mouth, and her teeth search for loose cuticles. Rob's is the one name she'd hoped never to hear again when he disappeared from town seventeen years ago.

"Rosie? Are you still there? Is something wrong?"

"Everett's calling," Rose says so softly she can barely hear herself. "I've got to go." She hangs the receiver on the hook and lingers a moment, as though still connected to Rob by Helen's voice. Her mouth tastes metallic, as if she's been sucking on nickels. She tiptoes into the bedroom, looks to make sure Everett is still sleeping, slips a dress from its hanger, and hurries to the bathroom.

She must have brushed her teeth, combed her hair and zipped the dress, but she only remembers turning the car key and wanting to hush the engine.

Her Galaxy heads toward town, slowing abruptly where the speed limit drops from fifty to twenty-five. Chief Dudley waits in his cruiser behind the same bush every day, clocking all the residents. She salutes as she passes him, then coasts toward the three downtown blocks of Eden proper, lurching from one corner to the next. It's silly to have so many stop signs in a one-bank town.

In the middle of one block she pauses for old Mr.

Cockburn to cross to Millie's Dunk 'n' Sip from the loading dock at the Feed and Seed. She forces a smile and tells herself to nod and act normal, though stopping directly in front of the donut shop is last on her list. Mr. Cockburn dodders in front of her car, his left hand trailing across her hood for balance. Rose oh-so-casually glances to her left. The hunched backs of the Saturday-morning regulars show through the window, middle-aged men straddling counter stools in their John Deere caps, chugging hot coffee as if June temperatures didn't faze them. She can hear them in her head, chewing on predictable topics between swallows—whether Reagan's new agriculture secretary will favor Ohio or if the plate ump in last night's Reds game was on the take. But even squinting she can't make out one back from the next. Can't tell if one of them belongs to Rob. Helen sounded certain, but Rose needs to see for herself.

At the corner one of Eden's single mothers leaves Duds-In-Suds with a laundry basket balanced on one hip. The woman brushes the hair off her brow, and two raggedy kids with green mouths come straggling behind her, sucking on lollipops. Rose slows, remembering the days when Valley was small and wakened early, when Rose, too, had finished her housework before 8:00 a.m. The woman steps into the road, then stops to make eye contact with Rose. The children bump into their mother's back. Rose takes note of the kids' health, as though she's assigned to watch over fatherless children everywhere. Welfare brats, Everett calls them. Rose winces every time he says it, his judgment slashing at her insides.

There's a parking spot one block up where she'll have a good view of Main Street but Helen can't see her. She turns around in the alley next to the theater and parallel parks facing Millie's. Then she pulls her checkbook and a pen from her purse, so if anyone wonders why she's sitting there, she can pretend to be balancing her account. But no one is outside except for the single mom, who piles the kids into her rusty boat of a Chevy. Rose strains to see if she can make out car seats through the windshield, though maybe the kids are too old for that. The Chevy cruises by, the kids standing behind the broad bench seat while their mother flips through radio channels. "Seat belts!" Rose hollers, but then is instantly ashamed. Everett regularly reminds her what's none of her business. Luckily the Chevy radio is blaring, so no one heard.

The street is quiet for long minutes afterward, and Rose considers where Rob might stay if he were really back in town. His mother's house sold—she saw the sign—so if he's there, he can't stay long. She once heard Phil Langston mention Rob's name in Millie's. She can't remember that they buddied around in school, but those things changed, judging from herself and Helen anyway. The two of them had hardly spoken until after graduation. Helen had smoked in the woods behind the school with the fast crowd, while Rose, who didn't own her own clarinet, had stayed after school to practice in the band room. Everett had hung out in that hallway, so she hadn't really been by herself. Rob had always been on a ball field of one shape or another, with all the girls going gaga from the stands. Since Rose hadn't been one of them, their night together was all the more miraculous.

Just then Millie's screen door swings open. A bunch of the regulars ramble out, turning and talking to the person holding the door, jostling each other and laughing. Then Rob steps onto the stoop in jeans and a tucked-in T-shirt. "Sweet Jesus," comes from Rose's lips unbidden, and she fingers the rayon of her dress, rubbing its silky softness over her bare thighs. Rob stands with his hands in his hip pockets, rocking slightly from heels to toes. She'd know that stance anywhere—a man version of the boy who, in the warm water of Kaiser Lake, first freed her body from more than her bathing suit. Rob's a little broader for all these years, but so is she. Still, gravity's been kind. His hair is shorter now, freshly washed and combed, and he's grown a mustache. He turns from the doorway, waves to the guys going the other way and heads up the street toward her. Her first instinct is to duck, and Rose finds herself sprawling across the front seat, wishing the hot-pink flowers on her dress would die. The plastic upholstery grabs at her legs, and the titillating mix of exhilaration and danger that kept her awake those long-ago summer nights grips her once again. Never mind she's thirty five and runs a household. Her schoolgirl foolishness is back. He still has that power.

She hears his boots on the sidewalk and can't resist opening her eyes. He glances down. Valley's smile flits across his mouth and eyes. Dimples pinpoint his cheeks. If she looks familiar, he doesn't let on. He walks on by. She blows the bangs off her forehead and assures herself he didn't miss a step. He smiled, yes, but anyone would smile at the sight of a woman lying on a car seat. She needn't feel foolish. It made perfect sense to lie down in your car when you didn't feel well.

But that's nonsense, and Rose knows it.

When enough time has passed that Rose is certain Rob is farther down the street, she sits up and searches her rearview mirror. She can't help noting how Rob's shoulders preside over his narrow waist and firm buttocks. Her hands cup as if around his bottom. Her palms remember.

Rob disappears around a corner, and Rose checks her reflection. She sees crow's feet, but her brow is still smooth. It's the one advantage of carrying a little extra weight. Her skin is young-looking, even if her hips and thighs make it hard to find a bathing suit. She stretches her mouth in a grimace to exercise her neck muscles, then relaxes again. Her chin looks tighter for it, she's sure, and she does the exercise a few more times. A double chin would spoil her looks.

Two car doors slam behind her. She watches Woody Mansfield and his son get out of the Mansfield Plumbing truck and jaywalk to Millie's, Woody catching the sleeve of Billy's Little League shirt to hurry him across. Everett has been working on a new house with Woody this week, making sure Rose has a good life and she wonders when she'll realize that Rob's good looks are no match for Everett's hard work. Whatever brought Rob back to Eden, concern for her welfare wasn't it. He probably doesn't even know Valley is a girl—

except that he's been in touch with Phil. She wonders what Phil knows and if he has ever talked to Everett. They've never been close, she's certain of that, but there was no controlling who sat down on the next stool at Millie's. At least Everett isn't in there this morning. She needs to get home before he realizes she's been gone.

Rose starts the engine and pulls out of the parking space.

In her bathrobe once again, Rose busies herself in the stuffy kitchen, parting the café curtains, then working to raise swollen windows. "Who needs him anyway?" she mutters, giving the wooden frame a whack. "Everett's the better man." She lifts in vain, then gives the frame another good thunk— as if, energetic enough, she might not only raise the window but send Rob back where he came from. By the time she's ratcheted the second window up, she's broken a sweat. The morning breeze feels fresh on her skin, though it holds the telltale heaviness of another humid day.

On her way by the drawer, Rose chooses a chocolate from the box of Fanny Farmer she keeps hidden under the silverware tray. Chocolate and mint mingle on her tongue as she runs cold water into her mother's old aluminum coffeepot, measures grounds into the basket and adds tiny pieces of broken eggshell to cut the bitterness. A whiff of propane wafts up before the burner poofs into flame. She centers the pot. Everett gave her an automatic coffeemaker on Mother's Day—the one with the timer so she could wake up to fresh coffee—but a month has passed and she hasn't unboxed it.

She can't think why she should change when the old way works fine.

Rose tiptoes to the stairs to listen for bedroom sounds. It's nearly eight o'clock, but Everett isn't stirring. Valley's room is silent. She climbs to the second floor, stops at her daughter's door and pushes it open. She can't see Valley's head past the enormous jar on the bedside stand where Valley farms butterflies. The current resident is a green caterpillar with a pink underbelly, nothing but a worm to Rose, but at least it's in a jar. It hangs from its twig by a silken thread so invisible, it might be floating in air.

Valley lies facing the wall, her body curled up. She's still dressed in the shirt she wore on her date and the sapphire pendant Rose passed down for Valley's sixteenth birthday. Rose cranes her neck to see the narrow chin with the wide brow that has always reminded her of the Flemish Madonna that hung in her childhood church. Instead she sees black mascara streaked down Valley's cheeks. "Mother of God, have mercy," Rose murmurs, wondering that she had fallen asleep before her daughter came in. Sex does that to Rose— makes her relaxed and irresponsible. She should have behaved herself.

She fingers the scapular she's kept in her bathrobe pocket since Everett insisted she take it off. The tiny picture of the Virgin is sweat-stained and talcum-furry, still attached to the shoelace she'd worn around her neck through childhood. Rose tucks the scapular in the zipper pouch of Valley's purse and puts it back on the dresser. Valley's stuffed animals sit lined up facing her music stand. Rose chooses a lamb with a tattered pink bow and tucks it in the nook of Valley's chin.

At her own bedroom door Rose sees the slope of Everett's bare shoulder peeking out from the quilt. She pictures him propped over her, broad and strong on straight elbows. But in the morning light his pectorals look flabbier than she remembered, and her mother's voice plays in her head: *Control yourself. Pleasure doesn't last. Eat only enough to know you've eaten.* It's the only tone Rose remembers now—since the night she was orphaned by a heart attack. She presses her thumbs into the pudge around her midriff, tattling, tattling on her. She used to be thin.

She kneels on the new waterbed and bounces. The mattress sloshes with the movement, and Everett's body teeters back and forth. The musk of his skin—heightened by his effort the night before—is slightly sour. His eyes are closed, but a smile plays across his lips. His hand sneaks toward her and tugs on her bathrobe tie.

"Not now, Everett. We have to talk."

He opens one eye.

"Were you awake when Valley came in last night?"

"I woke at one-ten and checked her room. She was asleep."

"Her mascara's streaked all down her face. I knew that boy was no good."

Everett closes the eye again. "When she cried last month

you blamed her hormones. Why is it suddenly the boy's fault?"

Rose rolls onto her bottom. The mattress water cuddles her hips. "When he picked her up, he wouldn't look me in the face."

"Rosie, you never had to go into a strange house and meet a girl's parents." He tries to pull her over next to him, to comfort her.

Rose resists. Someone has to get upset about these things.

Everett gives up with a sigh. "She's sixteen, Rosie. Nearly grown. You can't run her life or choose her friends."

You never did care about Valley, Rose thinks for the ump-teenth time. She scoots to the edge of the bed. The mattress undulates, and she wonders what silly whim made him buy a waterbed—one of those midlife things, she suspects. At least it's not some overpriced coffin, a motorcycle or a race car. Still. It has to be a sin to be so comfortable. "It will serve you right if she gets pregnant," Rose sputters.

"For god's sake, Rosie. She's not a tramp."

Rose hugs herself to hide her cringing. How's she supposed to tell him the truth when he says things like that?

Everett tickles her upper arm, then reaches for her breast. Rose pushes his hand off. "I *do* trust her. It's *you boys* I don't trust." She purposely bounces the bed and escapes his reach. "My mother was right. Men only want one thing."

Rose drives past the brick elementary school and adjacent park, then crosses the bridge over the Miami River. The

Catholic church, Our Lady of the Rosary, squats on the other side, a brick fortress facing east, bordered on three sides with blacktop, then graves, before the farmland picks up once again. She doesn't know where else to go. Her conscience—an entity so real Rose expects to see it on a diagram of the human body—rants in her head: *This is what happens when you fornicate and lie. You should have told Everett the truth before he married you.* Of course she should have. And she didn't. She's certain of one thing now: Rob and Everett in a town this small is one man too many. Maybe the priest can tell her what to do.

There are no cars in the parking lot, only an old woman with long gray hair—a Chippewa Indian (crazy, some say) who keeps to herself on Esther Dalrymple's land. The woman is picking through the church's Dumpster as if she's lost something. Stubby white disks lie around her feet. They look to Rose like burned votive candles, but surely the church wouldn't throw prayers for people's loved ones in the trash. They must be leftover biscuits from a church supper. The woman is hungry. All Rose knows is that Esther claims the Indian healed her roan calf and Joe Harper took his mother's sick dog to her after it was too late.

Rose parks away from the Dumpster and squeezes through the church's heavy oak-and-iron door. The smell of tallow hangs over the narthex, and she pauses there, inhaling deeply, as if wax has the power to sanctify her worldly thoughts. Instead it reminds her of crayons. She fumbles around in her purse for her grocery money, finds a five, folds

it in fourths and fits it through the slot in the donation box.
Then she lights a candle on the tiered table and asks Our
Lady to watch over her confession. Her statue is adorned
today with white roses. Someone in town has died. Still, she
finds peace in the Virgin's sweet face, as she had in the
months after Rob's desertion when only the Holy Mother
knew and appreciated how she felt.

The sanctuary lies beyond a carved archway. Rose pulls a
scarf from her purse to cover her hair. Father Andrew is at
the altar, tidying up the morning Mass. He is old and stooped,
as if burdened by the weight of the crucifix hanging over his
head. Rose hides her face with the scarf, stands before the
confessional, coughs. He motions for her to enter the booth,
then joins her, on the other side of the partition. The rote
learned in childhood pours forth. "Bless me Father, for I
have sinned. It has been one week since my last confession."

"Go on." His voice is thin and hollow and makes Rose's
voice sound shrill in her head. Her stomach gurgles and she
remembers the chocolate she shouldn't have eaten if she
wants Communion.

"There's something I haven't told you."

"Yes—"

"It happened some time back."

"Go on."

"I was seventeen."

"Yes—"

"In love."

"Yes—"

She can't bring herself to go on. How could a priest, being male and celibate, understand her terror?

"And you…?" He's starting to sound impatient.

"You have to understand. I was so afraid after it happened. I didn't tell anyone."

"That you…?"

Why must he make her say it? What other sin do you commit with someone you love? "I *did it*, okay? But it wasn't just that," she hurries on, afraid he'll get angry if she doesn't spit it out fast. "One thing led to another." Through the screen she smells the wine on his breath. There's a greater sin involved. "Oh, God." Her throat tightens. She can barely speak. "I've received Communion anyway. Every week."

She hears him shift in the booth and begins to babble. "I had to or my mother would have known. No one caught me and nothing happened, so I just, you know, forgot it was wrong, I guess." It sounds lame, but it just about sums up how she's been married so long—seventeen years almost—without telling Everett. If no one found out, she had reasoned, and nothing happened, telling the truth did nothing but hurt people. Even now she is only hurting herself with all this confessing. If she had any sense, she'd walk out this minute. She pulls the scarf down over her face, afraid the priest can see through walls, even in darkness.

The bench on the priest's side creaks. "Let's adjourn to the room next door. An open discussion, face-to-face, might help you more."

Rose's fingers press the backs of her clasped hands. Face-to-face indeed. Father Andrew is supposed to pronounce her penance and administer absolution, not insist she confess the new way. To risk an open discussion, she'd have to leave town. She hasn't even mentioned deceiving Everett. She can't imagine saying it in broad daylight.

"And if that's not possible?"

"Then your priorities are wrong. Nothing is more important than your immortal soul."

Rose struggles up from flattened knees, steadying herself on the walls of the confessional. She pulls the scarf closer. "Thank you, Father," she says, but she is anything but thankful. She is on to his game. He wants to see her face so he can deny her Communion. On her way out she wonders why she thought to tell this man anything. If she tells anyone, it should be Everett.

Rose drives back through town to the Safeway market, accelerating through the yellow light at the new plaza. Confession is needless. If she had been born Protestant, she wouldn't have to confess to anyone but God. Everett's probably right about the Pope. God didn't make him infallible, her mother did.

The plaza parking lot is full of people. Summer Saturdays are like this. Little Leaguers, Girl Scouts, Rotarians—all out raising funds. Rose checks the supply of quarters in her ashtray and tucks them in her pocket. She's searching for a parking place and scanning the lot for Rob, when a toddler appears out of nowhere, in front of her car. Her brakes squeal. The car shimmies, skids. A woman shrieks. The tires grab.

The car settles back into itself. The boy stands inches from her bumper, a wisp of blond hair visible over her hood. His mother stands in a puddle of groceries and torn bags, her face frozen in the scream. A broken bottle of apple juice is soaking the paper bag.

Rose slumps over her steering wheel. His mother steps from the rubble of groceries and snatches the child up. The child wails. Blessed, blessed sound. Rose exhales her anxiety. "Thank you, Jude, glorious apostle, faithful servant and friend of Jesus." She pockets her hands in the opposite underarm to stop the prickling sensation. The mother is sobbing now. Rose watches her rock the boy, holding that precious head in her palm and kissing his hair, as Rose herself might have held Valley this morning if her daughter were younger.

The woman carries her son to a station wagon nearby. Rose parks. She fetches a coffee can that's rolled under a fender and sets it near the jumble of groceries. She picks the boxes of macaroni and cheese from the puddle of apple juice and stacks them in a pile next to the instant oatmeal, the English muffins and the Peter Pan. She has to do something to make up for scaring them. If she had hit the child— But Rose refuses that thought. She's told Valley never, ever to speed in a school zone. If Rose ever hit a child, she would never recover.

But why wasn't the child up in the cart seat, where drivers could see him?

Rose heads for the store, breasts cradled in her arms as if

she were cold. Inside she finds the cereal aisle and wanders up and down, her heart drubbing hard as she is alternately the driver and the mother of the crying child. She can't find the Shredded Wheat. It's always a maze, this aisle—the store brand's look-alike boxes mixed in with the real thing—but today it's impossible. The priest's voice mingles with the woman's shriek: *Your priorities are wrong. Nothing is more important than your immortal soul.* Rose takes down one box, puts it back and takes another, finally settling for Cheerios. On her way to the cashier she adds a package of pink, yellow and brown sugar wafers—the ones Valley reached for when she was a toddler in the cart seat—and a palm-size red-yellow-and-blue rubber ball for the toddling boy. She breezes through the express lane, forgetting that she needs coffee cream, and takes off with her bagged stash.

Rose is searching the parking lot for the mother's station wagon when she's caught by a singsong refrain rising and falling over the rattle of carts on the blacktop. She traces the chant to the end of the plaza where the band parents usually hold their bake sales and raffles. It's some kind of auction. The auctioneer is gobbling away, badgering his crowd to bid higher. She hears him calling names. Sister Mary Theresa. That has to be a nun. Rose feels as though he has hollered her name. In a way, he has. Once upon a time, Theresa of the Little Flower was her favorite saint.

At the outer edge of the group she peers between heads. Steel bed frames stand in the back of a truck, bound into units—two metal end pieces with legs and a metal spring in each package—each labeled with the name of a nun. The auctioneer's assistant steps through the crowd to hand Rose a flyer.

Buy a bed slept in by a Sister of Charity
to benefit
Dayton's own
St. Agnes Women's Shelter

The Sisters of Charity, the flyer says in small print, have donated their old beds to raise funds. The St. Agnes Shelter will provide home delivery to anyone donating over twenty dollars per bed.

Only five frames remain in the back of the pickup. The auctioneer begins the bidding on Sister Mary Theresa's bed at twenty dollars. A woman in shorts and red canvas Keds raises her hand.

"Twenty, I hear twenty. Who'll give me twenty-five?"

A woman in jeans and a Notre Dame T-shirt raises her hand.

There's a hush and Rose feels the mounting excitement. Perhaps it's a sign, she thinks, the direction she'd wanted from the priest, delivered by an alternate means. How else can she explain it? It's not every day you find a nun's bed at the grocery. Everett would call it coincidence, but then Everett believes the earth came about after an explosion, which makes as much sense to Rose as throwing calico squares up in the air and expecting them to land in a quilting pattern.

Rose rummages in her purse. She finds the plastic grain of her checkbook. Thanks to Rob's appearance this morning, she knows just how much she has.

"Thirty," says the woman in red Keds.

The auctioneer looks left. "Will you go thirty-five?"

Rose raises her hand high before the Notre Dame woman can answer, recalling the details of a bedtime story her mother read to her often—a story about St. Clare protecting herself and her convent by holding the blessed host before a band of marauding soldiers.

The auctioneer asks for forty. Notre Dame raises her hand.

Rose looks at the woman to get some idea how high she might go. Her jeans are clean but frayed. Her hair is flat against her head. She is not the beauty-parlor kind.

"Fifty," Rose says defiantly.

The auctioneer turns right. "Will you go sixty?" Red Keds bows her head. Left. Notre Dame turns away. Rose has won. She puts her groceries down and fishes for her checkbook.

"Going once. Going twice. Sold to the lady in the flowered dress for fifty dollars," the auctioneer proclaims. "God bless you, dear."

Rose smiles at him. He is not a priest, but it will have to do.

CHAPTER 2

Since last Thursday when the doctor named his intermittent symptoms multiple sclerosis, Everett dreads morning. Not the whole morning, just that moment when daylight jolts him from his dreams, as if he's been cruising down the freeway in his Ford Fairlane—Rosie at his side and Valley, frozen in his mind at age eleven, prattling away in the backseat—when the car slams into a tree. His stomach flies forward; his body remains belted to the car.

Everett closes his eyes, tries to meld with the warm water in the new mattress and opens his eyes a second time. His vision is fine, today at least. The edges of the room, where walls meet ceiling, are clear, not fuzzy. The wallpaper's red and white stripes are as distinct as prison bars. He wiggles his toes and taps his fingers on the mattress, then flexes his knees and elbows. The mattress ripples beneath him. He reaches for Rosie.

Instead of her usual sleeping form—sprawled on her stomach, left hand beside her cheek—he finds a pillow. He smiles in spite of her absence. He loves her soft breasts, the curve of her hips, how her skin springs back to his touch like yeasty dough. She's all woman, not a skinny stick like Helen—always working out and picking at her food as if it's poison. But Rose isn't strong like Helen, either. When he can no longer walk, how will she wrestle him out of the bathtub, into a wheelchair? He likes being the caretaker. Carrier of suitcases and heavy grocery bags. It wasn't supposed to turn out this way.

The worst part is not knowing what will happen. Or when. He was fine two days ago, before he knew his episodes had a name—and a deteriorating prognosis. Now he feels like a goddamn time bomb. In his mind's eye, a lighted fuse snakes across the quilt connected to bundled sticks of dynamite. He's got to snuff that fuse. Somehow.

He hasn't told Rosie. The thought of her expression, eyes soft and vulnerable, brows lifted, makes his stomach turn over. But he can't keep it secret forever. Maybe it's best to just tell her—to get it over with.

He hears her feet pad along the hall carpet and into the room. He senses her closeness, smells her breath as she peers over the quilt. He pretends to be sleeping, but when she gets close enough he grips the tie on her robe. The front comes loose as he tugs. "Not now, Everett," she says in her daytime voice. "We have to talk." When she flattens her robe to her chest, her nipples protrude through the pink cotton. He'd like to push them like buttons, but then she'd know he can see them. Even at night she wants the lights out. Can she really be so modest after all this time? Or does she just think she's supposed to be?

"Were you awake when Valley came in last night?" she asks.

He tells her he got up at one.

"Her mascara's streaked all down her face. I knew that boy was no good."

There she goes again, jumping to conclusions. Everett tries to distract her, reaching under her arm to knead her breast, but she's not falling for it. When he won't jump on her worry wagon, she flounces off. Everett imagines himself slipping her robe down off her shoulders, watching it fall to the floor as she dances in the morning light. He rocks the bed to the slinky music in his head, tightening and loosening his hips.

It will never happen. The bed settles.

Until Thursday he'd told himself her modesty was fine. It brought back the feeling of the first time, kept her always new. Maybe she knows that. Maybe her shyness is just an act. His groin stirs. Nah. Rosie isn't clever. She is Rosie of the White Sheets. A goddamn Catholic saint. She doesn't know that time is running out. By next week she may not want him at all, even in the darkness. He's got to tell her.

Everett rolls back onto his side and pushes himself up. So far so good. Nothing is numb, though so far he hasn't wakened to numbness. Reading a pamphlet shouldn't make symptoms appear, but since reading it, he's tracking every twinge. His legs hold when he hoists himself onto them— not like last Tuesday, when his right leg buckled suddenly and he fell from the fourth rung of the ladder. He'd chalked up his bruises to the hazards of work when Rosie had asked. But it wasn't the first time he'd fallen without cause.

He listens to the water run through the pipes as she turns the taps on and off. The silence means she's dressing. "Rosie?" No answer. He raises his voice. "Rosie?" Silence. His speech may go someday. He'll blabber, and people will think he's retarded and avert their eyes. No one will hire a retarded electrical contractor. "Rooo-ssieee!"

"I have to run to the store, Everett," Rosie says, emerging from the bathroom fully clothed and wriggling her bare feet into heeled pumps. "We're out of cream."

"Wait." She's halfway down the stairs before he formulates what it is he really wants. "I thought we might go somewhere today. You know, take a little day trip. Spend some time together." Her shoes tap on the kitchen tile and the door shuts behind her.

Okay, he thinks. If that's the way you want it. See if I'm here when you need me. He pulls on boxers, shorts and a polo and ties his sneakers, plotting to exit before she returns.

In the bathroom Everett pushes the clutter of Valley's makeup aside. He wipes her blond hairs from the vanity with a damp sponge and wonders at the irritation he feels. Maybe Rosie is right. Maybe feeding, clothing and sheltering a daughter isn't all there is to fathering. But Rose doesn't know what it's like to be him. He's never admitted it to anyone, but from day one he and Valley were off-kilter. In the hospital he had looked at the wrinkled, slimy infant Rosie held, seen the adoration in her eyes, the protective curve of her shoulders, and felt like a stranger. He'd chalked it up to Valley's early arrival. He and Rosie hardly knew one another when Valley turned up. Rosie's growing belly had seemed a pleasant pacifier that compensated for her disappearing figure. The pregnancy slowed Rosie down after the agitation of their courtship. She'd laid quietly on the couch many evenings with her head in his lap, loaning his hands her nightgowned breasts and belly, a drowsy smile on her face. He'd led her off to bed easily after that, and she'd folded herself around him, accepting his attentions to the end. Then Valley arrived and he got lost in the chaos of feedings and diapers and crying in the night. Rosie's breasts weren't his after that. None of her was.

Now that Valley is grown, Rosie is paranoid. He can't make a living and still worry over every little thing. When Rosie harps about the things he doesn't do for Valley, he wants to withhold what affection he does feel. He rinses the sponge under the tap, squeezes the water out and scrutinizes its intricate structure of cell walls. Outnumbered by women, he feels like one of its holes—surrounded but not connected. When his walls break down, he won't exist at all.

He hurries through his shave, musing on places he might like to go. With Rosie at the store, he doesn't have much time to make his getaway. He's combing the hair over his thinning crown when he sees the copy of the AAA magazine on the floor next to the john. The Miami Valley insert features adventures on Lake Erie. A sportsman's paradise waits three hours north, and he hasn't sampled any of it. A photo of a man harnessed to a yellow-and-orange parachute particularly fascinates him. *Parasailing,* the caption calls it. The chute is pulled by a speedboat, but the man is flying high in the air. One step short of skydiving, it looks to him. He's always wanted to know how it feels—that moment of free fall after leaving the plane, before the chute opens. A lot like an orgasm, he suspects, a gigantic orgasm. He'll do it while he's still able. And if part of his body gives out while he's doing it...well, he'll go down enjoying himself. It will serve Rosie right.

Everett grabs his duffel from the closet and stuffs it with underwear, another shirt and swim trunks. He stops at Valley's door on his way by and looks in. On the other side of her latest caterpillar and the phone he added when her friends began tying up his business line, her feline form curls toward the wall. He watches the quilt rise and fall with her breathing. The distance between them grew when puberty hit. Valley became sullen then. Setting foot in her room felt like trespassing.

Maybe he'll wait to tell Rosie. There will be plenty of time later. Years. If he tells her now, she'll strap him to a wheelchair the way she wants to chain Valley to the bedpost. She'll insist on driving everywhere, and he'll just sit there watching life pass by as if it's television. If he doesn't hold tight to the checkbook, he'll lose control of everything. Thank God he's invested their money. Hasn't let her spend it.

He scribbles a note before he leaves.

Rosie,

I've gone out to make a bid. There's a big one on the line. I may be late.

Love,
Everett

He chuckles to himself. He hasn't lied exactly, considering what he has in mind. His sense of humor is one thing he won't lose. Not if he holds on tight.

As Everett backs out of the garage, he glances at the garden. Small shoots are pushing through the soil, but from a distance he can't tell if they're plants or weeds. At the end of the driveway he glances up the road nervously. Just his luck, Rosie will pull into sight before he can make his escape.

The air's heavy this morning, laying a haze over the horizon. He's grateful for his air-conditioning as he speeds out of Eden. He plays with the radio dial. An announcer's voice tunes in midsentence.

"...the British in their ongoing countersiege of the Falklands. Port Stanley is defended by some seven thousand Argentine troops.

"Israeli land, sea and air forces invaded southern Lebanon in retaliation for the assassination attempt on Ambassador Shlomo Argov in London on June third. Ground troops occupy the territory from Tyre on the coast to the foothills of Mount Hermon following Israel's June fourth air strikes on Palestinian targets near Beirut."

Everett turns it off. Air strikes are everywhere.

Ten miles north, he stops to tank up in Union City—

first at the McDonald's drive-through where he orders two sausage-egg-and-cheese biscuits with a large coffee, then at a Sunoco. Everett eats one of the biscuits, then gets out to pump his gas. It's hot. Dr. Burns said heat and humidity aggravate his condition, and this June has been a doozy, with all the rain. He checks his oil and tire pressure, though before the diagnosis he wouldn't have bothered. Now his car has to be dependable in case he has an episode.

"Find everything you need?" the attendant calls, stepping from behind the raised hood of a Thunderbird. He's just a kid, nineteen at most, in work boots and a baggy one-piece coverall that says Ben. Hell, if Everett were a car, this kid could rewire his circuits.

"Just need to pay my bill," Everett says, feeling connected to Ben by the cord strung across the concrete. He might like to take him aside. Buy him a coffee. Tell him not to waste his youth or take his health for granted.

Ben would nod his head, say yeah and light up a cigarette.

Inside the station Everett pays with plastic, buys cigarettes from a machine and heads back to the car. The driver's door stands open, and Everett is surprised to see a dog lying on the floor on the passenger side. "Hey, Fella," Everett says and puts his hand out, palm up, to a beagle mutt with brown eyes, droopy ears and a pointy snout. Fella has a biscuit wrapper crumpled between his paws and looks up at Everett with guilty eyes, cowering slightly. Everett laughs. "Teach me to leave the door open." The dog stops licking the grease-stained wrapper to lap Everett's fingers. "Good stuff, huh?"

"Hey, Ben, this your dog?" Everett calls. "A dog jumped into my car."

Ben walks over and peers in. "Not mine. I hate dogs. My kid sister got attacked by a Doberman."

A lopsided silence hangs between them, then settles on the kid's end.

"No shit." It's all Everett can think to say. He wants to ask if she's okay but couldn't stand to hear that she isn't. He'd have to feel worse for Ben than he feels for himself.

This dog is no Doberman. "Must belong to someone," Everett says finally. He turns up an ID tag on the dog's collar. "I'll get him out of here for you. Where's Morningside Court?"

"Over there behind the Baptist church," Ben says and points the way.

Everett raises the window, lights a cigarette, then circles the block with the church steeple. He parks opposite a brick ranch at 136 Morningside, where a man is out back throwing a football to a gangly boy, six maybe, in a Cincinnati Bengals cap. A Jeep and a riding mower sit side-by-side in the open garage, and a gun rack hangs in the Jeep's back window.

Everett watches the ball bump end over end when the kid fumbles it. The kid and his dad lunge after it and roll around in a snarl of bodies that knocks the cap off the kid's head. Everett takes a drag on his cigarette, watching its tip turn red.

He waits while the nicotine floods his blood and blows smoke out his nose. Everett and his dad had played together sometimes, but it was baseball. His father, clad in Sears coveralls, would set his empty Thermos in the sink. "Hey, Rett," he'd say. His father called him Rett. And if supper wasn't ready he'd ask, "Want to throw the ball around?"

Everett always said yes but wished for more players—to have a game. He would ask his mother to play, but she'd say someone had to cook—an odd excuse since she barely touched the meals she made. His mother didn't sweat. Little lines radiated from her lips in permanent discontent. She never even ate her lipstick off.

A dog would want to play ball. Everett had asked for one for his birthday. His mother had shuddered and given him fish instead. She hadn't seemed to get it—that he'd wanted to do more than just look at his pet. Despite his disappointment, he'd spent his allowance on snails and colored gravel and a ceramic castle with turrets for them to swim around. At fourteen, when his shoulders broadened and his hips narrowed and his mother shied away from touching him at all, he took cool baths and released the fish into the tub water with him. They'd flipped their fantails at him and chased one another around his legs.

Everett feels the dog's belly but finds no genitals. "Guess you're not a Fella," he says, rumpling her loppy ears. She stands on the seat, cocks her head slightly to one side and wags her tail as if she's known him forever. She doesn't seem to know he's driven her home. Maybe if the windows were down.

Everett removes her tag, shifts into Drive and steps on the gas. The kid is too young to catch the damn football. Any dog will do for him. And the man—he has a son, a house, a Jeep, a gun. He doesn't need a dog, too.

The entrance ramp to Route 75 is not far down the road. He speeds onto the highway as if he's being chased, checking his rearview mirror for police cars. After a few miles he relaxes and lowers the passenger window. The dog sticks her nose into the wind. He lights another cigarette. Her ears blow back as they pull into the left lane to pass an eighteen-wheeler.

CHAPTER 3

Still in bed, Valley jolts to the banging of the kitchen screen. Her mother's footfalls shuffle around the kitchen downstairs. A paper bag crackles and a cupboard door knocks shut, wood on wood. Her mother has been to the grocery. She knows all the sounds and can interpret their meanings. At her flute lesson last week Mr. Moore remarked on how acutely she hears. She relistens to his velvet baritone, shaping itself around those words.

Valley stretches, and her arching ribs strain against the elastic of her bra. Her phone rings, startling her, and she snatches it up. The bell is turned down as far as it goes without shutting it off.

"Sooo," Joanie says without saying hello first. "How was it?"

"Okay," Valley whispers back. Joanie doesn't want the truth.

"You're *so* lucky. He's *such* a doll. I can't believe you're dating a *senior*. Where'd you go?"

"To the movie." Valley glances down at the clothes she wore on the date. The waistband of her shorts is cutting into her stomach. She pops the snap and wriggles them off as she sits up.

"And…"

"Then he brought me home."

"No stop at Millie's? He couldn't wait, huh?"

"I wasn't exactly hungry."

"I bet. So what happened? How was it?"

"Fine."

"Come on. Tell me. Or is it sacred and you have to keep it to yourself for a while?"

Valley fingers the gold chain around her neck, searching for the star-sapphire pendant and centering it in front.

"If you don't mind."

"I can't believe you landed a football player. It's too cool. Does he have any friends he'd like to loan me?"

"Can I call you later, Joanie? I've got a babysitting job. I have to get showered or I'll be late."

"Sure, I'll be here whenever you're ready to unload the goods."

Valley puts the receiver back on the cradle. Joanie gets so wrapped up in the externals. The football. The guy's age. What *she* liked best about Mark Thorburn was the way he said "Hey, la-dy" with a funny Southern accent as she passed by his locker on the way to homeroom. There had been no question of a good-night kiss, let alone the stuff that Joanie hopes happened. Valley hadn't known the script—didn't know it was all about him. Mark would never ask her out again.

Glued, mounted and hanging on the wall beside her bed is a photo puzzle. Valley stares at herself, age three, sitting on her mother's lap in a ruffled dress, her hair gathered in a duck barrette and sticking straight up like a fountain. The jigsaw had divided her face in two, one eye and her nose on one piece, the other eye on its interlocking mate. Maybe that's her problem. She's dumb-looking and schizophrenic.

"What do you think, Gerald?" she asks her current caterpillar—a spicebush swallowtail who is snacking on a sassafras branch in his stocking-covered jar. "Am I crazy?" The caterpillar continues eating, his mandibles nibbling away on the leaf. He looks bigger today. She sees the split exoskeleton, marking the fourth instar she's counted. He'll pupate soon. She'll get some fresh leaves for him today. Maybe she can find him a buddy, too.

Valley throws the quilt aside and heads to the bathroom.

"You're going *where?*" her mother asks while Valley rummages around the kitchen for something to eat. From her mother's tone, Valley might have announced she's headed somewhere outrageous—like prison. As she pours Cheerios into a ceramic bowl, she listens to the plinking sounds, so different from the tiny thuds they made falling onto plastic.

"You know the Harpers. Over on Walnut. Mrs. Harper stopped me on my way home from school and asked me to babysit today. It's only for a few hours. I'll still have time to practice my flute." Valley opens the fridge for the milk. She hears her mother crinkle the box's paper liner, then grovel around in the box for a handful. Her mother's teeth crunch rhythmically on the mouthful as Valley pours milk into the bowl, scattering the Os to the perimeter of the dish. The no-eating-between-meals rule doesn't apply to mothers.

"You really should have asked me first."

Valley rolls her eyes. Does every little decision have to go before the governing board? She modulates her voice to sound like her father's—the voice of reason calming an excitable woman. "Her sister's getting married. Her mother-in-law caught the flu and can't babysit. Mrs. Harper is counting on me."

Her mother takes a package of chicken breasts from the fridge. "Mrs. Harper has an infant, Valley."

"Yeah. So?"

"So you've only watched older children. You don't know what you're doing." She removes the cellophane from the chicken and drops it in the sink. Watery chicken blood pools in the plastic tray beneath the mottled yellow pieces.

Valley's lip curls at the sight. "I'm sixteen, Ma. It can't be worse than the Johnson twins. I get one into bed and the other one's out running around again." Her mother is ridiculously cautious. She hadn't allowed Valley to go to overnight parties, either—until two years after her friends were allowed. Then when she finally went, it was no big deal. So you didn't sleep that night. You went home and took a nap.

The chicken has disgusting yellow fat in globs around the edges of the skin. Her mother pulls them off with her fingers. It looks nasty, but Valley can't tear her eyes away. "Do you have to do that while I'm eating, Mom? It's sooo gross." Why is her mother wearing a nice dress to do such a messy task?

Her mother runs tap water over the breasts. "It's only

chicken. How'll you change a diaper if you can't stand chicken?" The blood in the tray dilutes to a pale pink.

"Lots of my friends babysit infants, Mom. Half those girls aren't as smart as I am." Valley puts a spoonful of Cheerios into her mouth. Joanie is regularly left to watch the Cranfords' sprawling farm full of kids and animals.

"They have little brothers and sisters to learn on." Her mother strips the thick skin off a breast. The flesh beneath has a vulnerable bluish-purple cast. Valley's hand involuntarily flattens to her chest.

"Is it my fault I'm an only child?" It's a cheap shot, and Valley feels a twinge of guilt—but mostly satisfaction—poking at the soft spot in her mother's armor. Her mother would have loved a whole houseful of kids.

"Just don't expect it to be easy. You can't throw him in the crib and talk on the phone."

"I wouldn't do that. I'm not like that Diane Locklear. Why are you always lumping me with the crazy kids in the news?"

"I don't. I brag about you all the time. About your flute playing. And how well you speak French." She looks up, her face the picture of motherly pride.

"We speak English in this country, Mom. And no one in Eden cares that I play the flute."

It's true, what she's saying, why she will never be popular.

"What do you think? That everyone's going to gather at Millie's on Saturday night to hear me play Mozart? Or how about at the Pizza Carryout? I could toodle away in front of the road map while the dropouts sprinkle mozzarella."

"That's honest work, Valley. And I certainly don't insist you play the flute. You can quit this minute. I have more to do than drive you to Dayton every week for your lesson."

"I don't want to quit, Mom. That's not the point." What would she do without her flute? Being an only child is no fun at all. "And I could drive myself if you ever let me take the car out of Eden."

Her mother lets out a long sigh. "How was your date last night? Did that boy behave himself?"

"I don't want to talk about it."

"Don't get huffy. I just asked And take that necklace off. Babies break necklaces. You don't want to lose it."

Her mother now turns a bar of soap over and over in her palms and rubs it around between her fingers and under her nails. The suds drip on the chicken skins, and Valley grits her teeth, as if soap and chicken should somehow be kept separate.

Valley drops her bowl into the chicken mess. "I'm going to be late. Goodbye, Mom." She listens with satisfaction when the screen door thwacks shut behind her.

Joey Harper starts fussing the second his mother hands him to Valley. Mrs. Harper retrieves her pocketbook from the dish-cluttered table and wipes her brow with her forearm. "Will you be all right?"

Valley nods. Mrs. Harper has walked her through Joey's routine, demonstrating how to lower the gingham blind, raise the crib rail, fill the humidifier and wind the teddy's music box. "My mother's home in case anything happens,"

Valley assures her, though she has no intention of calling home. When it comes to nervous moms, she knows the script.

Mrs. Harper looks back at the two of them on her way out the kitchen door. "He's just been changed and fed. The phone numbers are on the wall next to the phone, and there's a Coke for you in the fridge next to his bottle. I threw clean rompers in the dryer. They'll be done in a bit if you need one."

Valley crosses her arms around Joey's diapered bum while he waggles his face into her chest. He's a cute little guy, especially when he isn't fussing. "I'll be fine. Enjoy the wedding."

Mrs. Harper sends Valley a tired smile. Valley goes to the door, shifting Joey to her hip so they can wave. She pumps Joey's arm up and down. Joey yowls and strains toward his mother. "Hush, Joey." Valley grips his chubby thigh. "Mummy will come back."

Mrs. Harper backs out of the narrow driveway, honks twice, and heads down the street. Valley's used to crying kids. At first the Johnson twins fussed when their mother left, but they're four now and cry when their mother returns. Joey scrunches his fists into his face. Valley thinks he's settling in, but he surprises her and exhales another loud howl. He sounds, in fact, as if he's just warming up. Valley jiggles him on her hip. A high-pitched squeal pierces his longer wailing, dividing it in sections. She stops jiggling. The squealing continues. The pitch ascends half an octave higher on the next breath. A sweat breaks out on her upper lip. She lifts him from her hip to her chest, cuddling his head under her chin, but his screaming is too close to her ear. "Jeez, Joey, you sound like Joanie's pigs." She imitates the pigs. Joey stops, looks at her, then takes a breath and yowls louder. Valley tilts her head away. The roots of her hair tingle. Just when she thinks it can't get any louder, he pulls out another stop. "This little piggy goes to market. This little piggy stays home," she chants in his ear. Joey shrieks back. She's heard of pitches high enough to shatter glass. Mrs. Harper will come home to a house full of broken windows.

She spies a vacuum cleaner on the dining room floor. From the crumbs on the rug, it looks as though Mrs. Harper never got to use it. Valley switches the canister on with her foot. Its whine breaks into Joey's crying. He snorts a minute, body shuddering, then lowers his pitch to match it, just missing. The interval is awful. Valley switches it off, heads to the living room rocker and sits down. He arches his back and flails his arms, toothless gums spread wide around his bawling. His legs pedal at her stomach and thighs. He is hard to restrain, but she rocks anyway. How can a four-month-old baby be so strong? With the chair still moving, she doubles over him and *shh*s in his ear, but Joey can't hear. His blue romper is damp with sweat. Tears streak down his cheeks.

Valley sings "She'll Be Comin' Round the Mountain" at the top of her lungs, clapping his hands and adding a "whee-ha!" at the end of each line. The Johnson twins love that. Joey wails.

Facedown at her feet is a fluffy teddy bear. Valley seizes its behind and snuggles it up to Joey. "Look, here's your bear, Joey. Let's name your bear." Joey bats the bear away, arms flailing. "How about Sebastian?" Valley has a bear named Sebastian. But Joey hates the name. He arches his back and howls. She tosses Sebastian on the couch.

Panic flits at the edge of her consciousness. What is *wrong* with him? With her? How hard should it be to rock a baby? The TV commercials with the mother smiling at her sleeping baby play lullabies in the background. It looks so serene. Chalk up another way television romanticizes everything. She should have known.

What if her mother is right? What if she can't manage an infant? Valley's arms feel numb, as if her blood is too thick for her veins. Her heart thuds, trying to push it around. Joey's voice rises and falls like a siren, its overtones playing tag around the edges of her mind. She can hardly hear the voice in her own head. He's too young to bribe with a Popsicle as she does when Mary Jane Walker has a temper tantrum. "Man, you're really on a roll." She tries to calm herself by laughing at him. "Ha, ha, ha, ha, ha." She bobs her head up and down as if he has her doubled over. He out-yowls her laughter. What should she do? Weddings go on and on. He's showing no signs of fatigue. What had her teacher said about this in Home Ec? She can't think. If Joey would shut up, maybe she could remember.

Valley gets up and tromps around the living room, jostling Joey with every step. Snot is smeared down his romper. His face has turned an ugly red-purple, and she wonders that a mere fifteen minutes ago she thought he was cute. Her toes curl with every shriek. She holds him away from her ear. He looks like a slimy beet. "Stop it!" she hollers. She's instantly ashamed.

She lays Joey on the couch next to Sebastian and watches Joey thrash while she takes several deep breaths and decides to try a bottle. His mother said he just ate, but anything is worth a try, and with all the hollering, he might have worked up an appetite. She runs to the kitchen, finds the bottle in the fridge and sticks it in the microwave. "Never mind. I'm coming back," she yells, though she doesn't know why it matters. Joey doesn't care. He cries whether she's there or not.

While the microwave ticks off the slowest minute on record, she goes to the living room door to check on him. Joey has scooted to the corner of the couch, his noise muffled slightly by Sebastian's fur. "Good job, Sebastian." It's mean to say it, but it's how she feels. Joey can't hear her.

In the kitchen the microwave is counting down from twenty-seven seconds. Joey's cranking isn't as loud with the microwave humming in her ear. Twenty seconds to go. His squalls are intermittent now. Maybe she's the problem, and he's better off alone. Maybe she should stay in the kitchen and let him work it out. The seconds count down. The turntable rotates, and Valley watches, mesmerized, as the bottle circles round and round. When the microwave clicks off, the house is quiet. Valley waits while the overtones of the humming die away, then inhales deeply, as if silence has become a component of air. She's done it. Joey has finally quit howling. The silence is more than a reward. It's heavenly bliss. She collapses into the counter. It's been a long morning, but Joey has finally, finally gone to sleep.

She tiptoes to the living room and peeks around the doorway at him. He is a different child. Her mother always talks about how she liked to watch Valley sleep. She pulls Sebastian away from his face gently so as not to wake him. She'll go upstairs and get his blanket. Let him nap right here. But as she's about to leave, something about him strikes her as not quite right. For a baby that was flailing two minutes back, he is awfully still. She watches his back. Surely his back should be moving.

Holy Mother of God.

Valley runs to the phone. Dials home. Hangs up before it rings. Dials the hospital. "Middleton Community Hospital." It's an older woman. Valley can't force words out. "Hello? Hello? Can I help you?" Valley hangs up. Runs to the window. Looks up and down the street. Old Mr. Carmichael is on his porch. He can't help. He can hardly get out of the rocker.

Images of Joey in a casket rise in her mind's eye. The room is closing in, but she refuses to faint. She snatches Joey up. His head lops to one side. She lifts him higher, his chest to her cheek, but can hear nothing but the ringing in her ears. His body is so heavy. "Oh, God," she shrieks, thumping his back. "Someone help me!"

Joey shudders. One leg pedals.

At least she thinks so. She may have jostled him. She thumps his back again. Rubs in a circle.

He sputters. Coughs.

Tears pop to Valley's eyes.

Joey takes a deep breath. A year passes while Valley waits. He exhales.

"Good boy, Joey. You are such a good boy." The tears break from her eyes and disappear in the nap of his sleeper. Joey inhales again. Exhales. Double shudders. Inhales.

He is breathing. In, out. In, out. He opens his eyes. Looks into her face. Screws up his face and mewls at her. She runs to the phone. Dials home. "Mom. I need you to come. Joey's having a bad time."

The familiar thrum of the Galaxy engine out on the Harpers' driveway comforts Valley—like the pendulum of the cuckoo clock over the couch at home. Joey is still sobbing when her mother bursts through the door. "It's awful hot in here, Valley," she says. "Take your vest off, lamb. You'll die of the heat." She takes Joey and cuddles him to her bosom, crooning lulling nonsense into his ear. He nuzzles into her like a favorite pillow, wiping snot all over her dress. Valley retreats to the couch, stuffing the guilty Sebastian behind her.

"Don't smother him, Ma."

"He's just rooting around, goosie. You don't have to worry." Her mother stands in the middle of the room, swaying gently. Joey's sobs, muffled by her breast, change to rhythmic whimpering, then slow to occasional gasps.

"Has he been doing this long?" Her mother looks straight at her for the first time.

Valley nods and looks away. She takes a *Good Housekeeping* from the end table as an excuse. There's a picture of Princess Diana on the cover, in a green maternity dress with huge white polka dots and a white sailor collar. Motherhood is everywhere.

"You should have called me sooner," her mother says. "A baby always knows inexperienced arms." She looks at Joey. "Hasa been 'creamin' and hollerin', lambkin? Whatsa matter widda big boy? Huh? Whatsa matter?" she croons into the top of his head, punctuating each question with kisses on top of his head. "I think he wants a bottle, Valley. Did Mrs. Harper make one up?"

Valley gets the bottle from the microwave. Her mother settles into the rocker and tickles his cheek with the nipple. He turns and takes it into his mouth, sucking eagerly. She sings "Rock-a-bye Baby" in her thin soprano as he sucks.

Valley pictures Joey dumped from the cradle and lying limp on the ground, blue as a Smurf. "Mom, don't sing that. It's awful."

"It's just a song, silly. He doesn't understand the words."

"Well, I do. Don't sing it."

"He got you real upset, didn't he, lamb? I don't know who needs the rocking more—Joey or you."

Valley folds her hands, clenching her muscles around the

knot in her stomach so it won't unravel and give her away. The rocker's creaking and the sound of Joey's sucking calm her. She suddenly feels exhausted.

"Look at him, Valley, honey," her mother says. "Isn't he precious? Look at his little wrists. Like someone put a rubber band around his plump little arm. And his knuckles. Little dimples. Everything perfect."

Valley looks at the two of them, Joey's body merging into her mother's flowered dress.

"And he smells so good. Aah. You smelled so good I thought I'd go wild. Your scent was all over your blankets, and when I went to put them in the washer, I'd stand there and grieve that I was about to wash you away. I had to go cuddle you as soon as I'd done it."

Valley can't imagine sticking her face in peed-on baby blankets. Face it—whatever it is that makes women go ape over babies and cancel their lives for slavery to poop and snot, she doesn't have it.

Joey falls asleep with the bottle in his mouth. Her mother removes it and gets up from the rocker, his head cradled in her elbow and his bottom in her other palm. "Sit down here, Valley. You take him. He's fine now." She motions to the chair with her head.

Valley seats herself in the chair and takes Joey back. He stays asleep, though during the switch his head lolls dangerously to one side.

"That's right. There." Her mother props Joey's head between Valley's small breast and her arm. Valley tenses so his head won't move. "Perfect." Her mother stands back and regards the two of them with her head cocked to one side.

Valley's arm aches, but she doesn't move.

"Now rock, lamb. Relax. It feels good. Enjoy the motion." Valley pushes off with her toe.

"You should be fine now. Call me back if you need me."

Valley wishes her mother would stay. She doesn't want to be alone with Joey. Doesn't trust herself. But now that Joey is sleeping, her mother will be suspicious if she asks her to stay. She can't risk that.

The Galaxy disappears down the road, and Valley is left with Joey and the creaking rocker. She looks down at the sleeping child. How long had her Home Ec teacher said a baby could go without oxygen before brain damage? Was it five minutes? Fifteen? Longer for babies than for adults? How long had Joey gone without breathing? Valley mentally retraces her steps once it got silent—to the living room, to the phone. She accounts for the time it takes to dial the two calls, allows herself some time to think. It can't have been that long. Not fifteen minutes.

Joey looks so peaceful, lying in her arms. The rocker creaks and Valley hears a rhyme.

> Little Boy Blue, come blow your horn;
> The sheep's in the meadow,
> The cow's in the corn.
> Where's the little boy that looks after the sheep?
> He's under Sebastian, fast asleep.

CHAPTER 4

Rose drives home in a daze, choosing to take the long way around. She can feel Joey's plump calf in the hollow of her palm and his hot breath on her neck. His body had grown weightier as he'd relaxed, like in Valley's infancy when the two of them had napped together. Valley nursed, then dropped off to sleep in Rose's arms. Rose dozed, too, in a blissful half sleep, wakened by Valley's slightest movement. Those were the days. She knew exactly where Valley was every minute.

Farmland stretches out for miles on either side of the roadway. The fields, usually nappy with soybean plants by the second week in June, are bogs of puddles. Rose wonders if the seeds have rotted in the ground. Her tires *zhush* through a puddle, throwing water onto the wild grapevine growing over the roadside fence posts. The stench of hen manure from Gabriel's turkey farm is stronger downwind. The sky arches overhead in a blue dome, its clouds unaffected by the humidity that rises from the swampy earth like bad breath.

The summer Valley was conceived was different—hot but not humid. The water in Kaiser Lake was silky and warm; the perfume of lilac and honeysuckle hung in the air. Dishes clinked on screen porches around the lake as people lingered late over coffee and dessert, listening to the hiss of locusts. On such a night, Rose thinks, no one should be held responsible for what happened. And though she'd been terrified at the time, Valley was a keeper. If a baby was the punishment for her sin, she should sin more often. It was no wonder she couldn't confess it.

Rose sees a woman standing in the road ahead, waving her arms frantically. She knows it's Helen from the long legs and hair even before she's close enough to see her features. Rose brakes and pulls up next to her friend. "I thought you'd be at work."

"My car's in the garage, so I'm walking home for lunch. Bethany's home alone."

Rose has never seen Helen eat anything but yogurt, standing at the fridge in the Laundromat office—unless you count the sunflower seeds she bakes to chew on when she can't smoke. To Rose, yogurt isn't lunch. Certainly nothing to walk home for. But that's why Helen has pretty thighs and hers are all mottled.

"Get in. I'll drive you. I meant to call you anyway. I may be gone for a few days—on a church retreat—so don't worry if you can't reach me." She's not really leaving home, but if she admits to secluding herself, Helen will think she's as crazy as the old woman robbing the church Dumpster.

Helen plants her tidy hips on the seat. "Oh, too bad. Just when Rob's arrived. Have you seen him yet? He stopped into the laundry with his stuff for me to wash, and guess what?

He recognized me!" Rose glances at her. Helen looks great in the sleeveless black tank she's wearing with her jeans. At times like this, Rose can't think what she likes about Helen. They wouldn't be friends if they hadn't been sitting together pregnant in Dr. Burns's office that year. Eleven months after she married Carl, Helen delivered Bethany and left the hospital wearing her jeans—which, at the moment, seems like a pretty good reason to hate her.

"He said he'd know my hair anywhere," Helen brags. Her hair really is pretty, but it's sickening how she relishes every little detail like Joanie Cranford. Helen wastes what little money she has on fancy botanical shampoos so her hair smells of windfall apples one day, ripe peaches the next.

"He called me Helen Dudley," Helen prattles on. "Maybe I should have changed my name back when Carl left, but after all those years of being called Milk Dud and Dudley-Do-Wrong, I was glad enough to be rid of it. He hadn't heard I'd married. He says he remembers the name Slezac, but only the name—he couldn't put a face to Carl. When you're not in the same class you don't really know each other. Anyway, he was sorry to hear about my divorce."

"Is he married?" The question comes out in a little half voice, and Rose clears her throat to cover, as if she's fighting a frog.

"He didn't say so." Helen prides herself on being the first to know the town gossip, and Rose eggs her on with a few more questions. "There's nobody with him," Helen says. "No woman, I mean. He's got some kid along, though."

Rose lets that sink in. "What do you mean *kid?*"

"Just some boy." To Helen it's a toss-off. "You know. Sixteen, maybe."

"Oooh, Bethany's age," Rose says, filling her voice with innuendo. Really she's worried that Valley has a half brother. What if he looks like Valley?

"You don't really think—" Helen says, though she's obviously conjuring a romance for Bethany. "Maybe I should invite them over. You know, for a friendly dinner."

Rose pictures the TV dinners she's seen Helen stack neatly in her grocery cart, filing each item as if she's lining up decimal points after counting the Laundromat's change. "It might be kind of obvious," Rose says, but when has Helen ever been afraid of being obvious?

Helen lights a cigarette and dangles her right hand out the open window. "If I'm not obvious, Bethany won't get it. I've never seen such a backward child. She never brings a soul home with her."

"Maybe she needs time alone. Some people do."

Rose turns off the main road and pulls over at the end of Helen's dirt driveway. The tree branches hang so low in Helen's front yard it's hard to see the brown bungalow Helen's grandfather left her. Her sunflowers and zinnias are spiking up already in the one sunny spot in the yard, the planter box over the septic tank. Gopher, Helen's chocolate Lab, comes bounding out to the car, tail wagging so hard his body wriggles all over.

Helen gets out of the car, patting Gopher with the hand holding her cigarette. "Flim Flannigan died last night. Did you know?"

"I knew someone had. He's suffered so long. And he had to be lonely after Louise died."

The dog's tail beats a knocking rhythm against the car door, and Rose fears dents. She wishes Helen would discipline her dog. Helen bends over to look in the window. "It's too bad you have to go right now. Rob asked for you."

Rose waits anxiously by the window for the deliveryman. She has cleaned the little room off the den that stores miscellaneous items: the boxed-up Mr. Coffee, albums of old photographs, a file box of bank statements and insurance records, a noisy window fan, two antique chairs with broken-out cane seats and three boxes of Christmas decorations. It took ten minutes to move the stuff to one side. Then she hung a picture of Our Lady with a mother-of-pearl rosary draped over the frame and a photo of Valley and herself stuck in its bottom corner.

The truck turns in, crunching gravel. Two men come to the door carrying the frame and spring between them. She leads them to the storage room and points to the corner where she wants it set up. They hand her the Mary Theresa tag, lay the metal spring between the head and foot frames and screw it together. They make a second trip to the truck and return with a thin mattress. This they lay in place, performing their duties solemnly, as if part of a ritual. Rose wonders where such men come from—men who don't roll their eyes at a woman's faith. Such a man would sit beside her in church. He would lead her up to Communion. Pray aloud at the dinner table. She can't imagine how that would be. It's not marriage as she knows it. She's not sure what it is. First Communion practice maybe, at age six. The boys and girls processed up the aisle, and the priest putting Necco wafers on their tongues so they could practice holding the host in their mouths without chewing.

Rose watches the men leave, then makes the sign of the cross over the bed.

She looks at the tag. Under Sister Mary Theresa's name is a quote in cramped handwriting: *True love grows by sacrifice, and the more thoroughly the soul rejects natural satisfaction, the stronger and more detached its tenderness becomes—St. Theresa, the Little Flower.* It's uncanny—exactly why she bought the bed. It even came with directions, in case she didn't understand.

This room, the simple bed, feels removed from her doubts about a God she cannot see. She covers the mattress with line-dried white sheets and smooths the rumples. She covers the sheets with a white-on-white quilt from her hope chest. It's one she made in Home Ec before she learned how to piece. Never before has she used it. The stitches are big and clumsy, but there's an innocence to them that helps her begin again. She tucks the overhanging edges under the mattress with perfect hospital corners. A clean envelope it is, and she the letter that will fit inside. A petition. To Jesus.

Rose kneels down and runs her hands over the quilt top. The fabric is soft like the batiste of her First Communion dress. After the service, her parents gave a party with a cake covered in white frosting roses. A photographer followed her around that afternoon, telling her to smile and snapping her picture in her white dress and lace veil. The veil was gathered on a plastic headband that pinched over her ears and made her head ache.

When she and Everett eloped, her only veil was the lace curtain she'd swiped from her mother's linen closet to wrap herself in for their first night at Beetley's Hotel on Indian Lake. She wore it wrapped sari-style and flung over her shoulder. Everett had unwrapped her gently, handling her like fragile lace, as if she, too, needed to be returned, untorn. Everett was different from Rob.

Oh, Rob. Only her head had been above water when they got to kissing. She had hardly noticed when the straps of her two-piece slid from her shoulders. They never found her bathing suit top, and she'd worn Rob's T-shirt home, her beach towel wrapped around her shoulders so her mother wouldn't notice.

Rose shakes her head. This is why she bought the bed— to purge those memories. She'll stay in this room and pray to the Holy Mother who bore a child and yet was without sin. She'll persevere until her heart is pure, not divided. Until her flesh is subdued. Maybe Rob will leave town meanwhile so she's not tempted. That would be a mercy as great as Everett's having left town for the day. That in itself was a miracle.

She ticks off the items she'll need for her retreat and rises obediently to collect them. Her missal is in the drawer of her bedside stand, dog-eared and stuffed full of the holy cards her mother collected at funeral homes and tucked into her birthday cards. They spill out on the floor—haloed images of Mary in blue drapery, Jesus with a lamb slung over his shoulders, Saint Francis feeding the birds and Saint Clare, barefoot and wearing sackcloth, placing the Blessed Sacrament between a soldier and the convent wall. Rose puts Clare on top to keep her marauder away.

The screen door bangs shut down in the kitchen.

"Valley? Is that you, lamb?" she calls down the stairs.

"Hi, Mom."

"How'd you make out with Joey?"

Valley appears in the doorway, pulling her fingers through her sweaty hair. "He puked all over me. I've got to take a shower."

"Babies spit up all the time. Especially formula-fed babies. That's why breast feeding is best." She likes to talk about these things with Valley, to pass on the womanly arts.

"Mom? How long can a person survive without oxygen?"

"How would I know that, lamb? I'm not a doctor."

"I just thought you might have read it somewhere. You're always telling me stories about kids getting shut up in old refrigerators or car trunks."

"Were you thinking of hiding in the trunk?"

There's silence for a moment, then Valley giggles a bit too loudly. "Bach didn't know that flutists need air. I wondered how long I can play without breathing. You know, without brain damage."

"I told you to take the summer off, lamb. You need a break sometimes."

Joey's mucous is all over the front of Rose's dress. She puts it in with the dry cleaning, removes her slip and looks down at the bulge of flesh pooching from the waistband of her satin panties. They're not exactly nun's underpants. As she peels them down her body, her belly protrudes with its silvery stretch marks, as if she's swallowed a winter squash. She pokes through the snarl of undies in her drawer, burrowing beneath the skimpy nighties Everett buys, and picks out a modest white cotton bra, panties and a plain half-slip. She stands behind the door to put them on, in case Valley should come barging in with more silly questions, then chooses a shirt and denim skirt as closest to what the nun's wear now that they've shed their habits. She likes skirts anyway. It's not that she thinks it's wrong to dress like a man, though her mother didn't own a pair of pants. It's that jeans dig into her waist and hug her thighs when she sits down. She's cooler and more comfortable in a skirt.

Her best rosary is under her pillow, one her mother kept draped over the radio through the fifties when Bishop Sheen came on every day to address the faithful. It was made by a monk in Normandy after World War II and feels like a piece of history. The beads are made of melted-down bullets, and large iron nails form the cross. The contorted Body is hammered from brass and welded to the nails at the hands and feet. As a child she liked to finger it, to peer through the tiny space between the Body and the cross.

Downstairs, she lays her supplies down on the table, next to the fabric she'd been cutting for a Jacob's ladder quilt.

Planning it seems long ago, though it was really only a day. She had been excited about the project, so excited she'd forgotten to eat lunch while she'd graphed it out. Then she made a cutting mistake on a flocked purple remnant she had been saving for just the right quilt. She won't get the ladder out of it now, and she feels like throwing it all away. She takes up her kaleidoscope, hoping another color combination will capture her. But every time the purple falls in with the blues she feels complete. There's nothing else she likes as well. It's all ruined. Tears spring to her eyes, and she swallows again and again. She'd been tired when she made the mistake, too tired to think straight and distracted by the boy who'd come for Valley.

She hopes Valley stays upstairs, because it's stupid to cry over a quilt. She's thankful Everett's gone. Neither of them understands that it's not just a quilt to Rose. It's the death of a perfect idea. Now, no matter who raves about the quilt—even if it takes another first at the county fair—it will always look second-rate to Rose.

She hears water rushing through the pipes. Valley is in the shower. Rose goes into the kitchen to get sandwich bags for her little piles of triangles and squares but forgets what she's after and opens the refrigerator. The sliced turkey will only go bad if she doesn't eat it. Everett isn't coming home and Valley doesn't like it.

She makes herself a turkey sandwich with cheese and lettuce, spreading mayonnaise to the edges of the rye bread with her favorite spreader. A bite at a time, she savors each mouthful as if it's her last. Rob asked for her. Helen said so. She washes her sandwich plate and pictures his backlit figure walking toward her down the sidewalk. A gold chain glints at the neck of his green T. His jeans bulge slightly at the zipper. But it's that moment when their eyes met she wants to capture. Her insides flutter as they had in junior high— before a test, when a cute boy walked by or whenever she saw Mary Sue Horton come toward her. "Stop it!" Rose says aloud to the dish brush. She dries the plate, puts it back on the shelf and hurries to her cell as if Rob is in hot pursuit. The air is close in the little room. That's okay. It's part of the discipline.

Kneeling beside her bed, Rose bows over her rosary. She says the Apostle's Creed on the crucifix—fingering the sharp angle of Christ's knees, the prickly points of the thorns on his brow—a Hail Mary on each of the little beads and an Our Father and Glory Be on each of the larger beads. She repeats them for Mr. Flannigan's soul. All of it is exhausting, her crying, her praying. She wonders if it's wrong to pray lying down. What did sick people do? Stroke patients? Mr. Flannigan? He certainly hadn't knelt. She lies flat on her back, her palms together, upright over her ribs. Her shirt absorbs the sweat on her back. She recites the questions and answers of the Baltimore Catechism, drilled into her by Sister Mary Thomas beginning in second grade. "Who made the world? God made the world. Who is God? God is the Creator of heaven and earth and of all things." When she's repeated all of lesson one, she repeats the Ten Commandments, the seven sacraments, the seven virtues and the seven deadly sins. She intends to confess on each one, beginning with gluttony and citing the box of chocolates, but before she gets to lust, Rose dozes.

In the dim light of consciousness she sees bicycle wheels turning, turning, revolving so fast the spokes become a blur and disappear. Valley is a baby, strapped into a child seat fixed to the rear fender. Rose is naked, perched on the seat, steering. She rounds a corner, bicycle leaning until it tips over and the curb reaches for the two of them, smacks her in the jaw and dislodges her teeth. She wriggles each tooth in turn, finds she can remove it, looks at the disgusting V-shaped root, then fits it back into its socket. Valley is sprawling on a lawn overgrown with enormous dandelions that make soft yellow pillows for her head. "Poor baby," Rose says, picking Valley up, but Valley cannot hear her. Rose looks in her ear. There's a dandelion inside. Rose plucks at it with her fingers first, then with tweezers, but only manages to shred it. Fragile yellow fibers stick to the tweezer tips like duck fluff. She digs deeper into Valley's ear, gouging at yellow, tweaking, pulling. But the dandelion is stubborn. It gives up its nap, but it will not budge.

CHAPTER 5

Port Clinton is new to Everett, but the AAA magazine has a good map. The air is much cooler by the lake. Drier, too. Good thing with the dog. Everett drives to the docks, parks in the shade of a large tree, rolls the windows partway down and pats the dog. "I won't be long. You'll be fine," he says in the singsong of doggy talk. She wags her back half, barks once and watches while he grabs a jacket from his trunk.

Everett buys a ticket to Put-in-Bay on the Jet Express, a jet-powered catamaran said to cross the harbor in twenty-two minutes. Onboard, he stands with the other tourists and watches wake spew from the engine before churning back into the bay. The passengers wear colorful windbreakers, orange and yellow, green and pink. Women pull hoods up over their blowing hair. Everett leaves his jacket hanging open. Cold is a woman thing.

Up ahead, the Perry Memorial rises from the center of downtown Put-in-Bay like a giant pencil, poised to connect the plump clouds into meaningful patterns. Everett thinks like that—connecting poles, configuring electrical circuits, though he rarely insists the patterns have meaning. Not like

Rosie, who finds significance in every event. He finds her interpretation of coincidence silly and trivial—the abracadabra of child play, like expecting sense of nursery rhymes or jump-rope chants.

When the Jet Express docks and its engines shut down, the organ band of Kimberly's Carousel—noted in the AAA guide for its all-wood horses—mixes with the seagulls' laughter. At King's Island Amusement Park Valley used to cling to the carousel pole, her neck craning to spot Rosie every turn round the circle. That's not what he came for.

He spies the parachutes billowing from their anchors down on the beach. He hurries to the dock to register, but when he arrives there's no line. The air is too chilly. He won't bother changing into swim trunks.

Everett pays his fee and signs the waiver before he loses his nerve. Out in the water, the boat motor revs while barechested boys with Greek letters on their caps snap him into a life vest. The boy maneuvering the boat keeps it pointing into the wind. The motor settles into a glubbing gurgle Everett can hardly hear over his heartbeat. He is about to do it. To take off…to fly…to soar with the seagulls—free of earth, gravity, his body. The boys tell him to step into a harness. He threads one leg, then the other through the leg straps. His bare feet look white. One boy tightens the cinch belt under his gut and adjusts the strap that runs between his legs. A red-yellow-and-blue chute billows out behind him, not yet clipped to rings on his harness. The wind riffles the edges of the chute. His mouth is suddenly dry. Two boys clip his chute on, holding him down with all their weight. "Hold on to those straps by your ears," the tall one says.

"Have fun, big guy."

They *halloo* to the driver. Release him as the boat takes off into the wind. Cold air rushes his face as the chute lifts him into the air. His weight settles into the sling seat. His knuckles whiten around the handholds. The beach disappears and he is over water. The waves reach for his feet, then curl into white fringe. He kicks his feet at the nothingness that suspends him. The water drops farther below. The waves look like ripples. He glances back. The shoreline forms a crescent behind him. The Perry Monument is not so tall after all. The red-and-white carousel awning rotates slowly, its pie-shaped wedges emerging from a stationary center point. Its calliope is silent now. Even the noise of the boat motor has faded away.

It is very still.

The article hadn't mentioned stillness. His skin breaks out in goose bumps. He'd expected rushing wind, rocking him in the harness swing, his hair blowing every which way. Everett has never heard such silence. Even in farm country in the middle of winter there are sounds—the echo of a car door slamming, a train whistle, the snap of icicles, the wind wiffling across stubbly fields or snapping frozen branches. The silence threatens to swallow him. He can't relax and enjoy the view in the face of such calm. How does he know he's still living? That he hasn't died of heart failure? Maybe he was wrong about heaven—all his visions of angels and cherubim, the many-headed monsters from Revelations, the only book of the Bible he's read. Maybe the giant throne room, the old man speaking in a booming voice amidst sulfur and magical creatures and terror and judgment is Oz, not heaven. Maybe heaven is a lot of nothing. A total void.

"Anybody home?" Everett calls into the stillness. The question goes nowhere. Maybe it's trapped in his head, like the sound of his voice when he plugs his ears with his fingers. Maybe he hasn't spoken at all. He lets go of the strap and holds his ears with his palms, then hollers.

The boat down on the water speeds around in circles. To his right a gull flaps its wings a few times, then glides, riding an updraft before circling around and descending to the water. For a minute it grazes the surface, then splashes and disappears. It surfaces and flaps off with a fish in its mouth. Everett envies its fluid movement, its freedom. He caws like the gull and flaps his arms. He pictures himself bailing out, as he had from swings when he was a child, then jackknifing into free fall, arms and legs spread wide to embrace the approaching earth like skydivers in James Bond movies.

Everett quells the urge. From this height, he'd never survive. Suicide is the coward's way out. But if he were closer to the water…the boat heads toward shore. He'll descend soon. He doesn't have much time. The buckles are locked into each other. He kicks his feet and plucks at the webbing threaded through the buckles on the crotch strap. Finally he pulls it free. The waist strap is all that remains. It's tight, and he can't see it over the bulk of his life jacket to loosen it. While he fumbles with it, jerking and cursing, the boat slows down.

Everett's chute drops like a reeled-in kite. His time is short. The wind blows him toward shore. The beach approaches. The frat boys gesture, pointing and waving their arms. They holler and motion to pull down, like a train engineer on the whistle. He pulls all right—at the strap under his gut.

The boat idles offshore. The chute drops farther. The engine glubs. The calliope frolics. He's almost too late, too close. Then the strap gives and he's free. He thrusts his head out to propel his weight forward, spreads his arms and legs, then smacks on the blue-gray mirror.

When Everett regains consciousness, a frat boy's face is enlarged in the center of an expanse of sky. "He's coming to." The boy's voice is soprano and distorted. Other faces appear in a circle around his. Water runs from the kid's sun-bleached hair down his neck and chest. The seagulls' cries no longer sound like laughter. The clamor of the calliope mocks at his pain.

"Back off, everybody," the kid orders. The perimeter of faces clears out. "You okay, mister?" His eyes look earnest, as though the answer matters.

Yeah, Everett mouths. He has no air in his lungs. His head aches. His skin stings all over.

"What the hell were you trying to do? Are you fuckin' crazy, man?"

Everett gasps to breathe. There's a crushing weight on his chest.

"That life jacket saved you. Lie still. The ambulance will be here soon."

Everett heaves himself partway up. The kid pushes on his shoulders to lay him back down, but Everett resists. "No hospital." He shakes the kid's hands off. "I'm fine."

"You're not fine. They have to check you out. Insurance stuff."

"Hell with insurance…They're not…checking me out… I'm outa here…soon as I get…my breath."

A siren is coming toward the docks. Everett rolls onto his hands and knees, struggles up and staggers in the sand. The kid is on his tail, fussing at him.

Everett waves him off. "Beat it, kid. And while you're at it, get a real job."

"Crazy bastard."

Everett grabs his duffel off the sand and heads for the bathhouse. When he looks back, the kid is staring after him. Everett hates the boy's sculpted chest and taut, square jaw.

Back in the car, Everett cuddles his dog. The wind was cold on the trip across the bay, and the afternoon sun feels good, baking him through the windshield. Now that he's been to Oz and back, he's decided to name the dog Kansas. She puts her front paws in his lap and licks the sweat from his palms. Her tongue massages his calluses, but its grainy texture feels a bit removed until she moves to the skin on his wrist. His skin stings all over where he hit the water. His stomach is sour, his saliva bitter, but he's not sorry he did it. The way that boy fussed to save him, maybe there's something of his life left to salvage.

CHAPTER 6

Valley stops playing scales on her flute and listens. The house is so quiet her mother must be out weeding. She puts the flute down on her bed, crawls across it to the puzzle portrait and lifts it off the wall. Her father hates this picture. They had it made at Sears when they were all dressed up for Mother's Day one year, but he had refused to do it again. He couldn't stand the photographer tapping his chin to adjust the angle of his head and telling him to smile. And he didn't like the way Valley's hair stuck up from the duck barrette. "You just don't know what's cute," her mother told him one night when they were both in her room, kissing her good-night.

"Hair doesn't grow up," he said. "She's cute the way she is."

Maybe the picture is why he never comes in her room anymore. She doesn't blame him. She can't think why she's left it up. She turns the picture over and removes the clips and the cardboard to get to the puzzle itself. Once it's free of the frame, she props it on her pillow for a last look, makes a fist and punches through her baby face. A puzzle bracelet circles her wrist.

When Valley withdraws her hand, her pillowcase shows through. Her mother's lap now holds a white balloon. Tears well up in her eyes, and through their watery blur, it is young Mrs. Harper sitting there with a hole in her lap. And Joey's body without a head. She screams, but no sound comes from her mouth. It stays trapped in her head.

She sweeps the picture off her pillow and puts her Sebastian bear there instead. Frantically she searches for a place to hide it. The closet and bureau are no good; her mother will find it when she puts the laundry away. The mattress. She puts the ruined picture under it and drops the mattress. It will do until she can find a better place. She straightens the quilt. Pieces of her face still lay on the quilt top as if somehow part of its bear-paw pattern. She tries to fit them back together, but where her fist struck, the cardboard tongues are bent backward. She puts them in her top drawer under the balls of matched socks.

If only she could go back to a time when she didn't know about today. One day would do. She'd been a better person the day before. A strange pressure in her chest, like a giant spring winding ever tighter, threatens to uncoil and wang her all over the room. She reaches for her flute, as if it might anchor her, prevent her from hitting the walls.

A Bach bourrée is on her music stand, but the endless eighth notes are more than she can face. She turns instead to a sinfonia, a slow, dreamy piece she can almost play by heart.

As her breath funnels through the cylinder, Joey is seated before her, propped on the pillow in place of Sebastian. At first he is huge, a burden she must drag behind her through humid air and acres of boggy farmland. She slogs through the complications and resolutions of the melody until her tone becomes full and the music takes over. She allows its power to lift her to the peak of each phrase before falling freely down the backside. Joey is now light, full of helium. He floats up from the bog and is borne aloft on the sound of her voice. Eyes closed and body swaying, she woos him, leaning into the phrases, rocking him gently on the melody.

The vision of Joey fades and she is playing for Mr. Moore, but his chest is expanding, his face reddening from inhaling for her without exhaling into a flute. She plays on, weaving through the andante. Mr. Moore's face is purple now, but still she plays on, bewitched by the sound she's making—until he turns blue and keels over. She drops her flute and runs downstairs. In the refrigerator are two bottles of her father's beer. She uncaps them both and downs the first, not thinking how she'll replace them. The taste is nasty, but she doesn't care. She's after the drowsy, calm effect she's seen on her dad, the way he cares less with each beer as a Reds game wears on. She holds her nose to down the second bottle. She takes the bottles out to the garbage can, not quite able to be as quiet as she'd like to be, though nothing like calm has come over her yet. She buries them deep in a green plastic bag. Her mother is nowhere in sight. The backyard is empty.

Their two-story Victorian rises behind her like an empty tomb. She wonders where her mother is, why her father is gone on a Saturday. The company of a caterpillar isn't enough. The spring inside her chest begins to tighten. Her breath comes in spurts. She can't go inside. It's better to fly apart in the wide world, where she'll bounce off the soft blue of the sky's dome. She heads down the driveway, one step, then the next. She'll keep walking, forever if she has to. It's the one thing she's certain she can do.

Walking helps. She focuses on her breathing. Inhale one, two, three, four; exhale one, two, three, four, walking and breathing in 4/4 time. She changes to 3/4, bending her knee on the accented first beat and then taking the next two counts of the measure on her tiptoes. She sings a polonaise and is surprised at the end to find herself in town. In front of the movie theater, a long-haired boy leans up against the brick, a boy she can't remember seeing before. He's watching her with a blurry, bemused expression, one thumb hooked in the waist of his beltless jeans. His mouth curves up in a lazy grin.

"Hey, babe. My name is Zeke."

She thinks he's said *Snake*. The hair on her arms stands up. He crushes the cigarette cupped in his palm against the brick wall, rolls his shoulders off its surface and walks over to her. "You like music?"

Valley pushes her hair back over her shoulder, hesitates for a minute, then nods. She feels the danger, knows she is playing with fire. As a little girl she had secretly played pickup sticks with wooden matches.

He mirrors her movement, brushing the hair off his forehead. "I've got a new Rick Springfield tape in my truck. Want to hear it?"

Snake's edges are becoming blurry, and Valley shakes her head and blinks. He's about her height and lanky. His jeans fall loosely from his hip bones. His long hair gives him the look of someone faintly artistic, someone who plays in a band that rehearses in his uncle's garage.

"I don't know you," she says.

He presses his lips together and shakes his head slowly. He's sorry he can't help her with that, she can tell. "You sure do sing pretty."

"You sure do smoke."

A corner of Snake's mouth turns up in a one-sided smirk. He drops the cigarette and crushes it into the sidewalk with his sandal, as though he's determined to quit on the spot, to please her.

Across the street a knot of Valley's classmates come clamoring out of the pizzeria. They mill around in a clump, then pair off to loiter, guys leaning against the glass with their hands clasped beneath their girlfriends' rib cages. Valley is prettier than those girls, but she'll never be one of them. She crosses her arms. "I bet you play in a band."

"Nuclear Sleeping Sickness."

Valley snorts and her hand flies to her mouth. "But that's disgusting."

He laughs, too, but later, when she thinks back, she hears it more like a growl. "Don't think meaning. It's *all* about the sound." The way he drags out the *all*, he seems almost wistful.

She glances across the street. "Let me guess. You practice in your uncle's garage on Thursday nights and Saturday mornings." She no sooner says it than she knows she's wrong. That's what her classmates would do—if they were creative enough to start their own band. But Snake bows at the waist, one hand front, the other back, as if deferring to her superior intuition. "You're too good, Babe."

So he's not like Mark Thorburn. He won't dismiss her for silly mistakes. She points to the pay phone under the marquee. "I have to call home. I need to tell Mom where I am."

But when Valley hears her mother's voice, she changes her mind. Her mother would never understand why she needs to listen to music in a strange boy's truck. "It's me, Mom. I'm at Joanie's. Mrs. Cranford says I can stay the night." Oddly her mother agrees, almost thankfully it seems. Without even asking if Joanie's folks will be home.

Valley follows Snake to a truck parked on the main street, telling herself she's out in public, telling herself Eden is safe, telling herself she can always blow the match out before she gets burned.

CHAPTER 7

Rose wakens from her dream, tongue sweeping her teeth for gaping holes in her jaw. Needles prickle down her arms, her hands still folded over her ribs. Pain isn't such a bad thing. It proves she isn't dead on the curb. Her eye follows a ceiling crack to a large water stain shaped like Africa, roughly. It's a map to Rose, the voyage of her life. She's an explorer in search of a sea route to India's riches. Only she wants the riches of the Kingdom. For Valley. For herself. For Everett.

Someone squashed a bug on the ceiling, and a black mark intersects with the water stain and the crack. That, she decides, is the day when she first suspected she was pregnant. She remembers the terrible loneliness she felt, the sense that she didn't belong—not with her mother, who'd had a child but whose marriage license made that legitimate, or with her unmarried friends. The person she belonged with was Winona Rexall, the only girl in her class not to march down the auditorium aisle to "Pomp and Circumstance" because she was seven months along and the school board declared her condition "unseemly." (Rose spelled their verdict u-n-se-a-m-l-y. It described the way her insides tore further apart each time she felt wetness between her legs and ran off to the toilet, only to find not blood but that her bladder had leaked.) Belonging with Winona was worse than not belonging at all.

Now she can't remember what Winona looked like. She sees the binding of her senior yearbook beneath the stack of old phone books she means to recycle. She is up and after it so quickly black spots dance in front of her eyes. She looks at her watch. It's eight-ten. The house is quiet. If she has to revisit old feelings, it's comforting to know she's alone. In those awful weeks of isolation, she had faked sleep whenever she'd heard her mother's footfalls outside her bedroom door.

Rose sits on the bed, back to the wall and feet stuck out in front of her. Inside the front cover, written every which way, is a jumble of autographs. Most of her friends wrote *To a great kid* and signed *Love* before their names in loopy letters, dotting their i's with little hearts. Laney Kirkhart, who ate chocolate bars in a bathroom stall instead of braving the cafeteria, drew a daisy after her name. And Bamber Bateman, whose face she can't recall—though who could forget the name?—wrote the letters of his name around a smiley face, to look like hair.

Hilda Dunagan, who got free lunches from the government, wrote, *When you slide down the bannister to death, remember me as the one who pushed you.* Rose snorts in disgust. Everyone else was swapping yearbooks that day, and Rose didn't know how to exclude Hilda. As usual, Hilda had let

Rose know she understood the terms. Permanently. Hilda was like that. Rose is secretly pleased to see she misspelled *banister*.

She turns the book upside down to look at her classmates, since that's how Rob had seen her through the car window. A girl in a long dress stands on her head—or on her diamond tiara, rather. It has to be Mary Sue Horton, because she was homecoming queen, though upside down, Mary Sue's smile forms a half circle over a nose Rose never realized was so wide. Mary Sue was her classmates' standard of beauty. You were supposed to want to be like her, but she went around after gym class showers yanking towels off the flat-chested girls. Being popular had nothing to do with being kind.

Mary Sue's face looks different upside down—just a design with no name. Rose turns to her own picture and looks at it upside down. She hardly knows herself. And she looks so different now. Rob didn't recognize her. No way.

She can't resist turning to Rob's picture. His smile looks smug, self-satisfied, like the day she approached him with the news. She'd gone to his summer-league baseball game and sat in the bleachers with the other girlfriends and Eden's ten-year-old boys who came out with the lightning bugs and never seemed to go home. Her stomach was so acid that night she could hardly follow the game.

Rob was the last to leave the field. Finally, when the last car door slammed and all that remained were hissing locusts, Rose descended the bleachers slowly, minding herself so a leg didn't fall through the boards. She seated herself at the end of Eden's team bench. Rob was pacing the third-base line, taking off in sprints at unexplained moments, playing a game only he could see.

"Rob?"

He pointed to the outfield fence. "Did you see that triple I hit to left field?"

Rose had been off in the bathroom trying to spit out the nasty taste when she'd heard the bat crack and the crowd cheer. "It was great," she said. He came close to the bench, and the smell of his cologne, heightened by his exertion, was so strong she had to move away so she wouldn't puke.

He wound up and delivered an imaginary pitch right at her. She didn't let herself duck. "That freak thought his fastball was hot stuff. The kid needed schooling."

"You were great."

At home plate he began swinging an imaginary bat, poking the air a few times before delivering a home-run stroke. He watched the invisible ball fly over the fence. "If anyone else could hit, I would have scored."

Rose drew a line in the dust with the toe of her sandal. "Your team won."

He poked the air, preparing to hit again. "No winning team leaves a runner on third. Just one measly hit. That was all I needed."

"Rob?"

He was busy, facing another pitch. She could almost see the bat. Feel its weight.

"Yeah?"

She wanted to get up, take the bat away. Instead she laced her fingers together and turned them inside out, stretching her arms out in front of her. She couldn't quell the shudder that shook her shoulders. "You know what we did that night? At Kaiser Lake?"

He turned toward her, though he hadn't dropped the bat.

She couldn't look him in the eye. This wasn't how she'd pictured it. He was supposed to sit down beside her and take her hand. "I didn't get my…you know."

In the silence she pushed backward on the base of each finger, first one, then the next, until the knuckle popped.

"Stop it," he said. "That's gross."

His eye was on the incoming ball and he watched it into the catcher's mitt. "Ball one."

Rose remembers the infield dust, how fine and silky it felt between her toes and the sole of her sandal. It left a film on every surface, including the bench. "Rob. What are we going to do?"

"*We?*" he said.

The memory of that single syllable gives her chills. But it was nothing to what came next.

He swung the bat. "How do I know it's mine?"

Rose doesn't know what either of them said after that. Only that she felt mercilessly whacked into left field. Her mind went completely blank. Without any memory of how she got there, she found herself at home in bed, watching her clock's second hand go round and round without ever registering the time.

Rose is lying on her stomach now, clutching the white sheets. Someone is knocking on her kitchen door. She finds her shoes and hurries to the kitchen, thinking Valley forgot her key. But when she opens the door, she finds herself face-to-face with Rob. One hand instinctively finds her chest, and she wonders if she's asleep. Such coincidences only happened in dreams and bad movies.

"Rose Townsend?" Rob says. His eyes are grave, his mouth set in a straight line. A muscle pulses in his jaw.

Rose's heart pounds.

"You know me, don't you?"

Her lips form his name, though her voice is stuck at the back of her throat.

"Helen Dudley gave me your address."

She crosses her arms. "Slezac," she whispers.

"What?"

"Her name is Slezac now."

"Oh. Yeah. She told me."

This is where Rose should say she's not a Townsend anymore, but she's watching the way his forehead creases when he raises his brows. He's more attractive than she remembered, though the way his brow bone protrudes, no one would call him handsome exactly.

"Can I come in?"

Rose steps back but forgets to open the screen door. He opens it just far enough to slip through and catches it behind him. The smell of his shampoo fills her space, and she watches his eyes move around the room, stopping at the dishwasher, the curtains, the maple cabinets. Rose checks for evidence of Valley. Her flute case is on the counter, under the wall phone, but Rob has no way of knowing Rose hasn't taken up the flute. There's also a hairbrush with blond hairs in the bristles. Rose backs up in front of it. A framed watercolor Valley did years back hangs on the wall. It's unsigned but childish-looking with its background of red, green and yellow circles covered with what looks to Rose like a giant black spider. "Stained Glass" is the title, written at the bottom in the art teacher's tidy print.

"Nice house. Helen says you married Everett Forrester. He must be doing well."

"We're comfortable," Rose says, though at the moment she is far from comfortable. Her mouth tastes as though she just woke up—which she did—so she can't let him get too close. Her back aches at a point under her right shoulder blade.

The phone rings. Rose is startled but picks it up.

"It's me, Mom. I'm at Joanie's. Mrs. Cranford says I can stay the night."

Rose presses the receiver into her ear so Rob can't hear Valley's voice. "Have a good time," she says and hangs up. It's a blessing. Valley won't walk through the door. She takes a glass from the cupboard. "Can I get you something to drink?"

He smiles shyly, an expression she doesn't remember. "Ice water would taste good. It's pretty hot out there. Your house is nice and cool, though."

"It's the trees. Oak trees. They have huge leaves. But you wouldn't want to be around in the fall when it's time to rake them." Rose is babbling, saying any old thing. Actually Everett hires the leaves raked, but Rose talks as though it's a task she handles alone.

A smile flirts at the corners of his mouth. "I'll be the judge of that."

This is the Rob she remembers. She rubs her arms to flatten the goose bumps. She should ask him to sit down, but first she'd like to search the living room for telltale signs of Valley. She fills the glass with ice and water, backtracking several hours in her mind to when she picked up her quilt squares, then sidles into the living room, putting herself between him and anything he might see before she does.

"So what brings you back to Eden?" Rose says to fill the awkward space between them. She isn't sure she wants to know, but she can't stand not knowing, either.

"Two things. Mom's house is one. I have to move her stuff before the closing."

Rose wonders what the second is. She sits on the couch to keep the coffee table between herself and Rob. "I'm sorry Everett isn't home yet. He'd like to see you, too." Rob reaches over the table for the ice water, careful not to touch her hand on the transfer. He sits down in Everett's recliner, and Rose can't help noticing how differently Rob fills it. There's room left for a second person. His stomach doesn't pooch out of his lap.

Rose tucks her hands under her legs. Her thoughts race. If he asks for Valley, wants to see her, what in the world will she say? What will she tell Valley? This is your real father? No way. This is your uncle Rob? Everett will know better.

"Rosie Townsend," Rob says on a long sigh. "Well, well, well."

Rose's skin tingles and she searches for something to say. Silence feels threatening. Out of control. "What made you decide to look me up after all this time?"

"My probation officer wants me to make restitution. It's part of rehab."

Rob has a *probation officer*. Rose scratches at a stain on her skirt, then smooths it flatter over her thighs before tucking her hand back under herself. It's too late for Rob to marry her, so what kind of restitution does he want to make? "Are you married?" she asks.

He laughs. "The slammer isn't the best place to find a mate. But I've got a kid along. Not mine or anything. I'm part of a pilot program, delinquents and parolees. It's like that experiment where they took kids into Rahway and let the lifers rip on them. You heard about that."

She hadn't, of course, and she shudders to think they would experiment on kids. "Rip on them? What does that mean?"

"You know. Tell 'em what it's like inside. This kid's a tough one, but my parole depended on my participation."

"How did they match you up? By the crime?" It's rude to ask, but she needs to know what Rob did. He ought to just tell her.

"I wasn't as far gone at his age. Zeke held up a discount

store with a gun. He'd be in detention except the gun wasn't loaded and he only took cigarettes, no money. Dumb kid. Cop nabbed him in the parking lot."

Rose feels creepy knowing there's a delinquent loose in Eden and a convict in her living room. "Where is Zeke now?"

Rob takes a long drink of water. The ice clinks on the bottom when he rights the glass. His lips are wet and look redder than before. "In a town this size, I can walk anywhere I want to go, so I let him have my truck for the evening. Kid needs a little responsibility, but he has to check in with me by midnight."

"Are you supposed to do that?"

"That's the beauty of the program. We make our own rules. When I was a kid, Dad let me sit in his lap while he drove. You know, put my hands on the wheel and pretend? Anyway, he needs to know I trust him. No one's tried that."

Rose might point out that he, Rob, wasn't too trustworthy at that age, but thinks it best not to mention a subject she doesn't want to discuss. "Does he live with you?"

"Zeke has foster parents, but they were glad enough when I proposed this little trip. He came to help me move boxes."

Rob is about to put his glass down on the table beside Everett's chair, on the magazine to protect the tabletop, when he hesitates. Rose watches him read the cover and the muscles in her bottom tense. It's Valley's *Seventeen*. The cover shows three girls in striped bikinis and heart-shaped sunglasses bending over toward the camera with their hands on their knees. "How to Keep Him Looking, Looking,

Looking" is the title of the lead article. Hardly reading material for a married woman.

Rob looks up and their eyes meet. Rose says nothing. He takes the magazine off the pile and lays it on his lap. She would leap the coffee table and take it from him if she didn't feel so faint. What does he want from her? From Valley? The unasked question sucks up all the air in the room. Daylight is waning. Soon it will be time to turn lights on. She wants him out before dark. "Let me take that glass." If she goes to the kitchen, maybe he'll leave. She rounds the coffee table, tidily laid with *Time, Ladies Home Journal* and a bowl of seashells Valley picked up in Florida, then walks the perimeter of the room as if skirting the question. She takes the glass from his hand.

"Time for me to be going." He follows her from the room.

She goes to stand by the door. "Thanks for stopping by." He is holding the magazine out to her. She grasps it, but he doesn't let go.

"I came to say I was sorry." He waggles the *Seventeen*.

Rose can hardly breathe. She stares at his hand. Wills it to let go.

"Look at me, Rose."

Instead she snatches the magazine and folds it to her breast. He pushes through the screen door. Rose pulls the handle behind him until the latch clicks.

"You look fabulous, by the way. Must be good advice you read."

She squints at the screen's woven wire to keep from seeing the man beyond.

* * *

When Rob has disappeared down the driveway, Rose turns the lights on. She feels dirty, as if she's been sprayed by a tomcat. She should never have let Rob in. She hides the magazine in a drawer, then rubs down the sides of her skirt, uncertain whether she's trying to rub the scent off her hands or her legs. At the sink she soaps her hands up to her elbows, then clasps them in prayer and watches the suds squeeze between her fingers. "Hail Mary, full of grace." She pictures the Virgin with her bouquet of roses, standing in the arched alcove at the entrance to the church. "Blessed art thou among women and blessed is the fruit of thy womb, Jesus."

Rose dries her hands and finds herself searching the fridge. She's ravenously hungry. Surely the Virgin will understand. A bowl of grapes sits on the top shelf, a few picked off so their bare stems point at her accusingly. She plucks a grape and pops it into her mouth. It's sour. She takes another and another, hoping to find one that's sweet. Then she's fumbling with the package of wafers, ripping at the wrapper. She chooses a vanilla cookie over a pink or brown one. Sugar washes over her tongue, and before she knows it, she's eaten four.

"Forgive me, Father, for I have sinned." It's only been seven hours and she's failed already. She hears rustling outside the screen door. "Who's there? Is somebody there?" she calls into the darkness, straining her eyes to distinguish shapes. "Everett? Is that you?" Only the crickets answer. A squirrel, most likely. Out in the lilac bush. Rose shuts off the kitchen light and heads upstairs to the bathroom, determined to begin again, once she's gone to the john. She'll plug her ears so she's not distracted by little sounds.

In the bathroom mirror she sees how provocatively her hair frames her face. She searches Everett's shaving kit for the scissors and, before she can stop herself, snips her bangs nearly to the roots.

CHAPTER 8

Everett drives south on Route 75 with Kansas sleeping beside him, her chin resting on his thigh below the hem of his shorts. He can barely feel his foot pressing the accelerator and has to focus to sense the tickle of her whiskers on his leg. The MS is having a heyday this time. He'll have to drive with his left foot. When he hoists his right leg onto the hump under the ashtray, the car drifts across the dotted line into the passing lane. He jerks the wheel to correct it and Kansas slides into the passenger door. She looks at him with hurt brown eyes, as though he's betrayed her. "Sorry, old girl." He rumples her droopy ears with his right hand.

Everett practices moving his left foot back and forth from the accelerator to the brake and strains his eyes for the next exit. He hopes it's one with motels. He's tired. Kansas laps his right leg. He can't feel the texture of her tongue. He can see her saliva but is strangely removed from the slimy wetness. He kneads the furry flesh around her throat. She laps his hand. His hand registers the sensations.

A rest area is coming up. He'd hoped for a hot shower, but the rest area will have to do. He exits the freeway. At least

Kansas is welcome here. There's even a dog walk. She needs water. Later he'll stop for dog food.

Everett parks as close as he can to the cement-block building. It has all he needs—food in machines, a telephone, restrooms. He can sleep in the car if he has to. He tickles Kansas behind her ears, rolls his window down, tells himself his right leg is there whether he can feel it or not and hoists himself out of the car onto his left leg. He inches his way around the car, steadying himself on the hood. A family is eating sandwiches on a blanket in the sun. Under the nearest oak tree, a trucker sits at a picnic table, watching Everett instead of the woman talking to him. The trucker nods. Everett nods back, palming his way past his headlights, then hopping over to the table, trying to keep his face composed and natural. "Bad leg," Everett says.

"Bummer," the trucker says. He scratches the two-day-old whiskers on his chin. His left arm is tanner than the rest of him and makes him look heavier on that side. The woman turns to Everett and frowns in sympathy. Two deep lines run vertically between her eyebrows like train tracks.

"Looks like trouble," she says in a soothing drawl. Kentucky is his guess. She's wearing blue jeans and work boots, and Everett feels overdressed in his prissy polo and shorts. He pulls his gut in—as far as it goes, that is.

"It's temporary," Everett says. He can't stand pity. He smiles at the woman, and she smiles back. She's pretty when she smiles, though her bottom teeth overlap some. The train tracks almost disappear. Her puffy shoulder-length hair adds

fullness to her cheeks and makes her look younger than the
lines suggest. Rosie cut her hair short after Valley was born.
Said she couldn't manage a baby and long hair, too.

"How about I bring you something to drink?" the woman says.

"Thanks. And can I bother you for some water for my
dog?" Everett reaches for his wallet, but the woman has
headed away from the pop machines. She must be one of
those Southerners who sips on home-steeped iced tea all the
way down the highway. Everett pictures the lipstick smudge
on the edge of her plastic cup, though he doesn't remember
that she wore lipstick. He finds the thought slightly erotic.

The trucker rises from the picnic table and steps deftly
from its attached bench. "I'm outa here," he says. "Good
luck."

"You, too," Everett says as though he is in no more need
of luck than anyone else on the road.

Kansas is hanging out the car window, paws over the
rolled-down window. He pats his thigh and calls her to come.
She hesitates for a moment, then backs down onto the seat
and launches herself out the window, scrambling a bit when
she hits the pavement and letting out a yelp. Everett winces.
But Kansas recovers quickly and comes bounding over, tail
wagging, to stick her nose in his lap. He can't feel her muzzle
on his leg but waffles her ears to greet her. "Sorry, girl," he
says. "I'd have come for you if I could."

Everett hears a door slam. The woman emerges from the
shadow of a motor home carrying two plastic tumblers and

a plastic tub. The motor home is pulling a horse trailer, which explains the work boots.

"Here we go," she drawls, stretching *go* into a two-syllable word. Kansas bounds over to her, sniffs at her legs, then barks once and backs off. "Hel-lo, sweet pea."

She puts the tumblers down on the table, then reaches out to Kansas. "What's your name?"

"Kansas," Everett says.

She reaches her hand out to Kansas. "Hel-lo, Kansas. I'm Fay. Pleased to meet you." Kansas backs into a crouch, haunches in the air, and barks, tail wagging. "You smell Patches, don't you, baby?" She pats the plastic tub on the ground. Kansas sniffs, then laps at it eagerly.

"You were a thirsty girl, weren't you?" she says.

"You have a dog?" Everett asks.

"A pony." She nods over to the horse trailer.

Everett takes a sip of the drink she's brought him. It's lemonade, though she hasn't added sugar and it's sour. He takes another sip, cheeks and tongue involuntarily sucking his teeth. It's surprisingly refreshing. "Thanks. It's real good," he says. No suited young clerk at a motel would have treated him so well. Compassion doesn't come with a degree in hotel management.

"No problem," she drawls. "My rig's broken down. We're kind of camping out here until I can get some help."

"What's the trouble?"

"Oh, I didn't mean that." She turns away as if she has embarrassed herself and reaches for Kansas again. The dog advances toward her cautiously, nose working overtime.

"But I mean it. Seriously. You've helped me. Maybe I can return the favor."

"You can hardly walk."

"I have some mechanical skill. Describe the problem."

"I was driving down the road this morning, goin' to a carnival in Troy—Patches and I give pony rides to the kids—when the air-conditioning quit. I didn't notice right away, so I'm not sure how long it was. Then I started to get hot and the radio went off and I saw the sign for the roadside rest. Nothin' happened when I hit the gas, and I was just coasting along, hoping momentum would get me here. It was a stretch with Patches on the back slowing me down."

"That's your alternator. Maybe I can drive over—climb in and take a look. At least you'll know what to tell the mechanic. Have you got Triple-A?" Everett instantly feels stupid for asking. People who run carnival concessions don't buy Triple-A. She's been kind to him and he's one-upped her. But she seems not to have noticed.

She shakes her head.

He puts on his hearty voice. "That's why I do. I'll just stick around till they come. You lead. C'mon Kansas."

Kansas looks up, startled. She has made herself a nest in the family's abandoned blanket. They are now playing volleyball with a beach ball and no net. Everett supports his weight on the table and gets to his feet. Fay takes his right arm and puts it around her shoulders and tells him not to be afraid to lean. She's amazingly strong. Her shoulders are sinewy and her upper arms much firmer than Rosie's. She'd look great in a skinny-strap tee. But what's he thinking? He shouldn't be looking at another woman's arms, let alone comparing. He mustn't notice the way Fay's breast presses into his ribs or the way her surrounding hand tugs on the flesh of his midriff. Kansas dances at their feet, circling around the twosome and wagging her tail. Fay puts her left leg next to Everett's right so they move along as in a three-legged race. When he gets to the car hood, he transfers his weight to the hood and tells Fay he'll meet her at the rig. When he opens the driver's door, Kansas jumps in ahead of him and stands expectantly on the seat while Everett eases himself in. "Good girl," he says. She wags her tail.

Everett parks as close as he can to Fay's rig and reverses the process. Fay waits patiently and rewards him with a smile when he makes it to the car hood, as though he's accomplished something marvelous they've been working on for weeks. Kansas runs to the horse trailer, her nose to the pavement, and barks. Patches stamps and the trailer shakes. Kansas barks again. Fay laughs. "Let's see how she likes my RV."

Everett waits while Fay pulls the step out and opens the door. "You'd better go first," she says. "I'll be right behind you."

Kansas charges into the motor home first and disappears from sight, nose to the carpet. Everett braces himself with hands on either side of the door and climbs in. There's a captain's chair on the passenger side in front, swiveled around to face the dinette, and he lunges toward it. The right armrest stabs him in the thigh and he teeters. Fay steadies him from the left. He tips into the seat. Thank god he didn't fall on the floor. He pictures himself in a heap, bruised on one side and totally numb on the other, as if one leg's been cut off. It didn't happen, but still, the blood rushes to his face.

Kansas is exploring the back of the rig. Everett can see an unmade bed through the narrow doorway. The sheets are yellow with roses, which surprises him, but he averts his eyes quickly, as if Fay's caught him looking down her blouse. Instead he looks around the room he's sitting in. The design is amazing, the way they've fit a kitchen, dining room and seating area in such a small space. If he bought one of these, he could ramble around the countryside with his house all around him. He wouldn't be immobile and dependent, even if he couldn't leave the driver's seat. Unless his leg prevented the driving, that is. Then Rosie would have to drive.

"Thanks for having me in," he says. "I've never been inside one of these."

Fay shrugs as if embarrassed for a man to admire something she owns. "I bought it at one of those bank auctions. It has a lot of mileage, but whoever lost it took good care of it. I keep thinking the guy got sick and they had terrible medical bills. That's probably silly. It's just a feeling I have."

The thought depresses Everett. Fay refills the water tub for Kansas and busies herself putting the lemonade back in the miniature refrigerator. Their used glasses are sitting in the little sink now. The gas stove has four burners, like a real stove only closer together. It's like a doll's house. Rosie would love it. Overhead cabinets line the perimeter of the ceiling.

Fay points to a carpeted box, wide as the space between the two front seats. "The engine's under there." She lifts the cover. He doesn't have to move from the chair. He tinkers here and there just to look official. He already knows the alternator's bad.

"Did your battery light come on?" he asks.

"Yeah. But I didn't see how the battery could be low while I was driving. Doesn't it charge as you drive?"

"Only if the alternator's doing its job." Everett reaches for his wallet. "Here. Take my Triple-A card. Call the 800 number and tell them your alternator's gone. You'll need the make and model of your rig and the mile marker for the rest stop."

She crosses her arms and shakes her head. "No way. I couldn't. No."

"Why not? I bought the coverage. I can use it how I want to. I just need to be here when they come, to show my license and my membership card. You've been good to me. Let me help you."

She reaches for the card. "Okay, but I'm paying you back."

He wonders what she means—if she thinks he's offering to pay the repairs.

When Fay has gone off to the phone, Everett snoops around his chair. A pair of wraparound sunglasses, a magazine called *Practical Horseman*, a few cheap ballpoints, some cassette tapes and two crumpled gas receipts block the defroster. Everett smooths one receipt to see what it costs to fill one of these vehicles. Forty-seven gallons. Whew. At least she has a Visa card, so he won't have to foot the bill. Her scrawled signature looks like Fay Quinelle. She should save her receipts to deduct from her taxes. Nah. She's a carnival act. She doesn't claim her income.

He glances at the cassette tapes. Roy Orbison. Patsy Cline. Hank Williams. Valley would hate this stuff. Everett likes it, but he wouldn't admit it. Valley would call him a briar hopper, same as everyone else in Eden.

Beneath the glove compartment are several thumbed copies of *Woman's World* and a worn paperback. *The Thorn Birds*. He picks it up and scans the jacket blurb—forbidden love in the Australian outback—and puts it back down. The glove compartment tempts him, but he resists. Hanging from the rearview mirror is a blond girl's picture. She's smiling and her teeth look too big for her head. Eight years old is his guess. Valley was about that age when her adult teeth finally came in. He looks for resemblance to Fay but in the moment can't recall what Fay looks like.

Kansas is sniffing at a door near the bedroom. It has to be the bathroom. He's suddenly got to pee. With the kitchen counter on one side and the table on the other, he can make his way back there bearing his weight on his arms. He looks out the window for Fay. She's still at the pay phone. He hefts his weight forward out of the seat. The rig lurches with his motion.

The bathroom is small and smells sweetly of a chemical toilet. The tiny washbowl and mirror are inside the shower stall to the left of the toilet. There's an oval of pink soap and a tube of Ultra Brite down in the basin. Rosie always buys Crest, which suddenly seems boring. Ultra Brite is about singles smiling at one another across a bar or a pool table.

Everett braces himself in the doorway and unzips. Kansas tries to worm her head between his knees. "Go away," he tells her. A small bathroom could be a problem when he can't walk at all. But surely it could be modified. A rig a few feet longer would have more space. He can afford to have it custom built. Everett finishes up and rinses his hands in the little sink. He opens the cupboard under the sink to look for a towel but quickly closes the door again. He's certain he saw a bottle of Old Spice. Fay is married.

Fay is walking back across the parking lot when he settles into the passenger seat again. He wishes his leg would wake up. Rosie loses her sense of proportion at dusk, as though darkness automatically brings evil down on the world. It's also when she gets sexy—but then, to Rose, sex and evil are two sides of the same coin. If his leg improves, he'll call and say he's going to be late. If not, he'll say he got tied up with business.

"How'd you make out?" he asks when Fay climbs onboard. She's not wearing a wedding ring, he sees. But then, he's not wearing his, either. His hands swell in the summer heat. The metal gives him a rash.

"Great," she says, exhaling deeply as if she's come a long distance. "They offered to tow me to a garage either tonight or tomorrow morning. I figured it might be better for Patches to stay here tonight since it's too late for anyone to work on the rig now. Besides, I can't leave you stranded. That dinette folds down into a bed. You're welcome to stay. I thought I'd let Patches out to graze after dark."

"Did you tell them you're towing a trailer?"

The train tracks dig deep between her eyebrows. "Will it make a difference?"

"I don't know. If it does, you could probably leave it and come back later. Nobody would drive off with a horse."

Fay bends down to pat Kansas. The dog sniffs at her pockets and noses into them. "Maybe she'll fit in here."

Everett strains to see her face—to see if she's kidding. She's not. He's sitting with a woman who would put a horse in the house. Rosie would never believe it.

"I can't worry about it." Fay pushes her hands away from her body as if worry has come too close. "I have a repair bill instead of two-days' income, but everything's worked out so far and I'm going to trust that this will, too."

Kansas laps Fay's hands. Everett arranges his right leg on the engine casing, ignoring what sounds like a request. He doesn't want to get that involved. He nods toward the picture. "That your daughter?"

Fay smiles adoringly. "That's my Janice."

"I guess she's home with her father."

The train tracks appear again and a little gust of air escapes Fay's mouth. "Her father flew the coop long ago. Took off with the Queen of Fried Dough. They deserved each other, too."

Everett looks up at the cabinets around the ceiling and estimates the storage space. He doesn't know what to say.

"Enough about me," Fay says the second before his silence gets so awkward, they won't recover. "How about some soup and a sandwich? It's not great, but it's better than pop and candy. I've got beer, too. And peanuts. They're my treat at the end of the day."

Everett pictures her slumped in the captain's chair, reading *The Thorn Birds* with her beer and peanuts. She looks old and tired. "Or we could go for a bite somewhere in my car. My treat."

"Are you kidding? This is Nowhereville. Besides, if you fall, I might not be able to get you back up."

She has a point. And he might like to have a meal in the motor home—to try it out. Maybe Valley liked the tree house for the same reason. Having home miniaturized and relocated made it seem special. "Okay," he says. "Thanks."

Fay nods toward Kansas. "What will she eat? How about some oatmeal? I have instant."

"Anything you got's fine. She's not particular."

Fay mixes the oatmeal with hot water from the tap. "Mom used to make hot cereal for our dog when she was a puppy. Farina, I think." Everett likes the idea of cooking for a dog. Rosie would think it was stupid. Fay puts the oatmeal down for Kansas and watches her gobble it up, then takes a beer from the fridge. She pops the top and passes it to him. "I hope the can's okay. It saves on dishes."

"The can's great."

She fishes a jar of peanuts from the fridge. He sticks out his hand, palm up. "No bowl, either." She smiles and shakes him a handful from the jar before popping a few in her mouth.

"You're a good sport." Fay points with the jar to a lever on the chair's stanchion. "That seat reclines, you know. I ordered it from Sears. A Christmas present from Mom."

Everett thinks back to the years he was struggling to get his business off the ground, when Christmas was the only excuse for buying nonessentials. Now he can buy what he wants, when he wants it. But Fay might never make it there. Most people didn't. He takes a swig of beer and thinks how much worse off he'd be if he had MS and no insurance. His attitude toward Fay has been nothing but selfish. Fay is raising a child alone and hardly fretted about what is probably a major financial setback.

She takes a box of sugar cubes from the cupboard and puts several in her jeans pocket. "I've got to feed Patches. Don't go away now." When she smiles, she looks young again. He swivels the chair and watches in the side mirror as she walks back to the trailer. Her buns are muscular and firm.

Fifteen minutes later Fay returns, a rag hanging from her back pocket. Earthy scents, hay and manure, cling to her clothing and hair. She fetches another beer from the fridge and settles into the driver's seat with it, swiveling it to face him so her legs are out from under the wheel. He can't help noticing that her thighs don't spread far, even flattened against the seat, and her stomach doesn't fill her lap. He forces his eyes to her face. Perspiration has glued a few stray wisps to her forehead, and a piece of hay is stuck in her hair.

Kansas has settled on the engine casing between the two front seats. Fay's been nice to let Kansas have the run of the motor home. "Will I get to see Patches?" he asks.

"I'll get her out after supper. She's an old pony, not good for much besides pony rides, but she's mine. Janice loves her."

"Couldn't Janice travel with you?"

"I don't really want her standing there while the carnies hit on me."

Somehow Fay can say this and he knows she isn't just bragging about being attractive. It's a real problem for her.

Fay sips her beer. "A kid can only go on so many rides before the fun wears off. I'd rather she stay with Mom—not that I don't miss her. I dread Fridays. She cries when I leave." The back of Fay's right hand wipes her forehead. She gets up, though she's nowhere near finished her beer. She takes Everett's empty can. "Talk to me while I make the sandwiches." She takes another beer from the fridge, pops the lid and hands it to him without asking if he wants it. "Turkey sandwich okay?"

"Whatever you have is great." He wonders how beer affects MS. His blood feels thick in his veins—as if it's moving more slowly. He's been afraid to drink since the diagnosis.

She stacks bread slices, two high, in two piles on the tiny counter. "Mayo or mustard?"

"Both," he says, though he usually has one or the other. Tonight is different. He drinks his beer and watches her ringless fingers stack the shaved turkey onto the bread. She peels a slice of Swiss cheese from a package of eight. The cheese looks cared for with its paper sleeves, not like the clumsy chunks Rose buys that you have to slice yourself.

She looks over at him. "Tomatoes aren't in yet. Sorry." Her eyes are brown and soft as a cow's. She lays leaves of iceberg—the kind Rosie scornfully calls hamburger lettuce—over the cheese, then the other slice of bread and presses down as she cuts it diagonally into triangles. The bread is soft, three loaves for a dollar. The knife grooves it along the cut. Triangles are more exciting than Rosie's rectangles.

He watches Fay crank around a can of tomato soup. The saucepans are stowed in the oven. He wonders if they rattle when the rig is moving. The soup falls from the can with a soft plop. Fay adds milk and stirs it over a low flame on the tiny stove. Her hips stir slightly in an unconscious hula as her arm circles. She stops stirring only to sip her beer. Her lips look moist in the dusky light. Finally she lowers the flame and gets two plastic bowls down from the cupboard.

"You getting sleepy?" she drawls. To Everett, her speech sounds slower now.

"Must be. I'm not very good company."

"We'll get a bed made up for you as soon as you've had your supper." She hands him a plate with the bowl of soup and the sandwich. "Another beer?"

He hasn't finished this one. He needs to call Rose. He looks out at the concrete block building with the nearest phone. One hundred yards is a long way. "Why not?" he says.

This one will be gone soon. He needs to wash the sandwich down with something.

They eat, watching dusk settle over the grounds. Fewer cars are stopped outside now. Except for the occasional car making a bathroom stop, his car and Fay's rig have the passenger vehicle section to themselves. The cars swish by on the highway, headed for motels presumably, farther up the road. Lightning bugs flash, here and there, close to the grass. The bees have abandoned duty at the teeming trash containers. Diesel engines drone in the background. Kansas naps on the engine casing between them, head down on her front paws.

Finally, Fay moves from the driver's seat, takes Everett's plate and stacks it on top of her own, then fits both in the tiny sink. "I guess it's dark enough to put Patches out."

Everett leans forward, forgetting he can't get up. "I'll do the dishes."

She pushes him back in the chair with an index finger. "You'll sit right there. I'll bring my girl around for you to see."

When Fay returns leading the pony, Everett opens his window. Patches is light brown with big white splotches all over her body. Her face is vertically divided—half white, half brown—with big, intelligent eyes set far apart and lids with real lashes. He's amazed at how small she is. Now he's certain Fay was serious. Patches *would* fit in the motor home. He tries not to think about the poor mechanic who would have to fix the engine with a horse watching over his shoulder. He wants to return Fay's enthusiasm for Kansas by admiring Patches, but he's afraid he'll laugh.

"She's real pretty," he says, unsure if *pretty* is a word you use for a horse. She's got a pink clip in the bit of mane that falls onto her forehead. It brings out a slightly pink cast on the white side of her nose and looks ridiculous—like the dumb things Rosie used to do with Valley's hair. He points to it and says, "A clip?"

Fay laughs, and Patches lowers her face into Fay's bosom as though she thinks the two are laughing at her. "Janice put it on before I left so I'd remember to come back. As if I'd forget."

The barrette looks different to Everett now. Still stupid, but he's glad Fay left it there. He watches her take a sugar cube from her back pocket and feed it to Patches. He wonders if it matters to Valley if he comes back. He might like knowing he made a difference to the girl, as Fay does to Janice.

Fay strokes Patches's nose fondly. "She's a paint. Indians ride them in Westerns."

"I thought she looked familiar," Everett says. "Do they all have pink noses?"

Fay laughs. "That's sunburn. She's out in parking lots all day. You'd get sunburned, too."

Everett takes a closer look at the pony's hide. The white splotches on her rump aren't pink. A tiny fly is walking along her flank and the skin covering the muscle shudders. Patches stamps one hoof and Fay shoos the fly off. He envies the pony. She can feel tiny fly feet, and he can't even feel Kansas's paws—but then, with all the flies around, Patches might like to go numb.

Fay points to an open grassy area where the motor home will block the truckers' view of the horse. "I'm going to tether her over there for a while." She leads the pony away from the window and bends down to screw a metal stake into the ground. Patches goes nosing for the sugar cubes in Fay's back pocket and nudges her off balance. Fay crumples in a heap, laughing. Then she scrambles effortlessly to her feet and throws her arms around the pony's neck as if returning the affection. Everett reaches for Kansas and strokes her hind end. She lifts her head off her paws and gives him a quizzical look, listens with her ears cocked and puts her head back down.

Everett turns back to watch Fay. She is digging around in Patches's hooves with some doodad. He is suddenly exhausted and wishes she would finish fooling with her horse. He takes another swig of beer and settles his head back on the chair. His hand dangles over the arm of the chair, and Kansas's nose pokes at his fingers. "Good girl. Whadda good girl." The rhythm of his doggy talk makes him even drowsier. His lungs inflate and deflate slowly. Her ears feel silky under his palm.

Everett dreams of a large underground cavern filled with bats. They're all over the ceiling, pairs of eyes, and all he has is a slingshot and gemstones, rubies and emeralds, all over the floor of the cave. When he manages to darken one eye, the bat flies away and he's unable to blind it completely. One of the bats lands on his back, picks him up and carries him to the top of the cave, where he, too, can see everything. The cave glows from the light of all the gems, and he sees a huge pit he couldn't see from the ground. The pit fills most of the cave's floor. He can't imagine where he sat that he didn't fall down it.

CHAPTER 9

A mile outside Eden, Snake pulls his pickup truck off Miller Road. The seat upholstery is all ripped and spilling out on the passenger side of the pickup, so Valley is forced to sit close to Snake. She's so close, in fact, she can smell the cigarettes on his breath. He snaps the cassette into the tape deck. The tape cues in near the end of "Love is Alright Tonight," and he puts his arm around her shoulder. She doesn't mind. There's really nowhere else to put it in such close quarters.

His tape isn't really new. Joanie has had *Working Class Dog* since Christmas, so Snake must have meant *new to him*. Snake sings along with Rick Springfield, his voice a soft baritone following the melody on "Jessie's Girl." Valley is too shy to join in, but she hears the harmony in her head and knows their voices would sound good together. At the end of the song, when his eyes are closed and he's flowing on the overtones of the last notes, he pulls her closer and whispers some of the words to the song. She drops her head against his so that they're listening to "Hole in My Heart" nearly ear-to-ear. He doesn't seem to know the words, but he hums snatches of the melody, and she can feel his breath on her neck. The way his body moves slightly, she knows he really hears, that the music means something to him. "Carry Me Away" begins, and his lips graze her earlobe. "You don't know how beautiful you are." She turns to face him. His eyes are focused on her mouth. His lips nip at hers.

So this is what Joanie means when she talks about "making out." His lips are soft and taste of licorice.

"Sit in my lap," Snake whispers between kisses. The music plays on, but the only words she hears are his. "I want you close." He draws her sideways across his lap, her feet trailing on the passenger seat. Her weight is nothing to him. He is either very strong or she is floating, literally "carried away." The steering wheel grooves her midriff, but she barely notices. The hair of his forearm tickles her neck. Rippling sensations race through her like sixteenth notes. Valley drops her head back against the driver's window and closes her eyes. She holds her breath and hangs in mid-air waiting for him to nuzzle her mouth with his.

Her T-shirt has pulled loose from the waist of her shorts and she feels his palm against her ribs. It happened when he pulled her over. He's just getting comfortable. There's so little room. His hand is under her shirt, kneading her midriff. It feels so good she hardly notices when the snap at her waist pops and the zipper teeth release. But then he shoves the band of her bra up over her breasts. She opens her eyes, tenses and twists her shoulders. His biceps harden. His mouth locks on to hers. Snake's eyes flash green in the light of a passing car. She can't speak, let alone scream. He is suddenly enormous. His tongue pries at the crevice between her lips, and warm saliva slathers her mouth. She tries to turn her head, but everywhere she turns, he follows. She can't breathe.

Valley pushes her shoulder into his pectorals. His muscles contract, rock-hard, gripping her to him. Her right breast flattens against his chest. His thighs cup her bottom. She digs her heels into the bench seat, but can't get the leverage to free her hips. Her heart pounds double time. She sees herself chewed up and spit out, dumped in a heap on the roadside with roadkill. The scream of a trapped rabbit roils up from her gut, bypasses her sealed lips and explodes into her head. With one enormous effort she forces her hand up past her chest and thrusts her fist upward at his jaw.

His head snaps back. His legs release. She scuttles from his lap. He grabs her wrist. Her teeth close on his forearm. He yelps and flings her off. She crashes into the passenger door, cheekbone hitting glass, fumbles for the handle, falls out and scrambles away, crouching doglike.

She hears him holler, "*Bitch.*"

Tall trees line the roadside, black columns against the dusky sky. She plows into the tangle of underbrush, flattens herself to the ground and pauses to listen. Nothing. He isn't coming. She gets to her feet and hurries deeper into the woods. A strange exhilaration fills her as again and again she sees herself hitting him in the jaw.

Headlights flicker off the tree trunks ahead like strobe

lighting. Route 4. She stops before stepping from the shadows, stands straight, pulls her shirt from her sweaty skin and picks burrs from her shorts. Her skin crawls with unseen insects. She rubs down each leg. Branches have clawed her calves and ankles. Her hands smear blood around. She sucks its sticky warmth from her fingers and scans the roadway. The light down the road has to be Wheeler's Store. Oncoming headlamps search her out through thick magnifying lenses. The whine and taillights of a black sports car disappear around a bend in the road. Valley crosses the road in darkness and turns north.

Now that she can breathe again, she begins to shake. She wonders that one minute she'd been enjoying Snake's playful teasing and the next she was nailed down. Valley hugs herself, kicks a stone, announces to the woods that she is okay. The sidewalk begins. She is at the edge of town. Ahead, streetlights cast ponds of light on the road.

Rural Ohio houses—predictable arrangements of white rectangles—line the street, sitting on napkins of grass. Fences and flower gardens, also rectangular, surround the lawns. Daisy petals gleam in the moonlight. At the house on the corner of Elm Street Mrs. Hinkle's bed sheets flap from the clothesline like fettered ghosts.

Valley wonders how she freed the hand that hit Snake. Maybe her mother is right. Maybe there are such things as angels—winged creatures who swoop to the rescue in the nick of time.

The uneven sidewalk ends right before her house. The

road turns and the land rises to their gingerbread Victorian in a gentle slope of lawn before flattening out to join acres of farmland. Light shines from the downstairs windows in a row of rectangles. She blurs her eyes to see her house from a distance. Her classmates envy her. She doesn't have to feed chickens, clean stalls or throw hay bales onto a flatbed truck. She doesn't have to scrub her knuckles with lemons or dig dirt out from under her fingernails every night. She can babysit for her spending money. They think babysitting is easy, that work isn't hard unless your muscles get sore. They've never witnessed a Mary Jane Walker temper tantrum. And the noise. Where were her friends today when Joey Harper screamed until she lost her mind?

Valley is careful to walk on the lawn rather than crunch the gravel in the drive. She crouches beneath the living room and kitchen windows. The kitchen door is open. "Who's there? Is somebody there?" Her mother appears at the door, squinting through the screen into the darkness. Valley scrambles into the lilac bush.

"Everett? Is that you?"

Valley imagines herself stepping from the lilac leaves, opening the screen, crying in her mother's arms and telling her everything—wrapped in the quilt pieced from her childhood dresses. But it wouldn't be like that. Her mother's eyes would get big and the ritual do-you-realizes and you-could-have-been-hurts would follow. Her father would hear the commotion, show up in the doorway and vow to string the jerk up by his fingernails. Her mother would want to call in the priest. Her father would call Ed Dudley and alert the police. Both would say they told her so. That it proved what they've always said: that she's always been one to learn the hard way.

Valley doesn't move from the lilac bush. The kitchen light shines off her mother's hair in a halo. Her mother's brows dip into a frown. Valley holds her breath until the kitchen window darkens and her mother disappears.

The tree house her father built the summer she turned eight still sits in the crook of the old oak. Of all the gifts he'd made over the years, the tree house had been the best—a place to get away with her girlfriends to giggle and talk, safe from eavesdropping mothers and their constant demands to practice instruments, do chores, get off the phone, finish homework. She heads there now for a different reason. Tonight she longs to be safe, surrounded by her father's self-made world, though the boards nailed to the tree as footholds are skewed now or missing. She tests one with her weight. It gives way, a bent nail sticking from its center. She tosses the slat aside and begins to climb the remaining rungs without trying them first. The limb that holds the tree house is only eight feet up. She can fall that far without screaming.

The floorboards are covered in last fall's broken acorn and walnut shells. The squirrels have been busy. She brushes the shells aside, wondering that life can skitter out of control as easily. The tree feels sturdy against her back. She fingers for her necklace. *It's gone.* Her stomach turns over and tears spring to her eyes. It's too much. All the privileges she's

waited to turn sixteen for—making money, driving, dating—
aren't wonderful at all. They start out fine—she's cruising
down route 68 in her mother's Galaxy, calm as can be—when
a hay wagon drops a bale right in front of her. Brakes squeal
and phone poles cross her windshield at crazy angles. She
ends up in the ditch. Valley rests her head against the bark.
So far she's gotten by—with the car, with Joey, with Snake.
In her mind's eye she sees Snake's head rebounding off the
headrest. She leans forward, closes her eyes and bashes her
head against the tree.

CHAPTER 10

Everett wakens in Fay's passenger chair. Red digital numbers leer through the darkness: 2:43. He forgot to call Rosie. It's too late now. She'll be asleep. The dinette booth has been collapsed into a bed and made up with sheets. Fay's light is off back in the bedroom, so she must be asleep. Everett stands before he realizes what he's done. His leg is back. He can actually feel it. On the engine cover, Kansas struggles to her feet, heads to the door, and scratches on it with her front paw. "Gotta go out, girl?" Everett whispers hoarsely, leaving the scratch in his throat to clear when he's outside and won't disturb Fay. He's not tired anymore. He walks to the door feeling powerful and competent. "Come on. I'll go with you."

In the cool night air, Everett looks up to the navy summer sky. Orion's belt and the Big Dipper are particularly bright. The moon is full and spherical, not flat like a cutout. Kansas squats on a grassy strip. Everett hears her stream of pee hit the dry ground and feels the urge to unload the beers. What the heck, he thinks, glancing around to see that no one is looking, and joins her. She sniffs the ground his stream soaked and laps his right ankle. He feels the texture of her tongue and wants to do a little dance. He'll call Rosie after all—not worry about waking her. He'll tell her not to worry, that life is good, and he'll be home as soon as he can get there. He puts Kansas back in the rig, then heads to the phone with the easy gait of one who takes one hundred yards for granted. He punches in his telephone and credit card numbers. The phone rings. She doesn't pick up immediately. He's glad she isn't waiting, all worried, by the phone. But then it goes on and on. He lets it ring, not wanting to hang up just as she gets there. But she doesn't get there. No one answers. Where could she be at three in the morning? And Valley. Where is she? He hangs up and walks back to the motor home, solitary and deflated. The fact that he can walk no longer seems so wonderful.

"You okay?" Fay says when he climbs back into the rig.

"Yeah. My leg's all better." That must sound strange to her. What injury comes and goes like that? What if she thinks he was faking it before? He can hardly believe it's the same leg himself. He flexes his knee to prove he can do it, stamping his foot up and down like Patches. Yep. All there.

Fay appears in the doorway, her figure backlit by the bedroom. He can see the outline of her body through a thin white gown. Her hair is messy and fluffed out from her shoulders, as in a scene from some movie. He can't see her face. "I forgot to give you a pillow," she says. She has dragged hers off the bed. She bends over to place the pillow at the head of the bed, and he looks down the gown's gaping front to the inverted V of her breasts. When she straightens up, his hands find her breasts through the cotton. She moans and tilts her face up to his. He nuzzles her nose, and presses his cheekbone into hers. Their mouths meet and linger. Her hands fumble at his waist. He backs up to the bed, feels it behind his legs. His hands burrow under her gown, one to her breast, the other to the nest between her legs. She is already damp.

She bends to slide his shorts and boxers down. He sits. Her tongue stripes his left leg. She lifts her head to ask, "Sure you're okay?" then laughs when she sees. He doesn't answer. There's no turning back.

Her gown is off and her knees are on either side of his legs. She contracts her stomach in a feline arch. His hands confirm that her thighs are slender and her buttocks firm. His boxers bind his ankles, but otherwise he's free. Her stomach and midriff are taut; her breasts reach for him. His pores open like flowers as she lowers herself onto his chest, her legs parted and her fingers guiding his eager penis. It slides easily into the groove, and in he dives, deeper and deeper. She tilts her hips forward and back. He matches her movements. The motor home rocks. The pans rattle in the stove. He blocks it out, rocks on, focusing on his body. "Come 'ere, girl," he moans into Fay's hair.

A cold nose bumps his elbow. Tries to burrow under it. He swats with his hand. Kansas shakes her head and her ears flap. She bounds onto the bed, knocks into him, throws his arm up with her snout. He opens his eyes to her face in his.

"Oh, hell," Everett says. Fay lifts her head from the nook

of his neck. Strands of her hair are stuck to his lips. He spits them off. "Damn dog."

"Go awa-ay now, baby," she says in her gentle drawl, pushing Kansas from Everett's arm. But Kansas wags her tail and comes back for more.

Fay slides over to one side, and Everett swats Kansas's backside. "Dumb dog." He heaves her onto the floor. Her head hits the stove. She yelps. Fay mewls in sympathy. Everett gets up, grabbing his boxers to his waist, and finds Kansas. "She's okay." He strokes her back and head.

The effort has broken the spell, banished all urgency. He's a paunchy middle-aged man again. Fay lies back on the bed, her breasts flat as deflated balloons. "I can't do this, Fay." He picks Kansas up. "I'm sorry."

Fay rolls onto her side and props up on one elbow. "You sure?"

"Look, I made a mistake. I'm sorry."

Fay pulls the sheet over herself. "Wife at home?"

"Yeah. And a daughter."

Fay's head turns toward the wall. "I hope Janice turns out better'n me."

"It's not that, Fay. Really. You're the best person I've met today. I mean it."

Fay sits up, holding the sheet to her chest like a shield. "I mean it, too."

It takes all his willpower to keep himself from putting the dog down and returning to her side. The pain of her loneliness has actual substance, the way his father's had the nights after his mother left. But the tiny bed made from the dinette table looks pathetic, a toy bed for pretend love. The woman lives in a factory-decorated tin can—a poor substitute for a home, especially with no one to share it.

It's not fair. Fay is a good person. She deserves better than she's getting, but as each jerk deserts her, she thinks she's worthless. It's a damn shame, and better that he caught himself than be added to her list of users. "I have to go home now," he says, not knowing how else to end it. He puts Kansas on the floor and disappears into the bathroom, stepping into the shower stall until she's had time to collect herself and go back to the bedroom.

His reflection stares back at him from the mirror over the sink. His hair stands on end. A shadow covers his cheeks and chin. Who is this slob? What the hell does he think he's doing? He runs cold water into the basin, puts his wrists under the faucet, splashes cold water on his face and combs his hair. It's not much improvement, and he wonders how hard he'll have to hit the wall before he learns.

Everett pulls out of the rest area, anxious to drive away into the night. He shouldn't have loaned Fay his Triple-A card. Can she use it to trace him? Hound him? Tell Rosie? He should have given her cash for repairs and made up a name for himself. Some name like Reginald, a name he'd never recognize as himself.

His right foot presses the accelerator. Kansas is curled on the seat next to his thigh. Her fur is satiny against his skin when the nap is flat, prickly when he pushes against the grain. It's amazing the way his leg is numb one minute and fine the next. Maybe this MS is a trick of his mind. A very bad dream. But the Technicolor is unbeatably lifelike—even in the dark.

Route 75 South. Home. He's out of cigarettes. He'd like to bite his nails, but his fingers smell as though he's been cleaning fish. The apricot tint of her shampoo lingers on his skin. He rolls the windows down. Kansas gets to her feet to sniff the warm wind. Everett wants to bury his nose in Kansas's neck and inhale pure dog. Anything's better than the stench of his conscience.

He pictures Rosie at home, sleeping on her side, breasts stacked like loaves of rising dough. Fay's teats were lean and pointed. Skim milk compared to Rosie's cream. Damn, he's been a fool.

The highway's broken white lines pass by him. Blip. Blip. Blip. It's soothing, really. He focuses on the lines and lets himself become one with the car seat, then the car itself, so he, Kansas and the other cars are all one unit moving down the highway.

The skyline of Dayton rises up ahead of him, dimly lit by yellow lights that line the freeway. The Art Institute with its circular stair and red roof tiles, the pencil-shaped carillon at Deeds Park, the Reynolds and Reynolds clock tower with its little blue roof. Five-twenty. He'll be home soon. Safe, if not sound.

The house is silent in the darkness. With Kansas tucked under one arm, he opens the door and heads for the

bathroom, climbing the stairs in darkness. Outside the
bathroom door he sets Kansas down and tells her to stay. Her
tail thunks against the doorframe, but he closes the door and
listens while she plops herself down on the floor to wait.
Then he peels his clothes off, examining his shorts and shirt
for telltale signs—a hair the wrong color, a lipstick stain. He
buries his nose in them, not sure whether the smell is on his
clothes or in his nostrils. He grabs Rosie's can of Secret and
sprays it into the air, holding his clothes below where the
mist will settle on them. Then he throws them in the
hamper.

For once, he is grateful for the Irish Spring Rosie loves.
He's never liked its peculiar perfume, thought it made him
smell like a sissy. Now he lathers it all over, making suds
while standing clear of the shower spray. When he's certain
he's covered every inch of skin, he steps into the warm water,
watches the suds rinse down his legs and then swirl down the
drain. He finds a clean towel in the cupboard under the sink
and rubs his skin until it turns pink and his hairs stand up.
Before the mirror is clear of steam, he dries a hole large
enough to see his face and tweaks his nose hairs with the
special trimmer Rose gave him for Christmas last year. Maybe
the smell is in his nose hairs. He brushes his teeth and takes
a swig of Listerine. He sloshes and swallows, waits while it
burns down his throat. It will kill Fay's germs. If only there
were Listerine for his conscience. He's showered, but he is
not clean. Fay's vagina is wrapped around him like a sleeve.

Everett shaves, then stares at his face. His mouth puckers

in little lines around his lips. It's his mother's mouth, small and pinched, not fleshy like his father's bedtime kisses planted squarely on his forehead. His eyes have a weird greenish cast, like lichen on an old tree. He's host to a parasite now. Fay will always be there, looking over his shoulder, never leaving him alone. The myelin sheaths around his nerve bundles will break up and float away, but Fay's vagina will never let go. Only good things shatter. His loyalty to Rosie. His myelin. His body. Like the day he sneaked into the kitchen from school to hide his report card, to see his mother sprawled on the couch with the Fuller Brush man, skirt up to her waist, her fleshy ass peeking from the satin of her garter belt. Everett doesn't know how long he stared at the open case of wares on the floor before ducking out and hiding behind the garbage can. He remembers feeling hollow as the big tree in the woods where he and his friends huddled, not quite daring to look up into the darkness above them. In his childhood dreams, that darkness was solid and threatened to fall, to flatten them all. Then he saw his mother on the couch and it happened.

Everett leaves the bathroom and searches for Rosie, Kansas at his heels. She is not in the bedroom. Valley's bed is also empty. He heads down the stairs, nearly tripping on the dog. Rosie is not asleep on the couch—where he found her when he got home late in the early days of their marriage. Back then she claimed she couldn't sleep without him. Maybe she and Valley went to Dayton for some reason. Maybe there was a crisis. But surely she would have left a note. He searches the usual place on the kitchen counter, but the only note there is his. When he sees that her purse is missing from the telephone table, the realization hits him. She's left him. Taken Valley and gone. He looks back at the note he left that morning and longs to be the man he was when he wrote it.

He searches the refrigerator for a beer—he was certain he had left a few in there—but gives up at last and climbs the stairs. Numbness of a different kind sets in now. On the bed, he fishes Rosie's nightgown from under her pillow and buries his face in it. The lavender of her sachet mixes with the spicy musk of her skin. She's left something for him anyway. Eau de Rosie. Kansas sticks her nose in the nightie and wags her tail. Then she yips, takes off down the stairs and yips again.

"Be quiet, Kansas." He no sooner says it than he realizes: if no one is home, it doesn't matter. If he has to be alone, thank God he has the dog. Everett follows Kansas down the stairs, anxious that she come back up to sleep with him. Maybe she has to go to the bathroom.

But Kansas is not waiting at the door. She's outside the storage room, scratching the door, then turning to him and wagging her tail. Maybe there's a dead mouse in there. Kansas turns to the door and scratches again. Everett turns on a light, tells Kansas to stay, and opens the door cautiously, not certain what he will find. A wedge of light falls across his sleeping wife, stretched out on her stomach, wearing only a cotton bra and a pair of underpants. What the hell? He wants to feel relief, but there's something so odd about the moment he can't fathom what it means. Kansas looks up at Everett as if asking permission to enter. He shakes his head, then examines the bed as carefully as he can given the hall light behind him. He's never seen it before, can't explain why it's here. Unless she *knows*. That's got to be it. She's left his bed because she *knows*.

But how would she have found out? It makes no sense. But then, Rosie has ways that bypass common sense. Like the Virgin tattled on him when Rosie's Rice Krispies spelled the word *infidelity* while they floated around in the extra milk. For that matter, how did anyone ever know the things they knew? By some means as invisible as electrons popping from one ion to the next so that current flowed. The same way he had known about his mother. You just got the feeling.

At least she hasn't left the house completely. There will be plenty of time to sort it out. Meanwhile, he'd better tend to Kansas. "C'mon. Let's get you outside before you have an accident. Bad first impression. You have to audition to live here, you know."

Out in the backyard, Kansas barely squats to pee before she takes off across the yard, tearing over to the big oak. Everett is bent over, picking up yesterday's paper off the driveway when between his legs, he sees her paws up on the trunk, her nose sniffing the air. A squirrel maybe? Kansas barks. The sound is shrill and percussive in the Sunday-morning silence. "Kansas. No!" he rasps. But Kansas keeps barking, and a blond head pops up from the floor of the tree house, just visible in the morning light. There's a catch in

Everett's breath. "Valley?" Kansas is making a racket. "What are you doing up there?"

Valley stretches and yawns. There's no way she heard him.

He crosses the yard and picks Kansas up. "It's okay, Kansas. Valley lives here, too."

"Where'd you get the dog?"

"You scared me to death. What are you doing up there?"

She waits too long before she says, "It was too hot in Joanie's room so I came home and slept out here."

"By yourself?"

Valley busies herself brushing acorn shells off her clothes and picking them from her hair. She takes a quick inventory to see if Snake's left any telltale marks on her body, bruises she'll have to explain. "Joanie was here, too. But she left early to help with the milking."

He bends over to put Kansas down before her squirming makes him drop her.

"What's up with the dog?" Valley is holding on to a branch while picking her way down the ladder.

Everett reaches up, ready to catch her if she falls.

When her feet are safely planted on the ground, Valley rubs the back of her head.

"What happened to your cheek?"

"What's wrong with it?"

"It's all black-and-blue."

Valley touches her cheek.

"It must have happened when that slat gave way." She points to the rotted board on the ground.

He picks up the rotten board, remembers pounding the footholds on to the tree, back before things got awkward between them. "I'll fix these if you like." He'd like to back up and start over—to have a relationship with the girl, like Fay's with Janice. Kansas bounces around like a windup toy, jumping in circles around their feet.

Valley crouches and stretches out her hand, palm up. Kansas sniffs her fingertips. "Hello, puppy dog. What's your name?" Kansas puts her nose to the ground and wags her tail.

"Do you like her?" He'll need Valley's support to combat Rosie.

Valley sits down in the grass Indian-style. "I've always wanted a puppy. Joanie has this cool border collie that herds their cows. But Mom says collies shed and bring in dirt. Can we keep her?"

"Mom hasn't met her yet. But if we like her, Mom doesn't have the deciding vote, does she?"

Valley looks up at him, a grin crossing her face. "You mean it? We can outvote her?"

He stuffs his hands deep in his pockets. "Why not? It's two against one."

"But Mom has more than one vote."

He winks at Valley. "Maybe it's time we changed that."

Valley's eyes shine. Kansas is tramping on her lap, fitting her legs between Valley's when she can, otherwise stepping on her thighs. Valley forms a circle with her arms to keep her there. "She is so cute. What's her name?"

"Kansas."

"That's weird. Why not Texas? She's got a brown star on her belly—you know, for the Lone Star State. Or Tennessee. That sounds like a girl's name." Valley squints her eyes up and scrutinizes the dog's face. "She looks more like an Alabama. We could call her Ali for short. Or Bama."

"She's already Kansas. That star on her belly is a sunflower. Her very own corsage. If we want to keep her, we have to present a united front to your mother."

"When do we begin?"

"Soon. But, Valley, have you got any clue why your mom's holed up in the storage room?"

Valley shrugs. "I don't know what you're talking about."

"She's got some steel-framed bed in there. She's sleeping in her underwear."

"Maybe she's lost it." Kansas is sniffing Valley's breath, nose practically in her mouth.

Everett feels a twinge in his leg. He bends the bad leg, props himself against the tree and supports himself on the other leg. It's the first time this morning he's even thought of his MS.

"She was fine when I saw her last."

"No telling what she's doing this time."

Valley bursts into laughter. Everett can't remember when he last heard her laugh out loud. "You mean it gets to you, too?" she says.

"I live here, don't I?"

Valley gets to her feet. "C'mon Kansas. Let's get this over with." She bends over to pick up the dog. "Whoa. You're heavier than you look."

Everett lifts under Kansas's haunches to lighten the load. "Remember, whatever she says, we don't give in. We have to stay united on this."

"Trust me, Dad. I can hold out. I have practice." Valley's grin stretches from ear to ear. "I can't believe you're doing this. You're always on her side."

A pang of conscience streaks through Everett—swift and sudden, as if Valley's delivered a sharp kick. First it's Fay and now it's Valley. On the other hand, Valley hasn't strung this many words together in his presence since she was a kid. He's actually doing what Rosie wants. Being a good father. He hopes she's satisfied.

Valley and Everett stand side-by-side outside the storage room door. Kansas squirms in Valley's arms. Everett knocks. "Rosie? Are you in there?"

"Everett. Where have you been?" Her voice sounds anxious, accusatory.

He's never been one to go drinking with the boys and end up on the barkeep's couch. "I'm the one that couldn't find *you*," he says. "Open up. There's someone I want you to meet." He winks at Valley and rumples Kansas's ears.

"I just woke up. I can't meet anyone now."

"Are you going to church? I might go with you."

"Me, too, Mom," Valley chimes in.

Everett wonders if they're overdoing it. Valley hasn't been to church since Easter. He hasn't been at all.

"Valley? You're home?"

"Open up," Everett says. "I feel stupid talking to a door. Are you okay?"

Valley tries the door handle, pushes it open and walks in with the dog in her arms. The room is hot and smells of morning breath, and suddenly Everett doesn't feel so dirty. He hangs outside anyway. Sees the crucifix on the wall.

Rose pulls the sheet around herself.

"What time is it? Where'd you get that dog, Valley? I've never seen that dog."

Everett's glad Valley is presenting the dog. Rose will have more trouble saying no.

Valley sits on the edge of the bed, next to her mother. "She's ours, Mom. Dad brought her home." Kansas sniffs toward Rose, but Rose pulls away. "Are you afraid of dogs, Mom?"

"I don't want fleas in my bed." Rose looks to Everett out in the hallway. "You said you were going to bid a job. Instead you bought a dog?"

Everett hates to lie. He only lies when Rosie asks if she looks fat, which isn't a lie because he likes how she looks, even with the weight. "I didn't buy her. I found her. Or she found me, rather. I was filling up the gas tank and she jumped in the car."

"That took all day?"

Everett shrugs. He's not lying if he doesn't talk.

"She must belong to someone."

"Hold on. I'll ask her." He enters and sticks his face in the dog's. "Kansas, do you belong to someone?" She cocks her head. "Come on, girl, you can tell me. Who's your owner?"

Kansas laps his face. "There you go. You have your answer, straight from the pooch's mouth."

Valley laughs and allows Kansas to range toward her mother. Kansas turns her head and laps Valley's face. "Mom, she's so friendly. Don't you think she's cute?"

Kansas sniffs at Rose's crotch. Rose pushes her away. "Don't let her lick your face, Valley. She's dirty."

Everett frowns. "You sound just like my mother."

"Some things are true no matter who says them. Valley, honey, what happened to your cheek? Your legs are all scratched."

Valley says that she and Joanie went walking in the woods.

"Better put some ice on your face." Rose struggles up from the bed, holds her T-shirt to her chest and goes to the door. "I'd get it for you," she says with sudden resolve, "but I'm not leaving this room until you get rid of that animal. It's the dog or me."

Everett and Valley file past Rose into the hall, Kansas still in Valley's arms. Everett turns back. "I've wanted a dog all my life, Rosie. You can hide if you want, but Kansas is staying. She's house-trained and obedient—a damn near perfect pet." He makes a show of putting his arm around Valley's shoulder, pretending they actually have a relationship. "C'mon, kiddo. Let's go to Millie's. It's the only way either of us is going to get any breakfast."

Everett knows his wife. Though her antics sometimes drive him crazy, Rosie is all about her family. She prides herself on keeping a comfortable house, cooking their favorites, being there when they get home. His ploy works. She follows them out of the storage room practically begging. "Please, Everett. Don't go to Millie's." She's in her bra and panties, but he won't let himself look. "What is it that you want? I'll make you eggs. Or pancakes. You don't have to go to Millie's."

But Everett isn't listening. He's wondering why she is giving up so easily on going to church.

Valley takes charge. "It's okay, Mom. We have to go out anyway. To buy food and toys for Kansas. I just need to call Joanie to get a list."

Rose repeats a Hail Mary to herself, grateful for the delay. While Valley's on the phone, she quickly assembles the cast-iron frying pan, a package of bacon, a dozen eggs, the pancake mix.

Valley hangs up and stuffs the list in her pocket. "Enjoy your breakfast, Mom." She's holding the dog under her left arm, though Kansas strains toward the bacon. Only the dog is interested in Rose's cooking.

Then Valley is out the door, the dog bounding along behind, ears flapping and tail wagging. When they have settled into his car, Everett backs out the driveway—faster than is safe, if you ask Rose. She stands at the kitchen window, helplessly watching. Rob will be at Millie's. If he recognizes Everett, he'll connect Valley to Rose. God knows what he'll say to them. And whatever happens, she deserves it—for lying to Everett.

Rose puts the food away and heads back to Sister Mary Theresa's bed to take up her rosary.

CHAPTER 11

Valley and Everett wait in line for a table at Millie's. With the screen door pressing into their backs, the shop seems dark compared to the bright sunlight outside. The fried-and-sugary smell of donuts hangs in the air, and the scent of fennel rises from a sausage coil cooking on the grill. A haze of cigarette smoke hovers in a cloud over the counter.

"Wow," Valley says. "This place is really hopping."

"Just about everybody drops in on Sunday," Everett says. "One way or another."

Valley hasn't eaten here in some time, but nothing has changed. The couples in front of them have little kids hanging off their legs. They mill in a gang having one big conversation, though they break into families when they claim tables and vie for one of Millie's two high chairs. Valley bites her thumbnail, watching the men particularly. From past experience she knows that each adult is tracking exactly who arrived first. Anyone takes a seat out of order and the mood becomes considerably less friendly. If sitting down out of order is such a crime, she wonders what they'd do if a person did something really bad.

At the counter the regulars (whom Valley calls the John Deere Society) are heatedly debating the Equal Rights Amendment, as if it weren't on its last gasp. Jesse Parker predicts hell will freeze over the day he sees his wife and daughters using restrooms with men, because that's what it amounts to, he swears. The other men nod and stab their eggs, layer bacon on their toast or hold their coffee cups out for refills. Ned Draper says he can't see his wife toting a sub-machine gun to defend the country, and they all laugh because his wife weighs at least two hundred and fifty pounds. Valley wonders how they can say this stuff over and over without boring themselves to death. They sound so stupid. Their opinions never change. They're also never wrong.

Only one guy sits there silent, no matter what anyone says. He's wearing a Bengals jersey. Valley watches him stub his cigarette in the egg yolk left on his plate and wonders that men have such terrible manners.

When Everett and Valley finally get settled in a window booth, Valley checks her watch. "It's been twenty minutes. You're sure Kansas is okay? She won't suffocate?" Joey's face rises before her.

"She's in the shade. I left the windows partway down." Everett pulls his wallet from his back pocket and thumbs through to make sure he can pay for breakfast. "She'll be fine."

Valley's mouth is suddenly dry. She pulls her list from her shorts and licks her lips. "Joanie said we need food and biscuits and a leash and collar. All that stuff is at Safeway in the pet aisle." She was careful to record everything Joanie said. After yesterday, she will never again assume she knows what she's doing. "She said we need a crate for her to sleep in—we get that at the vet's tomorrow—and pig ears or hooves for her to chew. The Feed and Seed has those, but it's not open until Monday, either."

Everett pulls on his earlobe. "Pig ears?"

"What they throw away when they slaughter the pigs. Joanie's collie loves them. The dogs might as well chew them, Dad. It cleans their teeth, too."

He unrolls his napkin, lays out the utensils and spreads the paper on his lap. "I'm not sure we need the crate." When he was a kid, his friends had dogs that roamed all over the house. He pats his pocket for his cigarettes. He's left them in the car.

"Dogs are burrowing animals, Dad. They like to be in closed spaces. It has to be one just big enough for her to stand and move around. She can stay in it when we're not home."

"Let's not get carried away. She's a really good dog."

"Dad, if we crate the dog, Mom is more likely to agree to keep her. When Kansas is muddy, she can go in the crate."

"How would you like me to put you in a crate?"

He looks so sincere that Valley laughs. "I'm not a dog, Dad. Can't we just try it? It's not a crate as in apple crate. It's like a puppy playpen. I had a playpen, didn't I? Joanie says it costs forty dollars."

"If you think it will convert your mom, we'll try it."

Valley breathes more easily now that she's convinced him.

She doesn't want to screw anything up with Kansas, but convincing her dad to do things by the book isn't easy. He's laid-back about everything but electricity. If she ever plugged a frayed cord into a socket, he'd blow a fuse.

Millie arrives to take their order. She has a kinky new perm, and her half apron is tied up under her bosom. "Now this is what I like to see. A father-daughter duet." Millie's half-glasses are partway down her nose. "What'll it be today?"

Valley looks at the menu board over the counter. "Is it too early for a cheeseburger?"

Millie swaps a look with Everett. "Kids." She shakes her head and scribbles on her pad. "It's too early, but I keep an electric frying pan over there for your kind. I s'pose you'll want me to throw French fries in with the donuts?"

"No. Just a cheeseburger, please. Plain. And a glass of milk."

"The burger comes with lettuce and tomato. If you don't want it on your burger, it's your garnish. The plate needs something."

Valley bites her lip to keep from laughing. Millie brags on her eye for design. The shop's walls are papered in dancing coffeepots and calico curtains hang in the windows. The colors match the plastic tablecloths tacked to the wood tables. Millie doesn't bother with the floor. The carpet is grungy from the farmers' feet in summer and slushy boots in winter.

"Everett?" Millie eyes him over the top of her glasses, pencil poised.

"Two eggs over easy, sausage and home fries. And a cup of coffee A-S-A-P."

"Asap's my middle name," Millie says. "Sounds biblical, don't it?" She heads for the coffeepot.

When Millie has returned to the counter, Valley meets her dad's eye and giggles. It's kind of fun being out with her dad.

Millie returns with a mug in one hand and the coffeepot in the other. She pours the coffee without spilling and reaches into her apron pocket for a handful of creamers.

"Hey, Joe," Everett says, straining to see around Millie. "When did you get in?"

Millie moves from their table to the next and a man takes her place. Valley looks up at a sculpted blue-eyed face that looks vaguely familiar.

"Late last night. Whew. What a week. It's good to be home."

"You know Valley? Valley, this is Mr. Harper."

Valley suddenly needs to go to the bathroom.

"Hey, Valley," Mr. Harper says, too friendly, as if he's met her before or as if he's one of those adults who thinks he can relate to kids. "Must be you that helped Ginny out with Joey yesterday. How many Valleys can there be in a town this flat?" He laughs and Everett joins him.

Valley sees nothing funny. She is sick to death of jokes about her name. *Valley* has a melodious sound, but she's the only one who appreciates that.

Mr. Harper switches his tone to match her seriousness. "Ginny had a real nice time at the wedding."

To Valley, the change is both abrupt and conspicuous. She picks at a hangnail and pulls it until it bleeds. "No problem."

He doesn't quit. "Ginny gets real tired, what with Joey still getting up at night. Going to that wedding meant a lot to her."

Valley wants to shut him up. She turns jocular to see what he'll do. "You mean he survived? No permanent damage?" She glances up long enough to see Joey's eyes in his father's face, then looks back at her hands. She knows she's being rude.

He doesn't take her bait. "You did a fine job. Joey needs to get used to someone else."

"Valley takes after her mother," Everett says. It's his bragging tone. "Rosie loves a baby more than anything."

Valley can tell he is smiling at her, though she is focused on her thumbnail now. She tears it down to the quick with her teeth. The flesh feels bald.

"Maybe you can babysit again next weekend," Mr. Harper says. "I'd like to take Ginny out for our anniversary."

Everett smiles. "I'm sure she'll be glad to help out."

"No," Valley says too adamantly, looking from her dad to Mr. Harper. She hears her tone and amends her "no" more quietly. "I mean, I can't. I'm busy." Her face flushes warm. She's given herself away. But no matter what anyone thinks, she won't trust herself alone with Joey. Never again will she agree to watch an infant.

Just then, as if to rescue her, Millie glides up to the end of the table with Valley's milk. "Excuse me, Joe." Mr. Harper steps aside. "Cold milk don't improve with age."

"Maybe another time then," Mr. Harper says halfheartedly. "Good to meet you, Valley." He nods at Everett, backs up a few steps and looks both ways, as if he took a wrong turn, but isn't sure where.

"Man, talk about pushy," Valley says too quickly. She pretends to be absorbed in the advertisements on the placemat. She's grateful when, five minutes later, Millie delivers their food.

Everett pokes his eggs with the tines of his fork.

She watches his yolk seep through the fork holes and over onto the hash browns. Mr. Harper saying Joey is fine means nothing. He probably wouldn't know if she'd replaced his son with a pork sausage. "He must be desperate." She tries to sound nonchalant, but inside her stomach has tightened into a fist.

"Valley, when someone speaks to you, it's considered polite to look them in the eye. Joe's a good guy. A little full of himself maybe, but that's the salesman coming out. He worries about Ginny. If he keeps that job, they really ought to move to Columbus, but she doesn't want to, and you can't blame him for that."

"Maybe he should stay home if he's so worried about her. He doesn't have to come down here the minute he gets home."

"A man can't stay home the way a woman can. You remember that, Valley. Men're wired differently. They go stir-crazy if you try to coop them up."

Valley moves the lettuce and tomato from her cheeseburger to the side of the plate. "You're the expert." She'd like to point out that *his* wife likes the coop so much, she's shut herself up in a storage room, but then she sees a scrap of meat hanging off the edge of her burger. It's a strange purplish color, like the little pendant at the back of Joey's mouth when he screamed. She bites it off, anxious that it disappear, and moves it around in her mouth, chewing but trying to keep it off her tongue. She washes it down with a swig of milk and puts the burger down. "I guess I'm not as hungry as I thought."

Everett wipes up egg yolk with a piece of toast. "You should have ordered eggs." He stuffs the toast into his mouth. "We'll have Millie wrap it up. You can eat it for lunch."

Valley is grateful. Her mom would have made her eat it, to teach her not to be wasteful. She looks at the men lining the counter—Mr. Cranford, old Mr. Cockburn, some stranger, Mr. Grangerford, but especially at Mr. Harper drinking coffee and talking to the other men while Mrs. Harper sits home with her fussy baby. Valley's skin begins to prickle. She'd like to tell him a thing or two. If he could find it in himself to stay home with his son, maybe Joey wouldn't be so fussy. She pictures herself planting a fist in the middle of Mr. Harper's handsome face. But just then the stranger stands up and blocks her view.

"Dad, who's that man in the Bengals jersey?" She tilts her head toward the stranger.

"You got me," Everett says without looking.

"They all seem to know him."

Everett continues to chew. "Probably went to school here."

"He looks kind of familiar."

Everett looks over to the counter. The man smiles and nods. Everett nods back. The man continues to stare. At Valley. Everett stands up. "Time to get out of here." He hasn't finished his breakfast, but he's fishing money from his wallet.

Valley doesn't move. "Sit down. I can wait till you finish."

The strange man makes his way to their table, pausing to high-five Mr. Harper on the way by. Then, without any introduction, he looks straight at Valley and says, "Did you happen to know Verna MacIntyre, by any chance?"

"Verna was old enough to be her grandmother," Everett says.

"That's true." The man reaches for his wallet and thumbs down into one of its pockets for a piece of notebook paper, furry on the folds. "I just thought, you know—it's just that she looks so much like her." A photo flutters from the paper. The man bends over to pick it up, then stares at it a minute before glancing again at Valley and back at the picture.

Everett steps out of the booth, in front of the guy. "Excuse us, please. Wrap your burger in a napkin, Valley. Kansas is waiting." He selects quarters from the change in his pocket and drops them on the table.

Valley plucks a napkin from the dispenser. "You said she'd be fine. Why don't you finish your breakfast?"

Everett pats his stomach to say he's full. "Time to go. Pick up your stuff. Your mom has been home alone long enough."

* * *

When Valley gets into the car, Kansas tramps all over her thighs. "Ouch, Kansas. Watch where you're walking."

Everett starts the car. "Better add toenail clippers to that list. What do you say we go to the Wal-Mart in Fairfield? They would probably have everything. How about it? A little trip?"

Valley frowns. "Wait a minute. I thought you just dragged me out of there because you wanted to get home to Mom."

"That was my excuse. I didn't like how Mr. Big Shot couldn't take his eyes off you." Everett pulls onto Main Street and turns toward the highway. "Besides, if we leave your mom alone, she won't have to stay locked up in that stupid room. She might be in a better mood when we get back. A good mood never hurts."

Valley wishes she had a dollar for every time her parents change the subject on her. "Okay, but tell me who was staring at me."

Everett frowns and glances at Valley. "You were there." He's silent for a moment. "Asking if you know Verna Mac-Intyre. Good god. Talk about obvious."

Valley doesn't see anything obvious. "I don't get it, Dad. Honest. What are you upset about?"

Everett glances her way again. "For god's sake, Valley. Don't you know when a guy's making a pass at you?" He glances a third time.

Valley turns toward the window so he won't see her eyes roll. Her parents are the ones that don't get it. If she's as beautiful as they say, why won't anyone worthwhile give her a second glance? "Really, Dad. What are you worried about? He's old enough to be my father."

Everett stops abruptly for the traffic light by the plaza. Kansas slides off the seat, lands on her side and has to scramble to right herself. Valley hoists her back up and holds her in place. "Do they make seat belts for dogs?"

"I don't know. They do for people. Better put yours on."

Everett is traveling south on Route 75. The Wal-Mart in Union City is closer, but he's afraid someone there might recognize Kansas. The dog, meanwhile, has curled up between them and fallen asleep with her head in Valley's lap.

"Dad, on my way to the Harpers' yesterday I saw that guy with Mrs. Slezack. He had his arm around her. I don't think he's interested in me."

Everett slips into the middle lane in front of a semi. It's hard talking about this stuff so he pretends that navigating the trucks takes more concentration than it really does. "There was a kid who went to high school with us, last name of MacIntyre. Seems like he got fired at the theater when Mr. Dougherty caught him making out with some girl in the projection room. He went for the cheerleader type."

They've never before had a conversation like this. Valley is being careful to look at the road ahead, not at him. "What is it about cheerleaders? From the guy's side, I mean."

"Think GTO. Sleek lines and extra pickup that hot-wires in a minute." Everett's face grows warm. But Rosie isn't going to tell her, and knowing how men think might prevent the trouble Rosie's so worried about.

"Am I the cheerleader type?"

There's a pause while he thinks how to soften what he's certain will seem like a blow. Good God. "I wouldn't want you to be." Even to himself he sounds fatherly and lame. He might as well have just said no.

Valley tosses her hair and looks out the window. "So what're you worried about?"

Everett feels like a fool and wishes Rosie were present. He should have known Valley was making a point, not asking for counsel. He wishes Rosie were present. They lapse into silence.

Field after muddy field stretches away from the highway on both sides of the road. There is water standing in the ditch, grass growing up through its surface. They pass a mileage sign. Fairfield is still five miles off.

"Dad?"

"Yeah?"

"If I'm not the cheerleader type, why would a guy ask me out?"

Now Everett's not sure what to think. She keeps switching it up on him. "Guys like other kinds of girls, too, you know. Friendly girls that are fun and easy to be with." He's not doing well. He isn't sure Valley falls into that category, either. She doesn't have much in common with the other kids in Eden.

"Can I tell you something?"

Everett isn't sure. His "Okay" is tentative.

"You've got to promise not to tell Mom."

Everett reaches for a cigarette and punches the cigarette lighter into the dash. "I promise."

"You know I went to the movies with Mark Thorburn Friday night."

"The guy who came by the house?" He tries to sound casual, as if hearing her confidences is an everyday event between them. He lights his cigarette, then rolls the window down. "I didn't know his last name. Is that James's son?"

"I guess. How many Thorburns could there be in a town this flat?"

They both laugh. Everett relaxes a bit, though he's not sure if it's the nicotine or having a joke between them. "James is in real estate. He uses me for inspections sometimes."

"Anyway."

"Yeah?"

"He wasn't very nice."

Everett glances at Valley's profile. "What does that mean?"

"It means he took me to the movies. Some dumb thing called *Cat People*. Talk about gross."

"And?"

"And he tried to...you know."

"What?"

"You know."

"Did you let him?"

"No, I didn't let him. I slapped his hand. Then he would hardly speak to me and didn't take me anywhere afterward.

When we got home, he didn't even get out to see me to the door. He's supposed to do that, isn't he?"

"I'm no expert on what kids do these days, Valley, but if you want a guy to walk you to the door, there's probably one out there willing. Mark Thorburn isn't the one, though." He exhales smoke, directing it toward the open window.

Valley is silent for a while. "You say I'm supposed to be friendly and easy to talk to." She strokes Kansas, though the dog is asleep. "I tried. I tried to talk football with him, you know, where he's on the football team. He let me talk for a while, then he said that I should know. I was Eden's biggest tight end."

Everett snorts, then coughs to cover. "Nice guy."

"Does that mean what I think it does?"

"It means he's an asshole and the next time I see his dad I'm going to—"

"No, Dad. You can't." She's looking at him now, pleading in earnest. "You can't tell anyone. I'd never live it down at school. You've always told Mom I have to fight my own battles. Let me handle it. Please. And you can't tell Mom, either. If you do, I'll never tell you anything again. Ever. I swear."

"Why'd you tell me if I'm not allowed to say anything?"

"I just needed to tell someone. Don't you ever feel like that? Like you just need to hear yourself say it out loud to a real live person?"

He does. But she's not the person he needs to tell. "Your mom says that's why she likes confession."

Valley is silent. He's been a coward, diverting the question.

"How come you offered to go to church today?"

Everett is silent for a minute. "I thought it might get your mom out of there." Everett changes lanes, to get out from behind a truck. He likes to see what's coming.

"Dad, there's something I've always wanted to ask you."

The exit to Fairfield is coming up. He doesn't want to miss it. He takes a drag on his cigarette. "Yeah?"

"How come Mom didn't marry a Catholic? I don't mean she shouldn't have married you. I just mean, wasn't it some sort of sin for a Catholic to marry a Protestant back then?"

"I'm not a Protestant. I'm nothing, really. My mother was a Catholic, which is probably why I'm not too keen on it."

"Did they make you sign that paper to let Mom raise me Catholic?"

"I signed it. It was important to your mom. I wanted to make her happy."

"Have *you* been happy?"

Everett's fried eggs sit heavily at the bottom of his stomach. "What kind of question is that?" The car is hot and he cranks the air-conditioning higher. He doesn't know what to say, though he wonders why she asked on this of all days. "Yeah. I guess so. Happy as I know how to be." He's got to play it cool. Act nonchalant. Maybe it's all a coincidence, the upshot of some crazy conversation she had with Joanie last night. If Fay tracked him down with the Triple-A card and called the house, Rosie might have answered, but Valley was with Joanie in the tree house. "You have to understand.

There are ups and downs, good times and bad, no matter who you marry. You marry the person you think you can weather the ride with. Someone whose faults you can stand." He watches Valley from the corner of his eye. If she's trying to trap him, she doesn't show it. She's not even looking at him.

"That's not very romantic."

"Don't say I didn't tell you."

"She's always harping at me. I hate it. Then she turns out to be right and I hate it even more."

"I love your mom, Valley. You do, too, whether or not you feel it right now. She devotes her life to us."

"Yeah, but I get sick of all the weird stuff. Joanie's mom doesn't lock herself up in storage rooms. Where do you s'pose she'll be when we get home? *Under* that weird little bed?"

"She'll be in the kitchen making a pot roast. Dog or no dog, she can't resist an excuse for a big meal."

Everett tries to sound confident, but he isn't so sure.

Valley and Everett wander around Wal-Mart pushing a basket with rickety wheels. It plays a *thunk-clunk*ing song as they pass gondolas of summer T-shirts and end caps with packages of tube socks in one-size-fits-all. Everett stops beside a sale rack of off-season gear, drawn to a bright orange shirt and some camouflage hunting fatigues marked down for clearance. He's not a hunter. Hasn't been up to now anyway. But that gun rack in the back of the man's Jeep and the fact that Kansas has a good enough nose to track Rosie to the storage room...well, it's made him think. He might like to try it. And here's a hunting shirt jumping off the rack at him for practically no money. If he were Rosie, he'd say that was a sign.

Valley points down the main aisle. "The pet department is over there by lawn and garden."

Everett tells her to go ahead. He'll find her in a minute. He waits for her to *thunk-clunk* away before he slips the bright orange shirt off the hanger. It's a size 2X, but too big is better than too small. He tries it on over his shirt. The shoulders hang off his, but the sleeves aren't that much too long. He checks the price tag. At nine ninety-eight he can't afford to leave it. If he never takes up hunting, he can keep it in the trunk in case the car breaks down at night or in a storm. You never knew when an orange shirt might save your life.

Everett glances around the sporting-goods department for anything else he might need. He walks past bicycles, fishing rods and cans of bright-yellow tennis balls. Hunting supplies are off-season in June, he guesses, but that means he'll have time to decide what game he'd like to target and find the gun he needs. Rosie won't like the idea, but it's the lesser of two evils, considering what he nearly fired off last night. A gun is definitely the answer.

Wal-Mart doesn't carry guns, not that he'd buy one here if they did. He pictures himself around a campfire with the guys from Millie's, Joe Harper asking him about his gun. "Yeah, she's a beauty," Everett hears himself say. "I picked her up at Wal-Mart." He chuckles to himself, picks up a Coleman flashlight to add to his stash and goes in search of Valley by way of the magazine rack. He picks up a copy of *Field and Stream*, then heads to the specialty-foods section. Next to an assortment of Planters nuts he finds the biggest box of Whitman's chocolate-covered cherries that Wal-Mart carries, skipping the sale boxes left over from Mother's Day in their special wrappers. Right now he can't afford to court her with anything less than top dollar.

CHAPTER 12

After trying unsuccessfully to focus on her prayers, Rose leaves Sister Mary Theresa's bed once again—this time to search the credenza for a honeymoon picture. That's the Everett Rob will remember. Hopefully seventeen years has taken its toll. She sorts through the jumbled contents of the drawer. Extraneous snapshots of other people's kids fall out, pictures of kids building snowmen, kids on sleds, from Christmas cards she'd felt funny throwing out though the kids have grown up and she can't place them anymore.

Stuck to the photo of herself in her cap and gown at high school baccalaureate she finds the five-by-seven taken the day after they'd eloped. At the Russell's Point amusement park they had stuck their faces through a plywood cutout painted with figures of Li'l Abner in an old-fashioned bathing suit and Daisy Mae in her usual polka-dot blouse and hot pants. Rose wonders how Everett has changed so much without her noticing. In the picture his chin hugs his jawbone, and brown hair spills over his forehead. His eyebrows are full and soft, not wiry and unruly like now. Only his eyes are the same. His eyes follow her no matter how she holds the picture—like the doll with peekaboo eyes she had as a kid.

Rose sets the photo down in his recliner, then glances at it sideways as if she were sitting next to him at the counter. She asks the Holy Mother what to do, but her mind's eye is scanning Main Street, watching Everett, Rob and Valley converge on Millie's. A fistfight breaks out and men fall backward against tables that skitter and collapse. Millie herself hides behind the counter, peeking over the top and ducking every time a coffee mug zings by her head.

Of course she's being ridiculous. Her mother said she could find drama in a can of beans—which was true after she read about a woman finding a man's thumb in a jar of apple-sauce.

She feels helpless sitting at home. Helpless and cowardly. Still, she can't go to Millie's. If Rob sees her with Everett and Valley, he'll know for sure. But how else will she know what's happening? Helen doesn't work on Sunday morning, so she can't call the Laundromat. Rose goes to the phone. She's called Everett at Millie's many times when his customers have needed him.

A female voice answers. It's not Millie, thank God.

Rose is suddenly fuddled. She can't ask for Everett. "Is Rob MacIntyre there?" Her throat is tight, her voice high and thin.

The waitress hollers for Rob over the clatter of dishes. A baby cries in the background and someone has a hacking cough. Rose can almost smell the cigarette smoke mingling with the fennel scent of sausage. "Just a minute," the waitress says. "He's on his way."

Rose hangs up and sits down. She mustn't faint. Not now. She drops her head between her knees and counts to ten. On righting herself, she knows what to do. If everyone's at Millie's, the rest of Eden is free for her. She'll go to the trailer park and poke around. If Rob is moving back, surely there'll be evidence. Boxes Phil won't have a place for. She gets dressed, finds her sunglasses in case Phil's at home and heads to the car.

Though she's lived in Eden all her life, Rose has never been to Shady Acres Estates. She heads toward town, careful to slow down for Ed Dudley's speed trap, then turns left at the first stop sign and drives a mile out. From the road she can see the trailers in among the trees, clustered in some semblance of a neighborhood. Their mailboxes are lined up along the entranceway. She had hoped to find Phil's name on one, but the boxes are numbered instead. Rose doesn't have time to go home for the phone book, so she'll have to figure out which trailer is Phil's some other way. She pulls to the side of the wide entrance road and looks around. The trees are full-grown, but strangely shaped with pitch-painted circles where a sawed-off branch grew into a trailer or a power line. The paved roads circle among the trailers. Many have a lawn and flowers in front. Rose drives slowly, crawling over the speed bumps.

Some trailers have stubs of rooms sticking out here and there off their long rectangles. The only person outside is a blond woman in a denim shirt and shorts backing a golf cart out of her driveway. There are several doorstep geese, one dressed in black-and-white-striped pajamas, like a chain-gang prisoner. One yard has a swing set. Children live there. Another has cement gnomes out front painted in primary colors. Along one driveway green plastic pinwheels whirl in the breeze.

Rose circles the park a second time. It shouldn't be hard to find one belonging to a single man. No swing sets, no flowers, no gnomes or pinwheels. She sees only two possibilities. Both are white corrugated metal with no decoration but the factory-installed metal shutters on the windows. One is propped up on cement blocks. The door has portable steps and looks like a trailer you'd see on a construction sight. Rose chooses that one because Phil's in construction. She pulls into the vacant driveway of the trailer next door feeling somewhat safe because it looks abandoned, weeds growing up among the day lilies. Two lawn chairs with broken webbing sit at odd angles on a makeshift deck. A bird feeder hangs from a metal crook at a rakish angle, the empty shells of sunflower seeds littered around the ground. A For Sale sign is propped in the window. She wonders how anyone expects to sell the place with weeds growing up in the flowers.

Rose checks her costume. In her denim skirt, she looks enough like a trailer-park resident to get out and move around freely. With the sunglasses on, these people won't know her. She'll pretend to be a buyer. She climbs the stairs to knock on the door. She's quite sure no one is home, but she has to make sure. On her way down the stairs she stoops to pull a weed from the day lilies.

"You lookin' for someone?"

Rose startles, her hand fluttering to her chest. She stands, scans the yard. Across the road a kid is lounging in the shade of an oddly-cropped tree. "What are you doing there?" she says. "You scared me."

The kid takes a drag on the cigarette he holds cupped in his hand. "I was here first." A sweet aroma like incense wafts toward her on the breeze. Her fear doesn't seem to faze him. He takes another long drag, then appears to suspend in air for a moment before he turns his head to blow smoke out his nostrils. A lazy dragon is what he looks like. He even has a jewel in his ear—hoarded dragon treasure.

"I was just looking. You know. It's for sale."

"Be my guest."

Rose points to the trailer next door. "Do you know who lives there?"

"It's a construction office. Goes from job to job wherever they get work."

Rose moves into the shade so she can see him better. His hair sits on his shoulders, but it's clean and combed. She likes it better than the skinhead style Valley's classmates wear. But then, she always did like Rob's longish hair. And something about the way the kid's lounging there, all slack-chested, as if he doesn't have a bone in his body—that's the way Rob was, too.

The kid rubs his shoulder blades into the tree trunk as if he has an itch. "You in real estate?"

Rose is about to say yes but hesitates. He's a kid. She needn't tell him anything. "Why?"

"You're not the trailer-park type."

Rose drops the weed and smoothes her skirt over her hips, pleased in a backhanded way that, despite her disguise, the difference shows.

The boy gets to his feet and ambles to the trailer's stairs as though time doesn't exist. She watches while he stubs his smoke out on the stoop, pockets it and then collapses onto the steps, once again going boneless. Rose has never seen anyone take such good care of a butt. She inspects a bag of rain-soaked mortar sitting beside the foundation and nudges it with her toe. It's rock-hard.

"Ruined," the kid says.

He seems to know the trailer, though he isn't remotely proprietary. "Do you go to school here?" Rose asks. "Maybe you know my daughter. She'd be about your age."

"What's her name?"

"Valley."

"I'm done with school."

Rose takes off her glasses and searches his face. He stares back without blinking. He doesn't look eighteen. His cheeks look soft in places, especially around his jawbone. His collarbone sticks out too far. She'd like to take him home, make him a grilled cheese sandwich and fatten him up.

"The truth is, I'm just being silly and sentimental." She

might as well say it. "Back in the day, I had a boyfriend who hung out here." She's amazed at how easily it rolls off her tongue to this kid she's never seen before.

A smirk plays around his lips.

"What's funny? You think I wasn't young once, too?" She's about to say she was thin in high school when he interrupts.

"What happened?"

"I gained weight. People do, you know, as they get older. It'll happen to you, too."

"No. What happened to your lover boy?"

She hesitates, then blurts, "He had to leave."

"And you couldn't wait?" He snorts his scorn. "Just like a woman."

"The baby needed a father." Rose flushes and looks at the ground. She hadn't meant to say that.

"Aah," he says. "You didn't tell me that." He leans back against the trailer siding, head tilted to one side. "But you're still carrying his torch, huh?" His tone is softer now, sympathetic even. "You come around here and pine, like you're visiting his grave or something?"

Rose searches his face, touched by the poetry of his notion. The boy is more of a romantic than she is. Father Andrew should take a lesson on how to hear confessions. But the thought of the old priest with a cigarette hanging off his lip makes her smile.

"Something funny?"

"I was just thinking you should be a priest, you being so easy to talk to and all."

The kid sniggers.

"I'm serious," Rose says. "Don't rule it out."

He rolls his shoulder off the trailer siding and bonelessly gets to his feet. "About the trailer. Someone's got a bid in."

"I don't really want the trailer," Rose admits, amazed at how telling one truth has freed her to tell another. Speaking the truth makes her feel light, airy even. She wishes she had tried it sooner.

An hour later Rose is back on Mary Theresa's bed, repeating the rosary with renewed fervor, when the dog's toenails click on the kitchen linoleum. She hears Valley's voice and the high pitch of Joanie Cranford's chatter.

"Is your mom away, Valley?"

Rose holds her breath.

"She's home. But she's not feeling quite herself today."

"That's too bad. I hope she feels better."

Rose exhales. Joanie is sensitive and considerate—a good friend for Valley.

"Let's go show Kansas my room, Joanie. She hasn't seen it yet." Valley calls the dog, and Rose hears them climb the stairs. She wonders where Everett is. The *thunk* of his chair reclining and crowd noise from the televised baseball game answers her question. She mumbles a Glory Be to help her concentrate.

"Look at your caterpillar, Valley. It's spinning its cocoon." It's Joanie's voice filtering down through the heat duct, as audible as if she were in the next room. "Let's show Kansas."

The box spring groans as they plop onto the bed. "Come on, Kansas," Valley says. "You can come up."

Rose has never realized how sound travels from Valley's room to this one. She feels guilty eavesdropping, but where is she supposed to go?

"I've got to tell you something," Valley says in a confidential hush. Rose moves closer to the heat duct, breathing shallowly. "I went out again last night."

"Two dates in a row?" Joanie's voice is shrill. Easier to hear. "You lucky dog. Mark must really like you."

"It wasn't Mark and it wasn't exactly a date. It just sort of, you know…happened?"

"You got picked up?" There's a tremor in Joanie's voice—an obvious thrill. Rose clutches her rosary. "Who is he? How'd you meet him?"

"Mom and Dad weren't home for some reason. The house was kind of spooky, so I headed downtown just for something to do, you know. Anyway, I walked past the theater and there was this guy standing by the posters of coming attractions. It was sort of unreal. He's nobody I've ever seen before."

"Was he cute?"

"He had long hair and an earring. He looked kind of, you know, artistic. Like someone from Antioch College."

"Probably gay."

"No. Trust me. He asked me if I'd listen to a tape with him in his truck."

Rose wraps her hands in the beads. It has to be the kid

she met in the trailer park. How many strange kids with long hair and an earring show up in Eden the same weekend? Valley describes the junker truck and goose bumps break down Rose's arms. The delinquent kid—what was his name?—had Rob's truck the night before. And it probably was a junker, because what else could a man afford after a stint in prison? When Valley describes how the kid pulled the truck off into the woods, Rose has to remind herself to breathe. Her daughter was alone with a *delinquent*.

"Did he kiss you?"

"Oh, yeah."

Rose would cover her ears if her hands weren't tied in the beads.

"Was he good?"

Rose sniffs. Maybe Joanie isn't the right friend for Valley.

"It didn't stop there."

Rob called him Zeke, Rose remembers. It can't be that Valley has repeated her mistake.

"Not—"

"He tried. Look at my legs."

Rose wants to run upstairs to see Valley's legs, but then she would never know what happened next. She twists the rosary, tight as her stomach.

"He scratched you?"

"Branches. I ran away through the woods. I was so scared I didn't even feel it."

She ran away. Rose's prayers have paid off.

"Does your dad know?"

"No, and you've got to swear you won't tell him. I'll probably never see the creep again anyway."

"You should go to the police."

"What would I say? Don't tell my dad, Chief Dudley, but—"

"You sure can't tell your mom."

"Are you kidding? She'd lock me in a convent."

Rose nods, a floor below. She likes the idea of walls and gates.

"Joanie, I need you to help me. You know my necklace— the one Mom and Dad gave me for my birthday, with the star sapphire? I had it on last night and now it's gone."

Rose squeezes her eyes shut. The sapphire is gone.

"Did he take it?"

"I don't know. We had a scuffle."

"Where'd they get it? You could save up for another one."

"It was Grandma's. I have to go back and at least try to find it."

"I have to be home to babysit at five, but that gives us an hour." Joanie's voice is too excited, as if Valley has proposed a grand adventure. "Can you find where you two parked? What if it's in his truck?"

Rose feels sick. The memory of Zeke's slack body lounging under that lopsided tree, his smoking, his earring, her sense of a dragon hoarding jewels—all of it makes her mad. He probably did take the necklace, right before he stole her daughter and her secrets. How had she been such a fool? He was probably having a good laugh this very minute at her asking if he knew Valley. She even gave him Valley's name. And how would he know about a bid on the trailer if Rob weren't the buyer? Valley's father is planning to settle in Eden. She needs to tell Everett, but at the moment all she can do is panic.

CHAPTER 13

The sun, hanging at half-mast in the western sky, lights the leaf awning beside the road and highlights each tree trunk. With Joanie chattering by her side, Valley passes Wheeler's store on Route 4 before beginning to calculate how far down the road she stepped from the woods. Joanie falls silent while Valley walks ten paces, then looks back trying to match the store's current size with the lighted one in her memory. Several hundred yards down the highway Valley stoops to inspect the soft ground near the roadside for footprints and broken twigs. What she knows about tracking she learned from watching fur traders in television movies where footprints and broken sticks figured largely in leading settlers to their Indian-kidnapped wives and kids. But here there's too much ground to survey. Ferns and saplings cover the woods' floor, masking footprints. There are too many sticks.

She gives up and steps in among the trees arbitrarily, Joanie at her heels. The air is cooler under the branches, the scent of damp soil and rotting wood strong enough to taste. With the woody vines and fallen trees, it's a wonder she made it through in the dark.

"Does anything look familiar?" Joanie whispers as though the woods—somehow active in their stillness—might be listening.

"It was really dark." A woodpecker streaks overhead, its red pate flashing in and out of tree trunks. Intermittently it shrieks a frantic *tuh-tuh-tuh-tuh-tuh*, like a stuttering lunatic gone hysterical. Valley approximates the pitch in her mind. Pain shoots under her one shoulder blade. Sweat breaks down the gully of her spine. She rounds her shoulders to ease the pain. Her shirt absorbs the moisture, stops the tickle. It's darker than she expected, but sunlight dapples the treetops. If she keeps the sun at her back, she should come to the dirt road where Snake parked the truck. Surely the truck left tracks. She pictures the necklace lying there on rutted mud, waiting for her to find it.

Valley stops suddenly and Joanie bashes into her. A fallen tree blocks their path, its unearthed roots reaching toward them. Valley sees a face in the gnarled roots—a horror-struck mouth, opened to scream in an O, and two hands covering its eyes. Valley points to the features. "Do you see that face?"

"It looks like a dog curled up in a tepee to me," Joanie says. "We should have brought Kansas. She'd be good at this."

As they circle the tree, Valley focuses on the ground, stepping over the knotty roots that stick up through the soil.

"Look over there, Valley. Do you remember seeing that?"

A dilapidated cabin with a tin roof sits off in a little clearing. It seems to have come from nowhere, as though they have followed a path of bread crumbs and entered the world of a fairy tale. Two windows face west, and a female cardinal flaps its wings in front of the glass, then throws itself against a pane. "It's going to break the window," Valley says.

Joanie shakes her head. "It's going to break its neck." As if on cue, the bird hurls itself against the window, then plummets to the ground. Joanie leaps over brush to get to the cabin. Valley picks her way more carefully, as if afraid to enter a world of magic. When she steps into the clearing, the bird lies twitching on its underside wing, head bent at an obtuse angle.

Joanie points to the glass. "She must have a nest around here. She saw her reflection and thought it was another bird, you know, invading her territory. Cardinals do that." Joanie kneels beside the bird and coos little mewling sounds that Valley doubts would comfort a cardinal. Each time the mass of feathers jerks, it turns a fraction of an inch, like a rowboat with only one oar. The breast heaves in sputters, each one weaker than the last. Valley sees panic in the bird's eye, the same panic she'd felt twice the day before—when Joey wasn't breathing, when Snake pinned her to the steering wheel. The bird begins to rotate faster. She blinks hard, but when she opens her eyes again, the bird's body is whirling and she feels herself drawn down a dark funnel. Her knees go slack right before everything goes black.

Joanie's voice sounds far away, as if she's calling down a hollow log. Valley's trying to speak, to tell Joanie she's there, but her voice is stuck under a weight on her chest and she can't squeeze it past. She reaches toward the voice, but her arm is too heavy to lift. She keeps trying, fighting off the weight. She's getting closer, but it's dark inside the log. It would be so much better if Joanie could see her. She struggles to speak, feels herself getting closer. Finally she opens her eyes to a canopy, like the vaulted ceiling at Our Lady. The chatter of squirrels is too soprano to be real. Perhaps it's the hiss of locusts. Then the weight lifts from her chest and Joanie's face is in hers. Her features are blurry at first, then they focus. "Thank God, Valley. You scared me to death. What happened?" Her voice is so high-pitched, Valley wants to hold her ears. Her arms won't move.

"I got dizzy."

"I thought you'd had a heart attack, but then I heard it beating."

The weight on her chest was Joanie's head. Up so close, Joanie's pores look enormous. Is this how she looked to Joey? She mustn't think about that. Another face appears, too, looking over Joanie's shoulder—a wrinkled face with brown eyes and a fringe of gray hair. A woman's face. Smaller than Joanie's but still huge.

I want to go home, Valley mouths.

"Take it easy for a minute. Wait until we're sure you're okay."

Valley feels chilly. Her stomach is a bit queasy, too, especially if she thinks of the bird's neck. She closes her eyes and collects her energy, then props herself up on an elbow and looks around. Everything's the size it should be now. A chipmunk skitters across the clearing, but the old woman is nowhere in sight. Valley pushes herself to a sitting position and scans the woods. "Where's the old woman? She was right behind you."

Joanie turns her head to follow Valley's gaze. "What old woman? We're by ourselves. There's no one here."

"She was right behind you. She had long gray hair, kind of ratty-looking, like that old mother cat in your barn."

Joanie sits back on her heels and crosses her arms. "Fluffy was pretty before she had too many litters." She gets to her feet. "I didn't see anyone. You must have hit your head."

Valley doesn't think so. She feels around on her head but finds no bumps. It's not inconceivable to see someone. There's a house here, and it makes sense that someone would live in it. She looks to the spot where the dying bird had lain.

It's not there.

Valley touches her collarbone, afraid the necklace might somehow have reappeared, just as the bird disappeared. Her throat is bare. "Let's get out of here, Joanie. This place is creeping me out." Valley looks to the treetops and points to where the sun shines. "West is that way. If we can just get back to the road, I'll be fine."

Joanie helps Valley to her feet. "I'd better follow," Joanie says, "in case you get dizzy again."

Valley picks her way through the underbrush, holding branches across their path and waiting for Joanie to take them from her. She wants to feel connected, to know she's not alone, but Joanie is quiet. The snap of twigs under their feet punctuates the chirp and chat of birds and squirrels. A mosquito whines near Valley's ear. She slaps at it but misses. The whine continues, like Joey crying from far away, and she wonders if she'll hear his voice forever.

When they step onto the highway, Valley is still dizzy. But Joanie's house is the other way. "It must be nearly five o'clock," Valley says. "You'd better go babysit."

"I'll walk you home. Mom won't mind my being late if I tell her why."

"You can't tell her why. You promised."

"What if you pass out again? You could get run over."

"Main Street is up ahead. Everyone in town knows me. What could happen?"

Valley hugs Joanie so she'll know it's goodbye. "I'm glad you were with me," she whispers in Joanie's ear. "Waking up alone, all sweaty and nauseous, would have really been scary." Especially since she's certain she saw someone. When she feels better, she's going back alone to check it out.

Joanie walks backward toward her farm, waving. "Call me when you get home so I know you're okay."

Valley is relieved. What she needs to do next she has to do alone.

From where Valley stands behind a tree across the street, the Harpers' house looks as though it, too, belongs in a fairy tale. It has a steeply pitched roof, shutters, a rose-covered trellis and gingerbread trim. There's a lead glass-and-lattice window by the door and a huge tree in the backyard that hangs over the roof. Tidy shrubs and flowers line the front of the house, so even if she came at night, she couldn't peek in the windows without leaving footprints in the dirt. There's an alley out back. Maybe she can watch from there.

Fairy tales never bothered with backyards. The house looks so different from the back, she's not sure she's got the right one and counts houses from the end to make sure. The back windows have no shutters. Tall grass grows along the chain-link fence, patchy in the shade under the tree. Garbage cans sit under the back steps, trash strewn around where a dog has scavenged. A weathered rocker sits on the tiny back porch next to the kitchen window.

The Harpers' garage is separate from the house, flush with the alley. Cobwebs connect the garage door to its molding, so Valley's certain it hasn't been used since winter. She tries the side door, finds it unlocked, and slips into the musty coolness. Faint daylight enters through a window facing the house. A plastic bucket containing a few crystals of rock salt will make a fine stool. She turns it upside down and sits three feet back from the window. The garage is so close to the house she can hear Joey squawking now and again, walls and curtains muffling the shrillness. If he's brain damaged, at least his lungs are healthy.

Not five minutes after Valley is at her post the kitchen window lights up and Mrs. Harper stands at the sink with Joey on one hip, facing out. Joey actually looks happy, waving a stuffed monkey around and kicking his legs. Not brain-dead at all. He looks cute, in fact. Mrs. Harper seems intent on something—and too tired. Strands of hair have escaped the barrette she's used to fasten up her pony tail. The overhead light sends a rosy glow off the red tones in her hair, like a tainted halo. Joey drops the monkey and strains after it, reaching for the floor. Mrs. Harper leans the other way to keep him balanced. Valley finds herself leaning, too, counteracting Joey's considerable weight as he drops his head toward the monkey. The bucket starts to tip, and she hangs for a second before she manages to right herself.

Mrs. Harper props him on the counter next. Joey strains over her arm toward the monkey and starts to fuss. Mrs. Harper's lips move, and frown lines appear between her eyebrows. She wrestles Joey to get his clothes off—romper and diaper—between adjusting the sink faucets, hot and cold. It must be time for his bath. "Give him the monkey," Valley whispers into the empty garage.

Mrs. Harper doesn't hear. She pins Joey against herself and untapes his diaper. His legs are stiff as he cries, and she can hardly pull it out from between his legs. Then she tries to bend him at the hips to seat him in the sink. He wants none of it. His will is undamaged, that's for sure. He bicycles his feet and water sloshes all over everywhere. Mrs. Harper backs her hips from the sink but holds on to Joey. She squints and wrinkles her nose. From this distance, with the sound muffled by several walls, Valley feels sorry for Joey—if he can see his mother's face through his tears, that is. No wonder he cries all the time with a mother who looks like that. "Just give him the monkey," she says, louder this time. "If it gets wet, you can throw it in the dryer." It suddenly seems so simple. Joey's desires are so small, so manageable.

Mrs. Harper's hand—the one threaded under Joey's other arm and around his back—grasps a flailing arm and pins it to his side. Then she immobilizes Joey, pressing him against her body, and soaps him down, rinsing him afterward with a plastic measuring cup full of water. Gradually Joey's screaming changes to a mechanical cranking. Probably the warmth of the water or its sound swashing around the sink. Valley can finally relax, as though Mrs. Harper is pouring warm water over her, too.

But Mrs. Harper is still frowning. She looks like a witch, her brows slanting upward from her nose. Joanie's face flashes across Valley's mind, too large and too close. She knows how Joey feels, helpless and immobilized with a huge face stuck in his. At least Joanie's expression was concerned. Poor Joey. She wonders if motherhood turns every woman into the wicked witch, if all mothers are angry that a baby is filling their lives with noise. Did her mother frown at her like this? If so, she never wants children of her own. She'll find a career, the flute perhaps, and skip this chapter.

A dump truck out on the street grinds its gears as it passes in front of the Harpers' house. Its rumbling weight sends vibrations through the neighborhood and up Valley's spine. The rocker on the back porch moves, rocking slightly. Valley is on her feet and out the door before she sees more.

CHAPTER 14

Sunday evening Everett finishes the last of the carryout pizza in his recliner, picking a loose piece of pepperoni and a rubbery string of cheese from the cardboard disk. He stuffs them in his mouth together and licks his fingers, while Kansas sits at his feet, nose in the air, nostrils quivering. It's not the pot roast with carrots and potatoes he's used to on Sunday, but it beats starving. Valley had moped around on the couch for a while when she came back from her walk, and when Rosie hadn't succumbed to making dinner, he listened at her door, then ordered out. He wonders what Rosie has been eating. He scratches another rib of melted mozzarella off the disk and drops it to Kansas, who makes off with it and wriggles under the couch to eat it in peace.

Rosie should come out to watch 60 Minutes the way they always do. She's so damn stubborn. He wishes she would put her grievances aside and go on, as he does. He's got MS for god's sake, and he's not holing up in some stupid room stewing about it. If Rosie has to be so goddamn righteous, he'll have to go back and find Fay.

A pang streaks through his stomach like a rogue current. Okay. Not Fay.

He hears Valley overhead, pacing the floor of her room—a strange method when it comes to studying for finals, but she makes grades, so he can't complain. If Rosie doesn't come out by bedtime, the heck with her. He can entertain himself. He will make the best of what is—take a lesson from Kansas and savor his solitude. It's not often, after all, that he gets time at home to do what only he wants to do.

He thumbs the copy of *Field and Stream* he picked up at Wal-Mart, looking for some know-how to go with his new orange shirt. The table of contents lists an article called "Hunting 101: An Introduction for the Lay Sportsman." He turns to page fifty-six and begins reading about the shotgun. There's a photo of a man standing knee-deep in marsh grass aiming his piece straight at Everett. A bevy of decoy ducks sit in the open water nearby, and a live fowl flies toward the camera in a blur of wing feathers. Everett is instantly that hunter. After the flying bird has fallen to the water, Everett sees himself pull a recently shot shell from his pocket and smell it, savoring the burned powder odor the way hunters do each fall on television shorts. He isn't certain how the powder smells, but the look on the guy's face, the way his jaw muscle tightens, looks the way Everett feels when he sniffs a good cigar.

Kansas, finished now with her cheese, approaches his chair, tail wagging, and puts her chin down on Everett's knee. He rumples her ears, glad he has her. Birds, dogs and guns—the trinity of manhood.

The sun casts its last glow through the ruffled curtains in the west windows. If Rosie doesn't come out, he'll get rid of her flowered couch, her quilted pillows. He'll redo the room like the one in the Absolut ad in his magazine—oxblood leather chairs, rolltop desk, fireplace with duck andirons, decoys on the oak mantle. Dark colors, leather and wood. A real man's room.

It's a good dream, but the thought of so much change is overwhelming. Maybe he'll buy a leather recliner for his office in the barn and add a humidor with Cuban cigars. It would be lots cheaper. Before anything else, he needs a gun. Rosie won't approve—she'll hate it, in fact—but if she wants to control him, she'll damn well have to come out.

Rose lies awake in Mary Theresa's bed, unable to stop her mind replaying and her body enacting the strain it took Valley to free herself from that nasty kid in the junker truck. She gets up one minute to straighten and retuck the twisted sheets, only to get back in bed and twist them up again. When she hears Everett's heavy footfalls climb the stairs and has given him time to fall asleep, she decides to go up and talk to Valley. Rose isn't supposed to know what happened, but surely Valley will understand that when a mother overhears her daughter describe a near rape, she doesn't plug her ears.

Rose hugs the wall so the stairs won't creak. Valley's door is cracked open, and she peeks in before knocking. Valley is sound asleep in the midst of her American history and

Spanish textbooks, a spiral notebook and a stack of note cards, each printed with a Spanish vocabulary word. Rose watches her daughter's breath rise and fall beneath her oversize t-shirt. Her legs look as though she's been lashed, and Rose is glad she knows the scratches were made by briars and not the punk's fingernails. She sits down on the edge of the bed hoping Valley will stir.

Valley takes one deep breath and heaves out a sigh, then goes on sleeping. Rose can't remember sleeping so soundly at Valley's age. After her night with Rob, she slept fitfully at first, then very little while she waited for her period. When it didn't come, she'd lain awake night after night.

After living through that misery, she'd never waken Valley. She searches Valley's arms and legs for bruises, but there's nothing remotely yellow or green. She wonders if Valley made up the story to impress Joanie. It's not likely. The lines of tiny pinpricks look like the work of sticker bushes, just as Valley said. She peeks under Valley's T-shirt. A greenish ridge between two ribs on her left side is turning an ugly purple. No bush made that bruise. The story is true. She'd like to touch the bruise, press on it to see if it hurts, but Valley needs her sleep. There will be time for talking when finals are over on Wednesday.

Meanwhile, she'll do what she can to get that kid out of Eden. Valley's not stupid enough to go near him again, but Rose herself fell for his line. He knows too much. And he's just the type to brag about his exploits. He's probably out there blabbing now, ruining Valley's chances for a nice boy.

Rose slides off the bed onto her knees. With her eyes open, searching Valley's face for signs of distress, she prays an Our Father, a Glory Be and a whole string of Hail Mary's, topping it off with the Memorarae before stealing out of the room and back downstairs. Tomorrow, when Everett's gone, she'll get into the cedar chest at the bottom of their bed and find that quilt—the one pieced in the pattern called Castle Wall—and put it on Valley's bed. Not a convent exactly. More of a prayer.

A hush covers the household when Everett wakens in the predawn darkness, startled by a groan. Half his face is buried in the pillow, but his left eye seeks the clock. The digits usually glare red through the blackness but are now a shade of gray. Nothing's stirring. Maybe he groaned in his sleep and wakened himself. But a strange awareness that things aren't quite right won't leave him. It's not just Rosie down in that weird bed. He lifts his head. The clock digits glow red when he adds his right eye. Four twenty-seven. He buries his right eye in the pillow. The numbers go gray. He closes both eyes. He wonders if this is what Dr. Burns is waiting for. Another symptom. Something other than the strange weakness in his leg to confirm the diagnosis. The literature Dr. Burns gave him— where did he put it?—said MS could affect one eye at a time.

He listens for Rosie's even breathing, hoping she might have relented and come to bed. He'll waken her if she's there. Tell her everything. He needs her to know, to be there with him when this weird stuff happens.

There's breathing, but it's faint, as if she's got a pillow over her head. He moves his foot to her side, probing for her legs, but the covers are flush against the mattress rather than arching up over her body. It's not a good sign, unless she's clinging to her edge of the mattress. She did that once at the Finger Lakes when they rented a guest cottage with a sagging bed. She called it sleeping uphill, he remembers, and came home grumpy, as if she hadn't been on vacation at all. He reaches out and pats the air on her side. His hand lands on the mattress, not her hips. Damn. He should have known. She can always hold out longer than he can.

He rolls over on his back. The mattress bobs and then Kansas is upon him, her tongue lapping his face. He turns away, but she's persistent and steps on his chest to get to him. Her tail is wagging. The mattress is a riot of waves. "No, Kansas," he hisses in a whisper. But there's no one to wake up except himself and she's doing a great job. He pushes her down under his arm. She bobs on the wave. "Lie down!" She does but sniffs around his underarm. It must be salty because she's immediately back on her feet, lapping his skin from his armpit to his elbow as if she hasn't eaten in a blue moon. He wonders if Valley forgot to feed her. He's not sure how many times a day a dog her size needs to eat. He bunches the sheet next to him to form a barrier so she can't get to his skin. Then he turns his back and pulls Rosie's pillow over his head. "Good night, Kansas," he says with finality, as if she were Rosie and he'd had enough.

Kansas circles twice, then plops down next to him and lets

out a long sigh. In minutes, she's breathing deeply, her sides expanding and contracting against his back. If only he could relax like that. He lies next to her all tensed up, alone once more. He closes his eyes but remains wide awake.

Rose is dreaming downstairs. She is sleeping in a cave when a dog comes upon her. She purrs to the texture of the dog's tongue lapping her skin, her thighs, her belly. She feels warm inside, filled with a well-being she hasn't known since carrying Valley—around the seventh month, after she was safely married to Everett and could relish the sensation of the baby rolling around inside as if they were tumbling together down some grassy hillside on a warm afternoon. Strangely, as the dog works his way over every inch of her body, Rose turns into a dog and the cave is her burrow. She might even be a rabbit and the fur all over her body is thick and soft. Her body is sinking in its own nap.

Rose wakens hungry, clutching her pillow, her right hand stroking a feather that's poked its way through the ticking. The day ahead seems long and hard. She wants to return to the burrow, where it's warm and soft and she's not alone to cope with Valley's dilemma. Maybe she should give up this foolishness, go upstairs and tell Everett. He'll know what to do, who to call. If he finds out about Rob, it's the price she pays to protect her daughter.

She sits up. Her pillowcase is missing. She feels around for it and finds herself nude, her bra wadded beneath her and her panties missing. The room is hot and very dark. She can't even control herself when she's asleep.

"This is ridiculous, Rosie," Everett mumbles under his breath when he tries the storage room door and finds it locked. Enough is enough. A gun and a humidor are scant compensation for her presence. He misses her. It's eight-thirty. Time she was up. Time to talk.

He thumps his fist on the door. Shower water trickles down his legs under his robe. The Harvest Gold he splashed on himself upstairs, hoping her favorite cologne would break down her resistance, fills him with a glorified version of his own presence. He's glad he thought to arm himself with Whitman's. The box is reassuringly heavy in his hand. It feels expensive.

Behind the door Rose stuffs her rosary under the sheet as if his knock has caught her stroking herself under the covers. Actually, she's been praying the Hail Mary, asking the Holy Mother to tell her what to do for Valley. But at the back of her mind, where urges lurk and loiter, she'd hoped he'd try something this morning. She's been listening to his footfalls since he got up, repeating her rosary to their rhythm. Every time he's come close to her door, her stomach has fluttered.

"Come on, Rosie. You're scaring the hell out of me. Saturday night I couldn't find you, for god's sake. Kansas scouted you out just when I was about to call the police."

Rose is intrigued. Images come to mind—of strange men with flashlights and barking dogs on leashes, spaced evenly and moving in a line across wooded land, all searching, each wanting to be the one to find her. She clutches the top sheet to her body and tiptoes to the door, opening it a crack, half expecting some leather-jacketed, grim-faced sheriff. It's Everett standing there, with that pleading look in his eyes that makes her want to repent for him. How is she supposed to stay mad at him, especially when he's holding the biggest box of chocolates she's ever seen? Damn him, anyway, she thinks, pulling the sheet around to cover her backside. She shouldn't have opened the door.

He holds the candy out to her. She takes it without looking at his eyes. He doesn't release the box for a minute, and Rose flashes to the moment when she and Rob were connected by Valley's magazine. A pang stabs at her conscience. Everett is such a good man. He doesn't deserve what she did. She's got to get Rob and the punk out of Eden.

She sinks down onto the bed, holding the box. "Where's the dog?" she whispers.

"Valley got a little cage for her, so she won't mess up the house when no one's watching her. Want to see?" Everett asks as he steps inside and shuts the door.

Rose knows what he's up to. She shakes her head. Without the dog as an excuse for her hibernation, she's not sure what to tell him. He'd laugh if she said she's doing penance. Everett doesn't believe in penance. And given how she can hardly keep her mind focused as she repeats prayers, she really can't blame him. Even if she were the best fast-and-prayer on the planet, she couldn't tell him. He'd ask what for.

He sits down tentatively beside her, as if not certain the bed will hold his weight. "How can you stand it in here all day long with only one little window?" He runs his hands along the bed frame beneath the mattress. "Where'd you get this thing?"

"It's secondhand," she says as if that answers the question. She can't say she got it at the grocery. She starts to giggle at the peculiarity of the auction but then crosses herself, pretending to push her hair off her forehead and adjust the sheet. She's tried to explain God to Everett. But exposing God to Everett's logic makes God look ridiculous. It's like explaining sex to a child. The mechanics don't add up to the experience. Everett would never understand what sleeping in Mary Theresa's bed means to her. Especially since she's not sure herself.

Everett's left hand moves from the bed frame to her right thigh. She can feel it there, though he's not touching her. He's wearing cologne today and its cloud envelops her. He has invaded her virginal closet, joined her in Mary Theresa's bed. A thrill races under her skin and chases around her body. She tries to skitter away from its grasp, chanting a Hail Mary in her mind. But her dream washes over the rote, bathing *Blessed art Thou among women* in the dog's wet tongue, then wrapping it in the warmth of rabbit fur. Everett lies down and pulls her down next to him, loosening her sheet. She feels herself open, as if her pores have fibers extending toward him. His breath quickens and she matches hers to his. Her head feels heavy and heavier still. She'll go mindless next.

"I know why you're in here, Rosie, and I don't blame you," Everett murmurs into her neck.

Rose's vision has blurred. His features are airbrushed in the dim light. His scent fills her head. *Blessed is the fruit of Thy womb, Jesus*. His damp skin against hers is all she wants.

"It didn't mean anything. Nothing has to change between us. It was just one of those things that happened."

Rose wonders what he is saying. That he knows? And he understands? She can't think when she's all goose bumps—doesn't care about anything but getting his robe off. *Pray for us sinners*. Her hand moves up his leg and finds its way to the gap of his robe. The box of chocolate falls to the floor with a thump. She scoots her hips over to make room. Pulls him toward her. *Now and in the hour of our death*. His hand works under the sheet and strokes her midriff, then kneads her breast. His lips nuzzle her neck, then latch on to her shoulder. She traces his ear with her tongue. One of them is moaning. She loses herself in the sound, descending to the ocean floor, where the stillness is so dense that she's only aware of him. His mouth latches on to her breast, and she starts swimming to the surface. Everett sucks, and she cups her breast so he gets all he wants. There's nothing she would hold back, that she doesn't want him to have. She strains with her legs, swimming toward him, toward him. Everett climbs on top. She scoots her bottom over to center their weight in the narrow bed.

He transfers more weight onto her body and pushes into her. The reality of metal springs, thin mattress, white sheets—it all slips into the fullness of his body joining with hers, holding her, rocking her. If this could last forever, their closeness, maybe what happened years back really wouldn't matter.

Minutes later Rose lies in the quiet of Everett's breathing. He came before she did, and she wrestles with the agitation of hanging there, nerves jangling. She's all stuffed up and frustrated inside, like after an unreleased sneeze. "What did you mean it doesn't matter?" she says. It had meant Valley, after all. You don't repent of the birth of a child. She will never wish her daughter away. "It changes everything."

He spiders his fingers up her arm and pulls her toward him. "It doesn't. I swear."

Rose rounds her shoulders to slip out of his grasp. She curls onto her side and rubs his touch off her arms. She can't imagine how discovering Valley is someone else's daughter can mean nothing to him. He must be in shock. When it hits him, he'll change his tune.

On his feet again, Everett wraps the robe around himself, tightening the tie below his belly. "We'll talk more tonight," he calls through the door. "I have to go to Dayton on business today. I won't be too long."

CHAPTER 15

As Everett approaches Dayton, fog hovers over the Miami River, spilling onto Route 75, softening the edges of the concrete. The Reynolds and Reynolds clock tower looks dreamy and unreal as it emerges from the gray-white—like Polaroid film developing before his eyes. He watches for the Third Street exit, threading his way between trucks to get to the right lane, then wending his way down the ramp. On Third Street men in suits are headed toward the county courts building. County prosecutors perhaps. Or civic-minded citizens showing up for jury duty. He accelerates to pass them, afraid they might look his way, pronounce him guilty and sentence him to a life without Rosie.

He has no appointments in Dayton, really, but he needs to drive. He thinks best in the car. What he doesn't understand is how Rosie found out. Fay must have traced him and called her. Women could be so vindictive.

But after twenty minutes of humming up the highway, sorting his thoughts, he knows what he's come to do. He's headed for Lazarus to find something expensive for Rosie. Not lingerie. Not hosiery and not perfume. All that stuff's too intimate and might remind her of what he has done. Today it will be jewelry. He doesn't know how to shop for jewelry, but the Lazarus salesladies are always willing to help. They don't make him feel stupid when he holds his arms in a circle—as if he's hugging Rosie—to show them what size, so today he will point out another customer who reminds him of Rosie, offer a price range and let the saleslady choose. If it's in a velvet box, Rosie will know he went all out. She can always exchange it if the woman goofs.

But Everett finds himself boxed in the curb lane by a city bus, obligated to turn right on Ludlow. The light is red, but the car behind him honks for him to make the turn. He accelerates before he sees a seated figure materialize in front of his bumper. He slams on the brakes and stops just short of the powered wheelchair's rubber tires. Likewise, the chair has stopped dead in the crosswalk. The stubbly-cheeked man driving it—one shoe positioned on the footrest, the other leg amputated at the knee—cowers to the far side of the chair, protecting his head in his folded arms. Everett sits there frozen, dizzy, his heart pounding, too shocked to think what to do. "I didn't see you," he whispers with what little wind he can muster. The man can't hear him. It doesn't matter why he nearly ran him down. "I'm so sorry. I didn't mean to scare you."

A man runs from the sidewalk into the street to help. He pushes on the chair handles from behind, but the chair won't budge. He throws his weight against it but only manages to jam his body into the back of the chair.

"It's motorized," Everett hollers, wanting to do something

useful, though he can't seem to do anything with his legs except press the brake. Shock? MS? He doesn't know, but if he lets the brake up, the car might roll. Even an inch and he'll hit the chair. "Use the power lever," he hollers out his window. "On the armrest." Battery-powered wheelchairs are a great new invention.

The pedestrian, a young man in jeans with long hair and a Jesus beard, leans over the chair and pushes the lever. The chair guns ahead, jerking the invalid's head back. It jumps the curb and nearly tips over backward, but Jesus steadies it in time, then stops it with the lever. With the road clear, Everett eases up on the brake and steers the Fairlane around the corner, inching along in case another wheelchair appears out of the foggy nowhere. He pulls the car over at the curb and waits for his heartbeat to slow. It skips a beat when the kid's hairy face fills the passenger window. Jesus's lips are moving, but Everett can't hear him. *He's okay, man,* Jesus mouths. *You okay?*

"Yeah." When the face disappears from the passenger window, Everett looks back to the sidewalk behind him. The wheelchair is no longer there. It has disappeared into the fog as mysteriously as it appeared. Maybe he's dreaming. Maybe the last two days—hell, the last week—are one big bad dream.

Everett's not wearing a seat belt. He pulls the lap strap across his stomach and buckles himself in, a sweat breaking out on his forehead. He wonders what the hell the guy is doing out in the fog. Doesn't he know no one can see him?

Everett cradles his head in his arms on top of the steering wheel. He nearly ran a man down—probably a Vietnam vet from the looks of him. Shit. Guy might as well have been shot down over Hanoi as come back home to get mauled by a car.

When Everett raises his gaze to the rearview mirror, he sees the future in his face. He's the man in that chair, helpless against whatever comes at him. He's such a selfish bastard. Why in the world would he court Rosie back to himself? She's better off to leave him now, whatever the reason, for all the good he'll be to her or anyone else.

An hour later, after he's calmed himself with a cigarette, swallowed a cup of coffee and soaked up the caffeine with a donut at the White Castle, Everett drives to a corner store wedged onto a pie-shape slice of land not far from Wayne Avenue. The windows are barred and covered with white paper, as if the gun shop might be a front for something else, a peep show maybe or an adult bookstore. Once he's parked out front, Everett pushes through the door. A heavy iron chain is wrapped ominously around the inside of the door handle. The store is small inside—a skewed rectangle, as if the sides have collapsed under pressure—and dimly lit. It feels crowded, not with people but with gun paraphernalia stacked above eye level in the middle of the floor: boxes of ammo, cases of gadgets, gun grips and scopes. The only walking space is a three-foot aisle along glass cases that display handguns like jewelry. Rifles and shotguns hang vertically on the wall behind the counter, price tags dangling from their trigger casings. The man behind the counter, a fortyish short-haired guy in a sport shirt, is assisting a twenty-something Hispanic kid who's fondling a silver handgun like James Bond's. "Pretty nice, huh?" the salesman says to the kid. "I've got one just like it."

Everett steps back from the counter, away from the kid and the salesman, to scrutinize them both. The kid, in his sleeveless T-shirt and long hair, looks as if he belongs in a big-city gang, and the salesman—well, put a vest on him and he could be the sheriff recruiting a deputy. But then, once in his wheelchair, Everett will be like the crotchety old men in movies, their skinny ribs showing through their undershirts, who ward off the bad guys by pointing a shotgun at them from their front porch, then firing it into the air.

When it comes to buying a gun, Everett doesn't know what to ask, and this store has no kind women to coach him past his ignorance. He checks out the prices of the guns on the wall and tells himself a shotgun is very different from a handgun—a veritable sporting good it is, like a golf club or a tennis racket. There are a lot more side-by-side shotguns than over-and-under. More of a selection. He'll choose something in the midprice range, the way you do with an estimate for a new roof. Not the cheapest or the most expensive. The middle ground, where he aims when he bids on a project.

The counter man turns to a middle-aged athletic type in a plaid shirt. He gets down a high-powered rifle with a fancy scope and a price tag that says nine hundred and ninety-nine dollars.

Joe Harper and Jed Peterson, who support the NRA lobby and hunt regularly, own guns like that.

"What did you have in mind?" the counter man asks Everett when the plaid shirt is happily holding the rifle up to his eye to sight down the barrel.

"You the owner?" Everett wants to deal with the owner. So he can dicker.

"Last I looked."

"I'm looking for a shotgun." He won't tell the man he hasn't pointed a gun since the rifle range at Boy Scout camp. The guy might try to take him for a ride.

"Twelve-gauge?"

"Yep."

He pulls an over-and-under off the wall. It's a Beretta marked sixteen hundred dollars. Everett dismisses it immediately. In his other hand the owner grabs a side-by-side Springfield Stevens marked two hundred and twenty-nine. "Here's the top and bottom," he says to Everett. "I've got stuff in between, too. What are you after?"

Everett is suddenly confused. "A shotgun."

"What game?"

Oh. His mind flashes back to the article he saw in *Field and Stream*. That's where all this started, after all. "Birds."

"Pheasant?"

"Yeah." That's it. He'll sit in the backyard in his wheelchair and shoot a pheasant for Rosie's dinner. She'll have the water boiling or the oven heated or whatever you do to cook pheasant.

"You want a twenty-eight-inch barrel, straight stock, high shooter, weighted slightly forward, six, maybe seven pounds."

"Exactly," Everett says, though he hasn't actually heard him. He remembers how Rosie had looked when he'd left her this morning. She'd been curled up in the fetal position, facing the wall, and that image superimposes itself over Rosie the pheasant cooker. His stomach bottoms out. She'll probably kick him out and he'll never get to give her anything again. At least he'll have the gun. He picks up each of the two guns in turn and lifts it to his eye. He can't tell the guy he needs the lightest one they make. If the MS takes off, he may not be able to lift it at all. He'll just sit there with the gun resting on the arm of his wheelchair, looking scary.

"Two barrels enough? Pheasant are smart and tricky. How about a pump?"

"What have you got?"

"A Remington, a Winchester and a Mossberg in a twenty-eight inch."

Everett picks them up as the owner lifts them off the wall, working the pump first to see how she slides. Then he puts each to his shoulder and aims as he saw the plaid shirt do. He should probably swing it around as if at a moving target, but the idea makes him nervous. He's not sure where the end of the barrel is really. He might hit something.

"I've got some automatics."

Everett shudders. "I like this one," he says, aiming the Mossberg. The walnut stock is a rich dark brown and smooth to his touch. The tag says two hundred and seventy-five dollars.

"Shot?" the owner asks.

"Sure."

The owner holds out a box of #5 and another of #6 three-inch shells. Everett doesn't know which to choose.

"I'll take 'em both," he says finally.

"Ohio resident?"

"Sure am."

"I need to see your driver's license."

Everett pulls it from his wallet along with his credit card.

The owner hands Everett a printed yellow form. He fills in his name, address, height, weight, race, date and place of birth, then reads through the questions about his record of felonies, domestic violence, alien status, addictions and mental institutionalization. He signs the form and dates it. The owner fills in the make, model and serial number on the gun.

"That it?" Everett asks.

"You're on your way."

Surely he can't just stroll in here and walk out with a gun. That's insane. "No waiting period?"

"Not in Ohio."

"You're not going to check my record before you let me take the gun?"

"This is a legal document. Do you know what the penalties are for lying on a federal form?"

"If I wanted to shoot someone, I might not care."

"Damn government. I had an eighty-seven-year-old black guy in here the other day, all crippled up with arthritis, who couldn't buy a gun because he'd done time for stealing food from a grocery during the Depression. They didn't jail whites for that in the thirties. State stopped the sale. What's he supposed to do to protect himself? These politicians blame crime on guns. As if a gun can shoot itself. Always blaming the inanimate object. Why don't they go after cars for killing people?"

Thoughts race through Everett's mind. A week ago he might have argued that cars are registered and drivers are licensed. Cars are already better regulated than guns. But he's not up for a fight. The black man who can't defend himself is more important than any principle. Good thing Everett isn't black on top of everything else. Nobody's telling him he can't have the gun.

On the way to his car, Everett feels sweat trickling down his back and realizes he's a little light-headed. He carries his gun hooked through his arm, muzzle down and close to his side so nobody gets the wrong idea. It looks ridiculous on a city block, but he's still glad he bought it. Neither Rosie nor Valley will agree, but if it's this easy to get a gun, he needs to have one—or only the criminals will be armed. That bumper sticker is right. It's a violent world out there. With the gun tucked safely in his trunk, he no longer feels at such a disadvantage. The world now is an altogether safer place.

CHAPTER 16

After Everett's departure, Rose lies in the narrow bed, listening to the stillness. In their lovemaking she missed the wave. Now her toes are clenched and one calf muscle threatens to cramp. She wonders how much Everett knows and how he found out. Her heart races. Her stomach is so empty and acid she feels as if it's starting to eat itself. The candy sits on the floor beside the bed, thankfully wrapped in plastic, tempting her to break her fast. She can't cave in now. Not when Everett's just found out. She can't understand why he wasn't more upset. Maybe Rob bragged that they were lovers, but Everett hasn't figured out about Valley. All Everett knows is that he wasn't the first. That might be a day's worth of disappointment but after all these years wouldn't matter so much. She doesn't know if she was Everett's first. And she doesn't care, though it seems men feel differently—more possessive. At least that's her sense.

Rose smells perspiration. She hasn't showered in two days. Her skin feels loose and smells sour, like hampered laundry. Surely cleanliness is no sin. She pushes the sheet aside, picks up the candy box and hurries out to the living room. She looks around, then stuffs the box under the sofa cushions. Anything to get it out of sight. Then she heads to the upstairs bathroom, eyeing the dog pen through the kitchen doorway. The dog gets to her feet and looks at Rose with expectant eyes and a wagging tail. She'd forgotten about the dog but has no time for it now. Everything is so screwed up. She concentrates on one problem, the kaleidoscope turns, and the picture is changed completely. She turns her back on the dog and climbs the stairs.

Rose sits down on the toilet. Getting rid of the pressure on her bladder is some relief. A soft breeze blows through the open window. The feeling on her bare skin is refreshing, like the morning air when her family vacationed at the lake during her childhood. When she wakened early, her mother led her down to the water, took her pajamas off and let her splash around naked before other people woke up. The water was cool before the midday sun baked it to bathwater.

Rose is slightly shamed by the memory. Why hadn't she worn a bathing suit? It wasn't as if she hadn't owned one.

Above the bathtub water droplets cling to the tile. Rose likes to shower first. There's something about the damp walls, the hair in the trap, that makes the room feel used and less refreshing. She considers toweling down the tile but knows there's no drying the shower curtain. She pulls it closed and turns on the water. It spurts cold at first, chilling her, but she makes herself stay. As it runs warm, she turns her face up and enjoys the pressure pounding on her skin. She turns her back on the spray and rotates her shoulders. Their soreness melts like candle wax, and she blesses their big hot-water heater. There's no skimping on water at their house. She'd like to stay all day.

Finally she begins to soap herself down. It's then that she discovers something odd. Her fingers find it first, an odd-textured depression in her skin's surface, like a dent in her right hip. She rubs at it, the soap in her palm, thinking it will go away. When it doesn't, she bends around to look, stepping from the spray to check it out. When she sees what it is, she gropes outside the shower curtain for a towel to blot the water from her lashes. She twists herself around again but nothing has changed. Her head goes light. She sits down on the side of the tub.

There, imprinted on her hip, is the figure of Christ on the cross. The thorns in his crown and his bent knees have drawn blood to the surface in pinpricks, though she isn't really bleeding. The tiny spots are red-purple, three thorn dots and a larger dot for his knees. The cross shape of his body is pale pink. She remembers the stories her mother read at bedtime, stories about Saint Clare and Saint Francis, how their palms and feet bled when they prayed. It was called the stigmata. But Francis and Clare lived in denial for years. She's only been at it for two days. And she's totally failed, considering she just had sex.

When her dizziness has passed, she stands up and rubs her side with the towel. She looks again. It's Jesus all right. The size and shape, however, is familiar. It's not the real stigmata. She owns the crucifix that made it. It happened in Sister

Mary Theresa's bed when Everett transferred his weight. It's like those ripples she found on her arms and legs as a child, after she napped on her mother's chenille spread. Nonetheless. She can't take her eyes off it. It's so clear—the drooping head, the bent-up knees. Her mind fills in the ladder of ribs and the cloth-covered loins. There He is, mortified in her flesh.

Rose faces the water again. Now the shower seems to be flooding her insides, too. Goose bumps break out on her arms. She's not cold—the water is warm—but her shoulders shudder. She turns the water off, finds the towel and rubs hard at her side with the terry. She'll erase the mark by making all her skin pink. Instead the mark turns a darker rose than the surrounding skin. It's so weird that it should have happened when she's been praying and seeking a sign. She looks again at the crucified figure. What more personal way could He tell her He died for her sins?

She sees the words in her missal, the bold type indicating where the congregation is supposed to speak. She whispers to the foggy mirror, "Did you know? He died for your sins." She rubs a circle in the fog and sees her reflection, wet hair washed back from her clean face. "He died for your sins." Her skin tingles. She hugs herself, rocking a minute, then breaks into a little dance as the meaning breaks over her. She wants to skip, throw her arms up and shout to the whole world. There's no one to stop her. She hurries to an open window in her bedroom and calls to the sparrows. "I'm okay. I'm forgiven." The tiny birds chirp back, and again she calls, "Did you hear? Forgiven!"

When she turns from the window, the sight of Everett's rumpled covers touches her. She gets in bed, wraps herself in his sheets and rocks purposely to make waves. It's really about Everett, too, the forgiveness. If Everett weren't who he is, so impatient and eager for her all the time, she'd never have received the mark. She inhales the musk from his pillow and returns to Everett sucking at her breasts. "Unless you eat my body," Rose thinks, but then stops herself. It's a blasphemous thought. Not at all what Jesus meant.

But the verse won't leave, no matter how she tries to dismiss it. She toys with the thought—how Everett consumes her—how Jesus insists that she eat His body. Maybe it is the same. Maybe that's what Jesus wants from her—a communion so close that it's somehow like sex. Nuns wear a wedding ring as the Bride of Christ, which had somehow seemed so chaste before. Could it mean they vow to become as close to Christ as she is to Everett? If so, Communion will never be the same. She has Sister Mary Theresa to thank, the Blessed Virgin and the Lord Himself. She wants to shout *Hallelujah*, like those women with big hair on Christian television, but she's Catholic so she contents herself with a good bounce on the bed.

When Rose is dressed and on her way downstairs, she passes Valley's doorway, sees the canopy bed and remembers she was going to search for a quilt. Back in her own bedroom she pulls quilts from the cedar chest until she finds the one she wants. It's in shades of blue, an intricate pattern, the center octagon surrounded with squares and elongated diamonds. But Rose sees that central octagon as a courtyard. The diamonds outlining the squares on four corners make turrets. Best of all are the trapezoids that connect the diamonds and form the actual castle wall. She had centered the castle on a huge square of deep-blue fabric, to represent the moat.

Rose begins to tidy up Valley's bed, careful to leave the papers in the same piles, though evening up their edges. Next to the bed the wormy caterpillar has spun a cocoon. His jar looks much tidier this way. She can't understand how Valley can sleep with worms watching.

Rose pulls the sheets taut and tucks them in, asking the Blessed Virgin to help Valley with her tests, when her fingers find an odd-shaped fragment of something under the mattress. It feels like heavy cardboard. The perimeter is uneven, like a puzzle piece. She pulls it out to look. It's mottled blue, like the background of studio portraits.

Rose lifts the mattress and finds the puzzle portrait, a few pieces broken out here and there, probably from Valley sleeping on it and shifting her weight. But the place where Valley's head used to be is now a gaping hole, unsightly, like an empty eye socket. Rose's stomach flops over. Her daughter is in pain and this is proof. She's got to get Rob and the punk to leave town, but short of writing poison-pen letters and slashing their tires, she's not sure how. It's best if they *want* to leave.

Rose smoothes the Castle Wall quilt over the bed. There's

a place where the piecing has pulled loose, and she finds her upstairs sewing basket to repair the rift. While she plies the tiny needle through the layers of fabric, her mind works on ways to breach Rob's wall. Just a tiny hole would do, a snag for a toe to get caught and cause lots of damage. She thinks back to the night he came by the house. She won't even have to make the hole. Rob's been to prison. He's already done it for her. Helen's twin brother is the police chief. He can run Rob out of town.

Rose lifts her skirt and slips her underpants down to examine the spot, as if Jesus might somehow endorse her plan. The crucifix has faded to a shapeless pink blur. With that bruise on Valley's side, though, she has to do something. The punk left his mark. Now she'll leave hers.

The police station is on the opposite side of Eden, beside the town garage. Rose parks next to Ed Dudley's police cruiser with its Kiss a Cop bumper sticker, and circles the yellow-brick building in search of the front door. She's not sure what she's going to say, but Ed had a puppy crush on her in high school, so getting him to do something shouldn't be too hard. Before getting out of the car, she checks the rearview mirror and arranges her hair so the stubs of the bangs she cut off won't show. "This is for Valley," she tells her reflection. She can't think of anything she wouldn't do for her daughter. She'd even die for her. Rose crosses herself and scoots out of the car before she changes her mind.

A yard fenced with chain link and topped with barbed

wire connects to the station—the evidence pound, she knows, from watching cop shows with Everett. But all the evidence Eden has collected is three picnic tables and a rusty trash barrel. Rose imagines a major heist from the state park. Her nerves make it seem funnier than it is.

She pauses a minute before entering. If people see her going in, they might think she's in trouble. But her only witnesses are knee-high corn plants and the headlight of an approaching train, nearly invisible in the sunlight. She enters a small waiting room. A buzzing fluorescent tube glows green on the built-in benches. She presses the spot where the crucifix marked her hip like some kind of lucky rabbit's foot, though she knows she shouldn't treat Jesus like a charm. "Bless me Father, for I have sinned," she mumbles as she steps up to the dispatcher's window.

"Call 1-800-GRAB DUI. Blow the whistle on drunk drivers" a poster on the far wall reads. Officer Mumford, a graying patrolman who reminds her of a friendly crossing guard, is manning the desk behind a sliding glass window. He looks up from his radio. "Hey, Rose. What brings you here?"

"I need to see Chief Dudley." Rose usually calls Helen's brother Ed, but today she uses his title so Mumford will know this is police business, not a personal visit. Still, the scent of pencil shavings takes her back to elementary school, and she feels ridiculous—like some fourth grader asking to speak to the principal. She uncrosses her feet and stands up straighter.

Officer Mumford reaches for the phone. "What business?" he asks matter-of-factly.

Rose hadn't planned on his asking. *Well, you see, Officer*

*Mumford, my old boyfriend is back in town, trying to buy Phil
Langston's trailer. You have to stop him.* The whole department
would have a good laugh over that, at those picnic tables,
eating carryout from McDonald's. "I can't tell you," Rose says
as inaudibly as the fourth grader she's become.

Office Mumford knits up his brows. "Are you okay?"

She looks at the floor. "Sort of." If she sounds upset, maybe
he'll turn her over to Ed without any more questions.

Mumford picks up the phone, waits, then announces her
presence. It's all for show, Rose thinks, since they could call
out as easily. Ed's just on the other side of the wall and his
door is open. Everything about her visit suddenly seems silly.
A staffed police department is silly in a town like Eden.
Other than some minor vandalism and a few kids picked up
for DUI, there's nothing for them to do.

Ed shows up at his office door in his starched blue shirt
and tie. "Well, hey there, Rosie," he says, obviously pleased
to see her. He's still slender, but much brawnier than the boy
she knew in high school. "Come on back." Roses scoots
through the doorway separating the waiting room from the
office, anxious to escape Officer Mumford's gaze.

Ed's office has paneled walls and sunlight pours through
his window. A small fan pivots in front of it, and his radio
terminal takes up the other side of his desk. A set of car keys
is pushpinned to the bulletin board map on the wall—stuck
to the street where they were found, Rose suspects. "What's
up?" Ed asks, sitting down at his desk and motioning her to
sit in the armless chair next to it.

Rose clears her throat and tries to look distressed and helpless. It worked once on Officer Tant when he stopped her for speeding on Main Street. She told him Everett wasn't home on time and she was worried about an accident. He then called the station for her, for accident reports, and forgot to write her a ticket.

"Do you remember Rob MacIntyre?" she begins. "He was in our high school class. Tall, thin. Kind of a bad boy?"

Ed leans back in his chair. "Funny you should mention him." He stares at a pencil poised between his two index fingers like a ruler needed to size up the situation. "I saw him down at Millie's yesterday. How long has it been since he left Eden?"

"Seventeen years," Rose says too quickly and twists the hem of her skirt. She should have waffled. Knowing precisely without a moment's thought seems too much as though she's been logging the years on her calendar. She hurries on so he doesn't have a chance to notice. "He came by my house the other night."

"Hmm. I didn't know you two were such good friends."

Rose shifts in the chair. "We're not. He wanted to see Everett." That's good. Believable. "Business or something." She forces herself to stop. She mustn't sound as if she's making excuses. She crosses her legs. "I just thought you should know something he said. For the record, you know. He's got a kid with him—a juvenile delinquent he met through the probation department." She lowers her voice and looks at him through her lashes. "Ed, Rob said he's been in prison."

Ed sits up again, frowns, bites his lower lip and drums his pencil on his desk the way the boys did in fourth grade. It drove the teacher crazy. Mrs. Murphy collected the pencils and broke them in two.

Ed stops drumming. "I can't say I'm surprised. Seems like Hennesey said all that tampering with public phones stopped when MacIntyre blew town, if I remember right. Nobody ever pinned it on him, but the locks were broke and there was money missing."

Hennesey was the police chief when Ed was a patrolman.

Rose leans forward. "Don't you need to know what they finally caught him doing? Prison isn't exactly your everyday address. Maybe you should look up his records."

Ed's chair creaks when he leans back. "I can't do that, Rose. Not without just cause. The state has procedures we have to follow. Curiosity doesn't justify snooping around in people's lives."

"But what if it was an act of violence?" Rose's voice is louder now. "You're here to protect the public safety. You might need to keep an eye on him."

"I hardly think he's violent." Ed looks out the window for a minute, then turns back to her. "I don't get it, Rose. What's it to you?"

Rose uncrosses and recrosses her legs, arranging her skirt in her lap while she thinks. She mustn't give him cause to poke around in *her* past, though she's never been to the police station before and can't think what he'd find besides a few parking tickets in Dayton. The incriminating evidence against her is in Dr. Burns's office, though even then she doesn't know what it would be.

"The man's paid his debt to society, whatever it was he did," Ed says when it's clear she's not going to explain herself. "I'm not a judge, and I'm not his probation officer." His voice has the hyperreasonable tone she gets from Helen sometimes. It always makes her feel stupid.

Rose opens her eyes wide and looks up at him, begging. "There must be a way. Can't you just do it—for me?"

"You're not the issue, Rose. Checking criminal records leaves a paper trail. I can't justify the check unless he does something wrong. Far as I can see, he's behavin' himself."

"He's trying to buy Phil Langston's trailer. He's planning to stay here."

"That's not a crime, Rosie. Why do you care?"

With that question, the room seems unbearably hot. Rose's mouth turns cottony, and the metallic taste is back. "Doggone it, Ed. How long have I known you? I'm your twin sister's best friend, and you can't do this one little thing without making a federal case out of it?"

"Helen's real fond of you, Rosie, and you know I'd do it for you if I could. I just can't."

"I just want you to look up Rob's record and I thought, you know, that you could make up some excuse. Can't you see how much it means to me?"

Ed stands and straightens the papers on his desk. "I can't help you, Rose. I'm sorry." He walks to the door to show her out.

Rose gets to her feet, defeated. "Everyone in town knows about your speed trap down past my house," she says on her way out. "You could at least change locations."

"I'm not trying to fool anyone. The kids and Mr. Cockburn don't always watch where they're going, and I want people to slow down."

Ed's right, of course. And she hates him for it.

The new dog is coiled on an old bath mat, sleeping in her pen, when Rose drops her purse on the kitchen counter. The dog lifts her head and looks at Rose with startled brown eyes, as if the purse has fallen on her head. "What's your problem?" Rose asks, though the dog demanded no explanation. The dog cocks her head to one side. Her eyes follow Rose as she fills the teakettle with water, sets it on a burner and searches the cupboard for one of those soothing apple-flavored tea bags she uses when she's on a diet—to fool herself into thinking she's eating something. "It seemed so simple," she tells the dog as she drops the tea bag in her favorite cup. She pours the hot water, watches the tea bag swell and pretends she's eating apple pie. The dog is still looking at her with soft, soulful eyes. She wonders what the dog's fur feels like. "You've been in there all morning. Do you need to go to the toilet?" Rose asks as if she were speaking to a person. She can't remember what it was Everett and Valley had been calling the dog. The name of some state. Nebraska?

The dog's tail thumps the pen floor a few times before she gets to her feet, stretches each of her back legs and walks to the little wire door. Rose slides the latch and opens the door a crack. Nebraska waits, tail wagging, then paws at the door to open it farther.

"Goodness," Rose says. "Aren't you a smart little thing?" Nebraska wriggles through the door and stands at Rose's feet, looking up. Rose stoops and pats her back tentatively, as if the dog is some beast that might suddenly go wild. Nebraska sits down. Rose pats her on the head. The fur feels silky, not bristly the way it looks. "Want to go outside?" The dog is on her feet, dancing over to the door. "Don't run away," Rose says, pushing the screen open. Nebraska trots out to the grass, squats, wipes her back feet, then looks back at Rose. "That's good. Come on back now." The dog bounds back, ears flopping. Rose is amazed. As a toddler, Valley always refused to use the potty before they left home, then needed to go in the middle of the supermarket. If Ed Dudley obeyed half so well as the dog, she'd be out of this mess, Rob run right out of town.

"Why won't anybody do what I want them to?" Rose asks the dog. Nebraska sits down and perks her ears. Rose looks to around the kitchen for something to give her. Next to the flour canister is the ball she bought for the child she nearly hit. She tosses it across the room. It bounces off the wall and rolls into the living room. Kansas bounds after it.

Rose follows her, but her thoughts return to her problem. On an impulse she pulls her skirt up above her waist and looks at her hip. Gone. There's not a single pinprick left—no sign that it was ever there. Her shoulders feel heavy and she sinks to the couch. It's her own fault. Everett is right. She puts way too much store in coincidence. It was a stupid accident, for heaven's sake. The exhilaration she felt when she found it is not only gone, she can't remember how it felt, then or ever. Only a fool hollered to birds and bounced on her bed. Or a lunatic. Her nun's bed and her prayers have all been for naught—a silly exercise she made up to help herself feel in control. Without actually paying a price.

The dog sits at Rose's feet, holding the red ball in her mouth. "What am I supposed to do now?" Rose asks her. "Tell them flat out that Valley is Rob's daughter?" Nebraska drops the ball and wags her tail. Rose is transfixed by the thought, hypnotized by the dog's tail going back and forth, back and forth. A calm settles over her. She hasn't known such peace since Rob came back, though the idea is outrageous and she can't imagine herself pulling it off.

The dog burrows under a couch cushion and is pushing and prodding it up as though she's trying to get under it. "What are you doing?" Rose asks. Nebraska drags the Whitman's box out with her mouth, pulling at it and falling backward when she loses her grip. Rose laughs. She rips the cellophane off the box, then opens the lid, inhales its heavy sweetness, pops one in her mouth and drops another one on the carpet for Nebraska. "Good girl," she says. "You know what's important." Rose slides down onto the floor next to the dog and takes another chocolate. She holds her hand out flat to Nebraska with a chocolate-covered cherry and watches the dog snarf it down. She couldn't find a girlfriend who would eat with more relish than this dog does.

She's decided now. She's giving up. She'll strip the sheets off Mary Theresa's bed and go back to sleeping with Everett. And she's really got to go see Helen. She doesn't need Ed's help to get rid of Rob. She can start a rumor. And she can count on Helen to pass it around.

CHAPTER 17

After plodding through her American history and Spanish finals at school, Valley heads for the highway. The day is hot. In her sleeveless shirt and shorts she feels trapped between the sun beating down and the heat rising from the pavement, as though she's been shut up in an oven to bake. Despite the heat, she hurries along, afraid she has waited too long. The woods, the shack and the old woman were so unearthly they may have disappeared by now.

A gigantic horsefly circles her hair, buzzing in her ear. She zigs and zags to dodge it. Nothing works until she darts from the blacktop of Route 4 onto the spongy soil of the woods floor, ducking under branches to the canopy of shade. The damp of rotting vegetation drowns the hot-tar smell, as if she's passed through an invisible curtain. Trouble is, it will be harder to find the cabin through the maze of tree trunks with no landmarks to get her bearings.

To Valley's surprise, though, she knows which way to go, as if she's somehow being drawn in the right direction, as if the old woman understands how badly Valley needs to know she's real. She picks her way between pine boughs and the slender boles of saplings, stepping over fallen trees until she sees the cabin's tin roof. The old woman is outside, stooping near the ground in a rare beam of light. Valley steps behind a large tree, where she can spy without being spotted. A natty braid hangs over the woman's one shoulder, and her head looks heavier on that side. *There*, Valley says to Joanie, nodding her head in an imagined conversation. *I told you I saw someone.*

The woman carries a grass basket hooked over one forearm and stoops to collect wild plants, picking flowers from some and yanking others up by the roots. Though the air feels warm to Valley, the woman wears jeans and a man's shirt, cuffs soiled and raveled with wear. A gray rat follows her around, chattering loudly, and Valley feels disoriented, like in those odd dreams where she's conscious of watching herself dreaming. The rat's fur looks shaggy like a squirrel's. When it sits up on its haunches and *chee-chee-chees* at the old woman, Valley sees that it *is* a squirrel, but it has no tail, like an imaginary animal in a mix-and-match game, waiting for her to choose between a peacock's feathers and a fish tail. The woman pays no mind to the squirrel's scolding but tosses an acorn his way. He holds it in his miniature hands and nibbles, his bright eyes darting alertly around the woods. He spots Valley and lets out an alarming stream of chatter. She tenses the way she does when she plays a wrong note in her flute lesson, but then, thinking the squirrel has announced her presence, she steps into the clearing, crackling twigs in- tentionally so the old woman won't be frightened. The woman doesn't look up. "Hello?" Valley says tentatively, as if testing her voice against the wilderness.

The woman continues to dig. She's on her knees now, her back to Valley, soles of her bare feet upturned and looking vulnerable in their pale contrast to the rest of her skin. Valley creeps closer. The woman is using a sharp stick to loosen dirt around a mayapple. She pulls long tentacles from the clinging soil along with the plant's fingerlike leaves and tiny white flowers. Valley remembers them from biology class. They'd done a whole semester on plants. She stoops nearby to pull another mayapple up, then offers it to the woman.

When Valley's shadow falls across the woman's work, she looks up in alarm and gets to her feet. Looking back over her shoulder at Valley, she scurries toward the house. Valley chases after her and catches her hand. "Wait." The woman frowns and cocks her head to one side as if she's listening to a deep inner silence. Then she pulls her hand away and hurries into the cabin but leaves the door ajar. The squirrel follows her in.

Valley stands in the doorway holding out the basket the old woman has left behind, waiting for her eyes to adjust to the darkness inside. Gradually the cabin's one room appears. The dirt floor is covered in broken nutshells, and dried flowers hang upside down from the ceiling. The woman stands by the far wall, clutching a long-haired tabby. Valley knocks on the door before stepping inside, to show the woman she has come for a visit. "I came to find out what happened to the bird that crashed into your window," she shouts, thinking the old woman might be hard of hearing. "I'm the girl who fainted outside your cabin."

The woman says nothing. Maybe she doesn't speak English? Valley can hear the cat purring. She takes four more steps and extends her hand, palm up, toward the two of them. The cat bats at it with a white paw but doesn't extend its claws.

Valley walks to the window. "The bird?" She locks her thumbs together and flaps her hands like wings. "Flew into the window." She flies her hands into the glass, then pantomimes the shocked bird falling to the ground as she drops to her knees. The old woman nods, her head at an angle. She puts the cat down and stoops next to Valley's dying bird. The odor of unwashed body saturates the woman's clothing, but somehow smells natural in this place. She cups Valley's hands in hers and walks her to the door and out to the edge of the clearing, where she kneels, still holding Valley's hands. Her palms are pale and leathery, like the soles of her feet. The woman kneels at a spot on the ground where the soil is disrupted, circled with a ring of white pebbles.

"I thought so," Valley says. "I didn't think she could live." She shakes her head and the old woman shakes hers, too. They agree. It's too bad.

"My name is Valley." The old woman stares at her with raised brows, and Valley understands that she is deaf. Valley grabs a stick and writes her name in the dirt in capital letters. Then she hands the stick to the woman. The woman smiles and draws lines, too. But her lines are not letters, just a design. If she knows English, she can't write. Or else she writes a different language. Valley names her Half-Moon, after pictures of the sleeping crescent in story books, always poised in the night sky at an angle, like a golden hammock. Half-Moon sounds Indian. There were Shawnees in Ohio, it seems, though she hasn't studied Indians since third grade. Tecumseh had some kind of standoff near Wilmington, Ohio. But there aren't Indians around anymore, so she's probably wrong. Not that it matters since Half-Moon can't talk or hear.

As Valley gets to her feet with the old woman still in a crouch, Half-Moon points to the scratches on Valley's legs. "Branches," Valley says, grabbing a woody shrub stem and passing it in front of her leg. She doesn't know how to explain why she was running, though she'd like to. It would be a relief to tell someone how frightened she was, though somehow she senses Half-Moon knows. The old woman gets up—nimbly, as if she's younger than she looks—and gestures for Valley to follow her back into the cabin.

In the shadows Valley spots unlit candles around the room, surprisingly manufactured looking, like the votives parishioners at Our Lady light to pray for their loved ones. Each candle is set in a jar like a jelly jar. Any recycling bin would supply those. The studs on one wall are lined with clay jars, each etched with a drawing. Those she must have made. On the ground beneath the jars is a large flat stone with a round rock the size of Valley's palm sitting on top.

Half-Moon takes down a jar with a picture of a tooth-edged pointed leaf. She removes several pieces of bark and runs her fingers along their soft insides, then fills a dipper with water from a clay jar near the fireplace. When she soaks the bark in the water, its soft pulp swells into a pasty ointment. She smears it down one of Valley's cuts with her middle finger. The paste is cool, her touch gentle. Valley smiles and Half-Moon smiles back. Deep lines crease the corners of her eyes, which don't disappear when her mouth straightens again. She nods and hands Valley the rest of the bark.

"Thank you."

Half-Moon sucks on her teeth, making a clucking sound. The squirrel skitters over to her feet. She picks him up and rubs the paste remaining on her middle finger on the stump of the squirrel's tail before putting him back down. The cat circles her legs in a figure eight, rubbing up against the woman's jeans. There's something strange about the cat's walk—as if his balance is off. Valley's never heard of a cat that didn't have great balance.

Then the cat brushes up against Valley's legs. The paste smears. Half-Moon emits a coarse snort that startles Valley until she sees her crinkling eyes and realizes she's laughing. While Half-Moon preens the cat, ungunking her fur with her thumb and forefinger, Valley looks around the room. There's a fireplace at one end. One corner is laid with corrugated cardboard and feed sacks stuffed with corn husks. Her bed.

Half-Moon pads to the fireplace and gestures for Valley to follow. There's heat coming from the ashes, though the embers don't glow until the woman stirs them. Half-Moon crosses her legs and sinks to the dirt floor, sitting Indian-style, then picks up a pipe from the hearth. She fills the bowl of the pipe from one of several clay jars nearby, then lights the leaves with a straw stuck in the embers. Her mouth spreads in a smile while she sucks on the stem. Valley inhales sour sweat along with the pipe's heavy incense. Half-Moon takes a deep drag on the stem and hands it to Valley, who sits down on the dirt floor, the packed earth cool beneath her bare legs. She hesitates. Her mother had taught her not to take food from strangers. Cigarettes were forbidden on other grounds, though Valley had not been tempted since she needed all her wind to play her flute. Pipes had never been mentioned. They were beyond question. And with good reason. Who knew what might be in that jar?

The cat rubs up against her thigh, then walks toward Half-Moon, still listing to one side as though it, too, has sucked on the pipe and feels the need to lie down. Once in the old woman's lap, the cat circles in the basin of her crossed legs and settles down, facing out. Valley's misgivings seem misplaced. The cat trusts Half-Moon. The old woman heals rather than harms. Valley takes the pipe, sniffs at its bowl, puts the mouthpiece to her lips and sucks deeply. With the drag in her mouth, she's uncertain what to do next. The fumes sit on her palate and rag on her throat. She's tempted to swallow but inhales instead. Her chest expands as though her lungs can now hold more oxygen. Half-Moon's upper body sways, and an unsingable sound, harsh and guttural, emerges from deep in her throat. She reaches for the pipe and sucks on the stem once again. The singing resumes once she's inhaled. Valley feels lighter, as though all the oxygen in her lungs has lifted the weight that's sat on her chest since she babysat Joey. That's when she notices an odd feature about the cat's face, though perhaps it, too, is part of the dream. The cat seems to be missing its whiskers. Big eyes, set wide in the inverted triangle of its face, look vulnerable, like Joey's eyes when he came to and saw her bending over him.

"I did a terrible thing Saturday," Valley says, amazed to hear not her usual voice but a pinched version come from her mouth, threaded between the rising and falling of Half-Moon's chant. Half-Moon's body is rocking, head swaying from one shoulder to the other. "I didn't mean for it happen," Valley says, fighting to sound earnest through her funny voice. "You have to believe that. I thought I could do it okay. I really did. All my friends babysit." Half-Moon's chant wanders up and down the scale. Her eyes are glazed over but fixed on Valley's face. "But the baby wouldn't stop crying no matter what I did. I tried everything I knew."

A pleasant hum clicks in and begins vibrating in Valley's blood, like the purring of the cat in Half-Moon's lap, a feeling quite opposite the horror of the deed she's confessing. Valley sings to her thrumming blood the songs she sang to Joey, then rocks back and forth as she relives trying to quiet him in the chair. "When nothing worked, I did an awful thing." Her body begins shaking and her throat feels as though it's been rubbed with sandpaper, but she has to force the words past it. To get it out. If she can't do it here, she'll carry it with her the rest of her life. "I left him to thrash it out alone," she blurts. Tears burst from her ducts and flood her eyes before breaking and wetting her cheeks. They taste salty when they hit her lips. "He stopped breathing," she whispers before her words turn to wailing that matches the sound coming from Half-Moon's throat. Her body weaves back and forth, in and out, swaying to the sound of her sorrow. When the image of Joey's face washes in on the tide, separate from his little blue body which bobs on a separate wave, huge bubbles rack up from her diaphragm and out her mouth, jagged and sharp, ranging all over the scale.

Valley opens her eyes, hoping Joey's defaced body will disappear. She sees Half-Moon stick a reedy wand with a thistle tip into the jar of water near the hearth. Valley's wailing stops midscale, and she lifts her face as the old woman drizzles water on her already wet cheeks. Half-Moon's cheeks are damp, too. The leaves of the thistle provide a surprising dousing. The singing comes once again from the old woman's throat as she waves the wand over Valley's head. With water dripping off her face, Valley reaches up to touch the thistle, as though it holds some healing power.

With the prickly purple thistle cupped in both hands, Valley hears a melody through the overtones of Half-Moon's wailing, deep and mournful, like Debussy or Ravel coming to her from underwater. The discord collects under her lungs until she feels as if they'll explode, then pushes, pushes up her throat, so that she throws her head back. Her torso flails like the dying cardinal circling in the dirt. When she thinks she can stand it no longer, it comes out her mouth in a loud shriek that somehow feels separate from any sound she's ever made. She chases the sound out the open door and through the woods in daylight, to the cab of Snake's truck, where once again she is struggling, trying to break from the bondage of his arms. She exhales hard, the way she did on Saturday night to make herself thin enough to get free, and a second shriek follows the first. Its sound tapers into breathlessness, and silence hangs in the room, thick with the terror of what she did first to Joey, then to herself.

When the silence thins, Half-Moon begins her tuneless dirge once again. It surrounds the silence and forces it out the door. A calm settles over Valley, and she wonders at what happened. A pleasant drowsiness overtakes her. The thought of stretching out on the cool ground and resting, sleeping until her scratches heal, overtakes her.

Half-Moon reaches into her breast pocket and pulls out a long chain. Valley sits still as the old woman weaves the gold links in a crown through Valley's hair. There's no sapphire on the chain, but Valley's sure it's hers nonetheless. The links are broken in one place and the large lobster-claw clasp has a blond hair caught in it. The sapphire charm must have slipped off when the chain broke.

Valley reaches up and fingers the gold links, touching tentatively so the chain doesn't fall. She holds her head very still and upright, as if Half-Moon's put a book on her head. The links slip from her clean hair anyway and slither to the ground. She slips it in her pocket. How had Half-Moon found it? How had she, Valley, come upon Half-Moon, then known to return to this place? It is as if Half-Moon has known all along and drawn her here. Is that possible? Are there people who know such things? Whose hearts bear burdens for people they've never met? Like the Blessed Virgin? The thought seems outlandish when she looks on the dirty creature standing before her. It doesn't matter. Valley's arms wrap around her Madonna's legs. She wipes her wet face on the worn denim and holds tight.

CHAPTER 18

Late that same afternoon Everett arrives home after installing a three-pronged, grounded electrical outlet in Esther Logan's kitchen to accommodate her new microwave. The kitchen stinks, and he's surprised to find that Kansas has messed her crate. It smells and looks like diarrhea, but once Kansas is released from the pen, she dances around his feet, so she must be okay. He's heard a change in dog food can cause diarrhea.

"Poor baby. Better get you outside," he tells her and wads up the newspaper in the bottom of the pen. Rosie won't like a dog that stinks up her kitchen. He heads out to the garbage can with Kansas. While she takes care of business, he'll inspect his purchase. It's still in his trunk. He can't quite bring himself to take a gun in the house, though the stinky diarrhea proves Rosie's still shut up in storage. That's how he thinks of her now, as if she's out of season or something. If he were going to hide the gun anywhere in the house, he'd bury it in the Christmas garland and move it come December.

He opens his trunk, picks up the gun, runs his hands over the walnut stock, slides the pump a few times. He'd love to fire this little baby. See how she blows.

Everett eyes the dead tree branch that hangs over the garden and picks out a few cans from the recycling bin in the garage. He'll just take a few practice shots. What the hell. If he hits nothing else, the noise may rouse Rosie from her roost. But he wants to make sure everyone is out of the way. He's not an expert marksman. Everett calls Kansas, puts her in the kitchen and closes the door tight. Valley's not home from school—probably at the library cramming for her next final—and Rosie…well, at least she's safe. Always complaining about the woodchucks in the garden, too. He'll say he's getting rid of them.

Everett opens the box of #5 shot and slides the little cylinders into their chambers. Loading her is fairly straightforward for a handy guy, and he's glad he didn't need the shopkeeper to show him how. There are some things a man can't ask. With all five chambers loaded, he lays the gun down carefully in his trunk once again, then paces his way across the lawn with the cans he's planning to line up on the tree branch as if he's about to fight a duel. He places the cans fairly far apart on the branch and chuckles to himself, thinking how the sound of gunfire will raise Rosie from the dead. As he walks back across the lawn, he sees Valley coming up the driveway. "Hey, kiddo. Where you been? It's almost five-thirty."

"Um, Joanie's house. Studying for English."

Everett doesn't notice that she's not carrying books. He beckons her to his trunk. "Come here. I want to show you something."

The gun is nestled in the Wal-Mart bag that holds the orange shirt. She has a weird look in her eye, as if she's not sure she's really seeing it. "Dad? Is that a gun?"

"That, my dear, is a Mossberg twelve-gauge shotgun. I've decided to take up hunting."

"Does Mom know?"

"She will soon. See those cans?" He points to the dead branch.

Valley giggles. "She'll say you'll shoot your eye out."

"Women." He wags his head. "How can a guy shoot his eye out with the gun pointing the other way?"

"Yeah, well, be careful."

He tries to look casual as he picks up the gun, puts the stock to his shoulder and aims down the barrel.

"Hold on. I'll watch from inside. If I don't warn her, Mom will go through the roof." She skips back to the house and pushes through the kitchen door.

That's when Everett spies the woodchuck among the green shoots in his garden. He raises the gun. Rosie will come out to see about the noise, and he'll have a trophy for her.

He sights the little fella's fat body down the barrel. Squeezes the trigger at the same moment that Kansas streaks after the woodchuck. *Blam!* A second after the blast Kansas crumples to the ground at the perimeter of the garden.

Everett breaks into a run, gun in one hand. At the edge of the grass he lays it down and stoops at her side. He's hit her left rear hip. The shot has made a bloody mess of it. Her breath is coming heavy and hard, her sides heaving. She doesn't lift her head, but the eye he can see looks at him re-proachfully.

"Oh, God. Oooh God," Everett moans. He hears himself praying, lips moving uncontrollably. "Don't let her die. Please God. I'll never shoot the stupid gun again." Everett looks back to the house, sees Valley's face at the kitchen window. Then Valley comes charging through the open kitchen door carrying a hand towel. Her face holds all the horror she must feel seeing her dog with blood for a hip, but she doesn't hide her face.

"God. Look what you did. Why don't you just shoot me next?"

"I shut her in the house, really I did. I thought she was safe," he says. "She must have escaped when you went in."

Valley rocks her one way to get the towel under her and then the other to hammock her in it. "Easy, girl. That's a good girl," she says in doggy singsong. "You're going to be alright."

Everett can't look, not at Valley's face or Kansas's eyes.

"Get me some ice and another towel," Valley directs. "We've got to stop the bleeding." She continues to croon to Kansas, how brave she is, how good, while Everett sprints across the lawn, forgetting he has a bum leg.

In the kitchen he finds a pan and bangs the metal trays hard against the counter until the cubes fall out, wondering where his wife is. She can't stay cooped up in there when he's brought the house down. There's no time to look for her now. On his way out the door he takes a handful of clean dish towels from a drawer.

Valley is where he left her, on her knees with her face close to the dog's ear. Kansas has closed her eyes. "Hang in there, baby," she says. "Mama's gonna take care of you."

Everett hands her the towels and the pan of ice. She presses a folded towel onto Kansas's hip. Its fibers turn red in splotches. Valley empties ice onto the bloodstains and wraps the length of another dish towel around the joint a few times, putting pressure on the wound by binding the towel tight. Everett wonders where she learned it.

"Okay, help me lift her. You take those two corners." With her head Valley indicates two corners of the hand towel beneath the dog. She takes the other two. They lift Kansas in her hammock. "Drive us to the vet," she says. "I'll sit with her in the back."

Valley backs onto the seat first, putting Kansas's head in her lap as Everett lowers her gently onto the seat. He pulls the keys from his pocket, closes the trunk and heads for the driver's side mechanically, as if he can do anything as long as Valley's voice continues to instruct him. Otherwise, he's completely numb.

On the town road Everett can see that he's going thirty-five, but the car feels as if its crawling. "How is she?" he asks periodically.

"Breathing."

Everett turns on his flashers and speeds down back roads, pausing only briefly at stop signs. The words *Help her, God. Please help her,* repeat over and over in his head.

The veterinary clinic is a one-story brick building with a flat roof. Everett pulls the car up close to the door and gets out to help Valley maneuver the towel full of Kansas out of the car and into the office. She opens her eyes when they move her, her vulnerable, betrayed look now given over to the blankness of resigned suffering. Everett hates himself.

"Go right in," the receptionist says when she sees the blood-soaked hammock between them. "The doctor is still here. Room two is empty."

Everett and Valley wend their hammock through the doorways, Everett grateful to whatever voice takes charge. He hears "Room two" announced over a crackly intercom, ending in the word *stat*. The treatment room is small, and the smell of alcohol replaces the lively animal odor of the outer office. Valley and Everett lay Kansas down on the stainless-steel table, Valley at her head, crooning in her ear. Kansas's sides flutter with rapid, shallow breathing. A blond woman in green scrubs enters by a second door, moving silently on her rubber-soled shoes, like a real hospital. She carries a needle and injects Kansas. "That should make her more comfortable." After a few breaths, Kansas closes her eyes and her breathing slows, which somehow makes Everett less comfortable. At least when she's awake, he knows she's alive. She looks dead now that she's unconscious.

Another woman in blue scrubs comes in with a mask dangling from around her neck. "I'm Dr. Weaver," she says, though Everett doesn't care as long as she helps Kansas. The vet removes the toweling from Kansas's hip. Everett makes himself look at the havoc he's made. The blood isn't gushing at least. It now mats her fur. "You did the right thing," the vet says. "You got the bleeding stopped."

Everett nods to Valley. "She did it. She did everything." He turns his head.

Valley is still standing next to Kansas, holding her head, still crooning a singsong in her ear. Valley is covered in blood.

Dr. Weaver asks how it happened.

"I accidentally let Kansas out when Dad was shooting gophers in the garden," Valley says.

"No, it was my fault," Everett says. "I should have put her in her crate before I started."

"Her name is Kansas?" The vet gets an IV bag from a metal locker and begins hooking it up, talking to Kansas all the while, telling the dog what she's doing, though Kansas appears to be asleep. Everett backs up to a bench along the wall and sits down so he's out of the way. Dr. Weaver's voice is gentle and reasonable, and while he doubts Kansas can hear, let alone understand what she's saying, he doesn't want the vet to stop talking.

"We can't do anything until we've treated her for shock," Dr. Weaver says to Valley and Everett. "When she's stabilized—twelve hours is my guess—I'll X-ray the hip. I can't plan the treatment until I see where the shot is lodged, how deep, how her bones are affected." She bends over the dog, shaves a patch of fur from Kansas's front leg and inserts the intravenous needle there, talking to her all the while. Everett buries his head in his hands and once again sees her little body streak into his site, ears flapping, just as he squeezes the trigger. The *blam* shakes the earth, louder than a sonic boom, and he watches Kansas crumple to the ground in slow motion. The look on her face when he knelt beside her— well, it's like a crime committed against a child. Better he should have shot himself. Moaning fills his ears, disconnected somehow from the noise coming out his mouth. Then Valley is beside him on the bench, her arm around his shoulders. He rests his head against hers and stares out the window at the indifferent sky, tracking the almost-imperceptible movement of clouds across the blue canvas. Seeing them move is suddenly so important, he forgets to blink. His eyes dry, then begin to water, and still he can't blink. Watching the clouds move is the only way he can stand how angry he is, the only way he can stand the sadness of seeing his dog and his daughter covered in blood. It's not only for Kansas that he grieves. He grieves for himself, too. For everyone on earth who suffers something undeserved.

Everett doesn't blink until Will Sweeney pulls his green Jeep up to the clinic door and gets out with a black Lab. The dog bounds around the parking lot, then follows Will inside as if he'd follow him anywhere, even into the vet's office. Will comes out a minute later with a big rawhide bone, the Lab bouncing along beside him, nose toward the treat. Will is a tender of life. He, Everett, a robber. If Kansas survives, he'll take the gun back to the shop. Sell it. Be thankful for the things he has. For each day that he has. Everett looks back to the examining table.

"I need to keep her here for several days. We'll try to save the puppies," Dr. Weaver says.

Valley lifts her head from Everett's shoulder. "She's going to have puppies?"

"Feel right here," the vet says, directing Valley's hand to Kansas's abdomen. "How long have you had her?"

"Only since Saturday."

Everett, too, is at Kansas's side, wanting to feel the puppies. First he touches the pink insides of Kansas's ear, lying flopped open on the stainless-steel table like another open wound. His hand finds the spot where the vet had guided Valley's hand, but all he feels is a balloon belly inside. He'd expected junior tennis balls or something. Kansas doesn't look big enough to deliver babies, but then, he doesn't know how you judge that on a dog. He does know that if she dies, the puppies will die, too. He'll be a murderer five or six times over.

"There's nothing any of us can do for her until this drip takes effect. I want you to go home and do something relaxing. We'll take good care of her."

"Will someone be watching her tonight?" Valley asks.

"My assistant will check her regularly."

"Can I see where she'll be?"

The vet nods and gestures for her to follow. Everett stays with Kansas, watching her ribs, willing them to keep rising and falling. When five minutes have ticked by on his watch, Everett wonders what's happened to them. He listens to the air conditioner click off and can hear voices through the wall. The treatment room smells faintly of kibble, as though they've been using it for sweeping compound. He sits again and watches Kansas from the bench. Another five minutes pass. He wonders what they could be doing. Suddenly he's certain Dr. Weaver is telling Valley she can't save Kansas, that this minute Valley is sobbing into the vet's smock. He wonders what kind of a father he is to let his daughter handle her dog's death with a stranger. Rosie is right. He *is* negligent.

Just when he's about to pick Kansas up and take her to find Valley, the assistant comes back in with a little cot, rolls Kansas onto a clean towel and has Everett help her move the dog onto the stretcher. They carry her to a room with two more tables and a stainless-steel tub. One wall is lined with cages. Several dogs, different sizes, lie inert on wire floors with trays underneath to catch their pee. Kansas still looks dead and Valley is nowhere. Once again the assistant leaves him with Kansas. He lays his hand on Kansas's ribs to make sure his eyes aren't playing tricks. He counts the breaths, up and down. When he gets to ten and is sure her little body is alive, his fingers smooth her bloody fur. She looks more comfortable that way. Again he touches her ear. The fur is especially silky on the thin rounded flaps. He flops them the way they do when she's running, willing her a future of bounding around again. She doesn't stir at all. He folds her ear down over the pink convoluted spiral inside, as if tucking her in with a blanket.

He has no business feeling sorry for himself. He shot his own dog, for god's sake. It was an accident, yes, but Kansas is suffering the same as if it'd been intentional. There ought to be a distinction. Unintentional injuries should hurt less. But they don't, and he's to blame. Not so undeserving after all. He's certainly not innocent like Kansas, on earth being loyal and obedient and only giving pleasure. Who's to say his disease isn't God's judgment on his misdeeds? When he thinks of it that way, maybe he got off light. The disease may not even develop, according to Dr. Burns. He may remain only partially affected part of the time.

Everett has resigned himself to partial paralysis when the veterinary assistant enters and hands him a card with a phone number. "The doctor says to call in six hours. We'll know more then."

Everett turns his face to the cage, suddenly afraid he's going to cry. "Have you seen my daughter?" he asks.

"Dr. Weaver's showing her the X-ray and operating rooms. She wanted to see where we'll be working on her."

"Thanks." He doesn't know what else to say. He watches while she pulls a tray out from under a Labrador retriever's hulking body. It's full of pee, and she glides to the back door so it won't spill.

"I'll get that," he says, hurrying ahead to open the rear door. Her watches her measure, then dump the pee out back, then goes out as she comes back in. "Tell my daughter I'm waiting in the car." He steps carefully through the grass to avoid stepping in poop. This is where Kansas will do her business when she's back on her feet. And she will be back on her feet. He can't stand it otherwise.

Everett heads for the blacktop parking lot. A hundred feet from the car his right leg buckles. He reaches for the ground to break his fall. He wishes he were still on the grass the instant before his hip hits the pavement.

CHAPTER 19

"Helen? It's me," Rose hollers as she opens Helen's front screen at five o'clock that afternoon. Helen hasn't got the new trim color on the screen door yet, but the storm windows—propped on the tree trunks on either side of the garden—look real nice in their new coat of dark green. The place looks fresh and clean, though God knows, Helen doesn't have an extra penny to her name. Rose glances through open doors off the front room, looking for her friend. "You work so hard," she mumbles. "You really deserve to be thin."

A country-and-western song is coming from the kitchen. Gopher bounds into the front room, barking and wagging her tail. "Down, girl. Stay down," Rose says in the firm tone she used that afternoon with Nebraska. Gopher sits, looking up at her expectantly, tail wagging, and Rose wonders that she never tried it before. She pats Gopher's head. Gopher drops her ears back and raises her snout into Rose's palm, then sniffs at Rose's legs and dress, nose working double time. "That's Nebraska you smell," Rose says. "She lives at my house now. Maybe you can come meet her." Gopher wags her tail. With her tongue hanging out, Gopher might be laughing. Rose's heart expands. Now that she's taking in orphans, she needs more room.

"Helen?" Rose calls again, heading for the cubbyhole kitchen. The boom box is blaring out the window, and Helen is pouring two glasses of lemonade.

"I thought you were away," Helen says when she sees Rose. There's something slightly hostile in her voice. Helen sets the lemonades on a tray next to two champagne glasses—His and Hers etched onto the sides—filled with red wine from a jug on the counter.

Rose settles her hip into the doorjamb. "Company?" she says. Rose had seen the truck in the driveway but assumed it was a loaner. "Sorry. I should have called first. I'll scoot on out. I just wanted to tell you I was back."

Before Helen can agree, a shriek rises above the music. Gopher pushes her way through the back screen door, and the wood frame bangs shut behind her. Rose sidles over to the sink and peers into the backyard. Bethany is seated in a webbed lawn chair with Zeke hovering over her. "Never mind them," Helen whispers, grabbing Rose's elbow to pull her away from the window. "They're just having fun."

Rose resists. Bethany is holding her hand to her head and laughing. Her eyes are following Zeke's every move. "Hey. That hurt!" she cries. "I didn't say you could pull out my hair." Despite her objections, Rose can tell Bethany is pleased.

Zeke finds one end of the hair. His eyes cross slightly,

as if he's trying to thread a needle. Then he does a strange pouncing act, hand landing cupped on the lawn chair webbing. Whatever he's after, Rose can tell from his grin that he caught it. With the catch in his hand, he makes a loose fist and shakes his hand hard, as if he's about to throw dice. He bends over the picnic table briefly and comes up with a fly buzzing around his hand in a perfect circle. "Ta, daaa!" Zeke says. "And now—the one and only—Trudy, the trained fly!" He parades around the chairs, a black fly buzzing along next to him at the end of Bethany's long brown hairs. Gopher prances after him, snapping at the fly.

"Can I hold her?" Bethany begs, following Zeke, the fly and Gopher around like another puppy. "How'd you get it on there?"

"You shake them silly till they don't know which end is up, then tie the hair to a leg while they lie there all goofy."

A low chortle comes from beneath the window. "Where'd you learn that?" a voice asks. Rose freezes midbreath. She knows that voice.

"Rob's here," Helen says now that he's given himself away. "He brought his young man along. Maybe it would be better if we catch up another time. No offense. It's hard enough for Bethany without people watching."

Rose pictures Bethany struggling in the truck with Zeke— only Bethany might not be strong or savvy enough to get away. "We need to talk, Helen. Now."

Helen pours a bag of pretzels into a basket with one hand and waves Rose off with the other. "I'll call you in the morning." She crumples the cellophane loudly before pitching it, as if to make her point more emphatic.

"Helen. You've got to listen. It's that kid. Zeke." Rose doesn't sound urgent without raising her voice. "He was with Valley Saturday night." She glances out at Bethany's undeveloped body. Bethany is so thin she looks more like thirteen than sixteen, but then, if Rose remembers correctly, Helen did, too, at that age.

Helen frowns and speaks at normal volume. "What are you saying? You don't want him two-timing her?" Her eyes narrow. "Why don't we just leave that up to him?"

"*Shhhh*. You've got it all wrong."

Helen picks up the tray and heads to the back door. "It's not enough that Valley has a father, a nice house and a mother that doesn't have to work?"

Rose backs up to let Helen by, caught off guard by the hostility. From the sound of things, Helen's been simmering for a long time.

"Rob is the first eligible man I've come across in a while, and I don't need you here ruining that for me," Helen whispers. "Goodbye, Rose." Helen bumps her hip into the screen to let herself through hands-free.

Rose follows Helen through the door. "You don't understand—" she says and finds herself standing in the middle of the circle of chairs, all heads turned her way. "Get that fly out of that poor girl's face," she tells Zeke. Helen giggles and serves Rob his drink.

"Hey, Rose," Rob says.

Zeke straightens up with his leashed fly, grinning ear to ear. "If it isn't the trailer-park lady. Picked any weeds lately?"

His insolence is as thick as the humidity. Imagining his grubby hands on Valley makes Rose crazy. "Pull. You pull weeds," she says, hating how stupid she sounds. Sweat breaks out on the back of her neck. She glances at Rob to see if he's laughing.

"Hear, hear," he says under his breath, raising his glass toward Rose as though toasting her vocabulary lesson. Maybe Rob's had it with the kid, too. Helen is looking from Rob to Rose to Rob again, as if they've chosen up sides behind her back and she's not sure which team she's on.

"But I've missed something here." Rob bends over slowly to put his glass down beside his lawn chair. It's the one that says *Hers*. "What makes Rose the trailer-park lady? I didn't know you two had met."

Zeke points at Rose and steps forward. "She was out snooping around Phil's trailer yesterday. She's still hot for you and fools herself with some notion there's something between you two." Zeke moves to catch Rose's eye. "Or should I say *someone?*"

Rob looks at Rose as if she's the one who has spoken. His eyes are that piercing blue she remembers so well. "What is he talking about?" Rob asks.

Zeke is smirking. "She thinks nobody knows. Watch her try to deny it now, in front of her friends."

Rose wants to slap the smirk off his face. "That was my daughter in your truck Saturday night." Her voice is so fierce it's hardly audible. "Wait till I tell Chief Dudley. You'll be out of here so fast—"

Rob holds one hand up to Rose, palm flat like a traffic cop. "Stop the bus," he says with such authority that Gopher jumps to her feet and barks at Rob.

"Quiet," Rob demands. Gopher slinks to Helen's feet and sits, yipping sounds escaping from her throat. Except for the yipping, a busy silence descends while each person mentally fires off another round. Rob settles back in his chair and turns to Zeke. He has already taken charge. "What did you mean about her being hot for me, as you so crudely put it?"

"That's what she said when I caught her snooping."

Rob turns to Rose and raises his eyebrows.

"I'm a happily married woman and these two—" she points to Helen and Bethany "—can vouch for that."

Rob waits.

Helen and Bethany say nothing.

Rob tilts his head at Rose. "After I saw you the other night, I thought sure you'd moved on."

Rose wonders how she's somehow been called to defend herself in public. She points to Zeke. "He tried to hurt my daughter. She has scratches all over her legs."

Zeke works his hands into his hip pockets and rocks. The fly buzzes off, dragging the hair behind it like a kite tail. "I didn't scratch anybody. I don't have the slightest clue who your daughter is."

"Go wait in the truck," Rob says. "Let me sort this out."

"You think she's going to admit to any of this? She's a liar."

"*Go wait in the truck,*" Rob repeats in a throaty hush.

"Whatever," Zeke says with a snort, waving a hand to dismiss them all. "But you be careful. She's gonna hit you up for frigging child support."

Then Rob is on his feet with a stone in his hand. "Shut the fuck up and get going." He hurtles the rock at Zeke's back. It hits dead center, and Zeke skitters off through the woods.

Rose's back stings between her shoulder blades. The stone had to hurt. If it were anyone else, she'd feel bad for the kid.

Rob faces the women again with a forced calm. He shakes his head and shrugs. "What did I do before I had him to run my life?" He's quiet now, but there's an edge to his voice. He sits down and rubs his hands up and down his thighs. They wait while he collects himself.

"You're sure it was only scratches?" he says to Rose.

Helen gets to her feet. "Why don't we leave you two to work this out," she says, handing Rose the glass of wine she had poured for herself. "Come on, Bethany. This doesn't concern us." Helen nudges her daughter toward the house, though clearly Bethany would like to stay for more.

Rose clutches the stemmed glass. She isn't sure she wants them to leave her alone with the man who threw that stone. Never before has she known Helen to think anything was private.

"I'll be in the house if you need me, Rosie."

When Helen closes the door, Rose backs up to stand against it, ankles crossed. Rob is tracing a patio brick with the toe of his sneaker and ruins an anthill built in a crevice. The ants scatter helter-skelter. Helen is rustling around in the kitchen. Rose suspects she is listening, but doesn't mind for once. She watches an ant scurry across the top of Rob's shoe. "I guess the cat's out of the bag," she says.

Rob leans forward and searches her face. "When you came to the ballpark that day, you mean that was true?"

Rose looks at him askance. "Why would I have lied about that?"

"I should have known." He rubs his forehead with his eyes squeezed shut, then drops his hands into his lap as if in defeat. "You may not believe this, you being you, but girls say that stuff to guys all the time. To trap them. I didn't know it was true."

Rose traces the etched letters on the glass with her finger, *H-i-s*, over and over. In all her fantasies of this moment, Rob had never said he didn't know it was true. Sometimes he said it was her fault. Sometimes he said the baby wasn't his. Sometimes he said it was her problem and had nothing to do with him. Awful as those answers were, at least she could defend herself. But for this answer she's unprepared. "I wouldn't have made that up. Not then. Not now." Her voice comes out thin and strained.

Rob looks toward the kitchen window. The boom box is off now, and he motions her to follow him to a crumbling brick barbecue, out of sight and earshot. Rose follows, but only because Gopher is still outside. She snaps her fingers behind her back and the dog follows after them. Gopher circles and lies down within two yards of where Rob indicates Rose should sit on a lichen-covered brick ledge. Rob stands over her, one foot on the ledge, leaning on his raised thigh. "I can't lie to you. I probably would've jumped town even if I had believed you. I wasn't ready for a family then, Rosie, but I'm different now. You've got to believe me. Why else would I hang out with that kid?" He upnods toward the driveway.

Rose watches a slug slither from a crack where the mortar has crumbled. It leaves a line of slime behind, and she wipes her fingers with her thumbs, though she hasn't touched it.

"After I was locked up, Mom went a little crazy—probably because I was locked up. There I was, all alone, in a prison in Pennsylvania. The other guys had families, you know, and once or twice a week they'd come to visit. But me? Nobody." His voice is rising. "Did you hear me? Nobody came to fuckin' visit. I was thirty-three years old and I had no one. You can't know how that feels."

The slug has made it to the edge of the slab. Rose watches it turn a slimy corner and head down vertically. "You don't know how it feels to be seventeen and pregnant and all alone," she says. The long nights are uncomfortably present to Rose— lying alone, in the dark, praying to bleed. She holds her voice firm. "I'm married, Rob. I'm sorry you're alone, but I can't help you."

He shakes his head and changes tactics. She can feel the shift. "I saw her, you know. In Millie's. Your daughter. My daughter."

Rose cringes. He can't be serious, claiming Valley now.

"She looks exactly like Mom's wedding pictures. I can't believe Mom never noticed, except after I was sentenced, she shut herself in the house and wouldn't even see her friends. She even opened a post office box in Middletown so her mailman wouldn't see the prison stamp on my letters. Can you believe that? I told her to move if she couldn't show her face in Eden. But no. She stayed, and made sure word never got out. She gave her life to *that*."

Rose pulls a mayapple up by the roots and wraps its stem around her hand. "I believe it. No one in this town knows that Everett's not Valley's father—though now that Helen knows, it won't be secret for long." A mosquito settles on her unwrapped hand. She slaps it, then flicks it aside.

"Everett doesn't know?"

Rose shakes her head. "I've got to tell him, before he hears it from someone else."

"I'll go with you."

"You most certainly will not," she says without hesitation. It's one thing Rose is certain of.

Rob doesn't give up. He crouches down and looks up into her face, his eyes soft and adoring like Nebraska's. "Rose, do you have any idea how much time you have to think in prison? I couldn't believe how I'd screwed up my life. Every night the dayshift guards walked out—went home to dinner with the wife and kids—and I ate off a plastic tray with a tableful of thugs and rapists. You can't know what this means to me—to discover I have somebody."

His eyes are too much. She shifts her gaze to her wrapped hand. There's her wedding ring. "Where were you when I needed to know I had somebody?"

Rob looks toward the setting sun, then back at Rose. "I'm here now. I can make it up to you."

"Are you crazy?" She wipes her palms down her skirt. "You think I'm going to turn my back on Everett. After he took care of us all these years?"

"No, no. I wouldn't ask you to do that. But couldn't you just include me—since you have to tell him anyway, I mean."

Rose pictures the three of them in bed together and lets out a snort. What Rob's asking is absurd. Everett is supposed to accept that Valley isn't his daughter and include the man who is? If Everett doesn't kick them out, he'll never want to see Rob again. She shakes her head. "Go away, Rob. Back where you came from. There's nothing for you here."

"Rose." He takes her chin so she can't look away. "Listen to me. Valley is my daughter. Mine. Not his. All I'm asking is to be part of her life."

Rose jerks her chin free. "Rob. She thinks Everett is her father. She loves him. How would you like it if your mother suddenly came home and said, 'Surprise! Here's your new father. The old one doesn't count'?"

Rob laughs, a short, forced sound—more of a snort than a laugh—then stares off at Helen's house and shakes his head. Gopher lifts her head, perks her ears, yips in her throat. "I'd've been thrilled. The old one beat my mother. Why do you think I worked out non-stop, played a sport every season?"

Rose sees how the flesh is just beginning to soften Rob's chin, how his face is rounder now, and more boyish, than when he was seventeen. His frame, squatting at her feet, is small for a man's. "Oh. I didn't know," she says.

"Yeah, well."

A moment passes. Rose wishes she didn't know. It's easier to stay angry if she doesn't know. "This is different," she says. She makes herself think about Valley, in the truck with Zeke. What Rob wants is impossible. "Everett is good to Valley. He built her a tree house and a canopy bed. Just the other day, he bought her a dog. You should see her with that dog. She's totally in love with the little thing."

"I'm not threatening the dog."

"But you're threatening the man who took care of us all these years."

"Rose, an ex-con is no threat to a successful man like Everett. Just think about it."

She is rocking now, arms crossed, kneading the flesh on her ribs. "I can't."

It's clearly not the answer he wants because Rob is on his feet, pacing the short space in front of her-frantic, gesturing. "She is my daughter, you know. I don't need your permission to claim her."

Rose stands to go. He can't threaten her. She'll call a lawyer. She'll do it right now. From Helen's phone.

Rob catches her arm. "I didn't mean that, Rose. Oh, god.

I'm such a jerk. I wouldn't do that to you. I just want to know my own daughter."

He is standing so close, she can hardly breathe. The scent of his skin, the way his lips move when he talks, she feels his presence—his passion. Her body sways toward him and for a split second, they're seventeen again, back in Kaiser Lake. But only for a second. She sees Valley in the truck and stops herself, steps back. He lets her go, though he's stronger and wouldn't have to. "I'll think about it," she says. "But you have to promise one thing. You have to leave me alone while I decide. And whatever I decide, that's it. No more."

"I promise."

"Starting now."

He backs away, turns, and obediently heads for the truck. She's amazed that he obeys.

Gopher gets up and ambles over to where Rose is standing. Before Rob is ten yards away, Rose hollers, "Wait." He turns halfway. "I have to know where you've been all this time and why you were in prison. Before I can decide."

"I bummed around the country, doing odd jobs to pay my way. One night I robbed a convenience store at gun point. Two whole years for a measly two hundred and change."

"Only two years?"

"It was a squirt gun."

Rob continues toward the driveway. Rose rumples the dog's ears, but her thoughts are mounting the truck with Rob, too startled to know what to make of him.

CHAPTER 20

Back in her car, Rose can't drive home fast enough. Helen will spread the word quickly, and no matter what Rose decides about the future, she wants Everett to hear the truth from her. Getting it from someone else would be too shaming. *She* might deserve that, but he doesn't.

As she drives, she practices different openings for the moment when she walks into the house and sees him in his recliner. "Everett, we need to talk," she says, glancing at herself in the rearview mirror as she speaks and driving onto the wrong side of the road. She jerks the wheel to the right and ignores Everett's response, talking deliberately to the yellow stripe down the middle of the road. "You know I've been on a little retreat. I want to tell you why. I'm sorry I've kept it to myself for so long. That was wrong. I'll do anything I can to make it up to you."

Anything? She wonders if she means that or if she is just saying it to soften the blow. And which blow is she thinking of? That Rob is Valley's real father? That Rob wants to stay in Eden and be part of their life? The farther she gets from Helen's house, from Rob himself, the more the complications pile up. If she opens the door a crack, how far into her world will Rob worm himself? What else will he compromise? And what kind of father will he be? He threw that rock at Zeke. Was that outrage—because Zeke hurt *his* daughter? Even if it was, is violence ever acceptable? What would Everett do under the circumstances? It doesn't matter. Whatever Everett would do, Rob just did the very thing he hated in his own father. Maybe Valley needs to be protected from him.

But what if Everett doesn't want them anymore? What if Rob is the only father Valley will have left? Will she say no to him then? There's no way she can decide until she knows what Everett's going to say.

Everett. A flood of warm feeling washes over her fear. He's so good to her, the way he refolds the paper after he's finished so she can find the page she wants, the way he runs her bath when she's come in late and the supper dishes aren't done until nine o'clock, the way he puts her vitamin pill on a saucer every morning when he takes his. She can't imagine Rob thinking to do such things. Even the new Rob.

Apart from telling Everett, there's no predicting how he will react, considering what his mother did. She's got to think of a way to tell him so he won't kick them out.

Rose pulls into the driveway. Everett's car isn't there. The garage door is open, but the garage is empty. The lightning bugs are flashing over the grass out back. He's always home by now. She walks to the road to check the mail. It's still there—bills mostly and a few ads. Everett usually picks it up on his way in.

In the house there's no note on the kitchen counter. The ice-cube trays are sitting out empty, puddles melted around them. The towel drawer is standing open. She didn't leave it that way. But where she's been cooped up for the weekend, Everett probably didn't think to let her know where he was going. Wherever he went, he took the dog. Her cage is empty, too.

The house is silent, no flute practice, so Valley must have gone out, too. They haven't been able to count on Rose to cook lately, so maybe they're off together getting supper. She drops the mail on the counter and opens the fridge to see what they have for food, spying the chicken breasts she had skinned sitting in a pool of their own blood, a bit grayer for the weekend that's passed. She should have frozen them. She draws them halfway up her nose before the gamy odor takes her breath away. She'll freeze them before she puts them in the garbage on trash day. Rose labels the bag Garbage with a marking pen before tucking the bag into the freezer. It's easier to diddle around than to figure out how to tell Everett.

The coffeepot is still on the burner from Saturday morning. If Everett doesn't want her, she will take it with her, she supposes. It was her mother's. But the idea of splitting the other household goods, divvying them up—well, how were you supposed to do that? You get the fry pan, I get the saucepan? What will either of them do with half a set of pans? Where is Everett and why doesn't he come home?

Just as she's biding time, filling the ice-cube trays, one in each hand, she hears a knock at the door. "Just a minute," she hollers, the water sloshing onto the floor as she carries them across the kitchen to the freezer. The water continues to run. She fits the trays into their tiny space next to the chicken, when the knock repeats a second time, more insistent this time. She wonders who is inconsiderate enough to drop by at dinnertime. Not Rob. He's promised to leave her alone. Helen would just walk right in.

Rose drops a dish towel on the floor, skates around on it to mop the spilled water, then kicks it off out of sight before she hurries to the door. "Hold your horses, I'm coming," she says under her breath.

On the other side of the kitchen door is a young woman, disgustingly slim in tight black jeans. Like Helen but curvier. She's wearing a white tank top that shows off her tidy cleavage and tan. A red bandanna circles her neck.

"Oh!" the woman says as if she hadn't expected anyone to answer the door. She steps down off the stoop and crosses her arms. "Everett Forrester. Does he live here?" Her speech has a gentle drawl.

"Do you have business with him?" Rose asks, cautious but not offensive, in case this woman turns out to be someone important—like a client with a big contract.

"We haven't met. I'm Fay Quinelle." Fay extends her right hand but keeps her left over her ribs.

"Marjorie," Rose says on the spur of the moment, shaking Fay's hand, but only to be polite. "Come in." Rose pushes the screen door open and steps to the side.

"Just for a minute. My daughter's waiting. Everett isn't here?"

New clients call him Mr. Forrester unless they grew up in Eden. "Are you from Eden? I don't think I've seen you around," Rose says as though she's greeting a newcomer after church.

"Eden? No," Fay says. She doesn't say where she is from, as visitors at church do to fill in the awkward silence. Fay looks around at the cabinets, the appliances, as if she's never seen such things before. Then she spies the mail on the counter. Rose follows her eyes. Everett's name is on the top envelope.

"Your water is running," Fay says while staring at the phone bill.

Rose feels her skin flush. Who is this woman, coming into her house, asking for her husband, inspecting her mail and telling her what to do with her own water? "So it is."

"Don't you want to turn it off?"

"Not especially." She's not going to take orders from a stranger.

"Okay," Fay says and takes a final look around as if memorizing the room. "When Everett gets back, please tell him I stopped by."

"Would you like to leave him a note?"

"No. I just wanted to return this," she says, flashing a Triple-A card she's fished from her jeans pocket. "He loaned it to me last Saturday."

Rose knows her husband and Everett would never do that. He must know this woman from somewhere.

"Tell him thanks for everything, too."

Rose wonders what all everything might be. And how she

can find out without letting on she has no idea where he went on Saturday. "He does like to be helpful," she says, her tone rising to lead Fay on.

"Well, you tell him he was right. It *was* the alternator. He knew even before he looked. My hand-squeezed lemonade was hardly payment for keeping those mechanics from fixing things that didn't need it." Fay turns to leave, pausing for a moment to say, "They do that, you know."

Rose nods and follows her to the door. She closes and locks it before hurrying to the front window to watch where the woman goes. A motor home is parked along the curb. She can't see much of the daughter in the passenger seat— only a shadowy silhouette—but the girl can't be much older than third or fourth grade.

Something is wrong. A woman in a motor home, not from Eden, who doesn't know Rose's name isn't Marjorie, stops by to return Everett's Triple-A card. What *was* Everett doing last Saturday? She was so busy getting set up in Mary Theresa's bed she never pursued the question.

Rose's stomach is suddenly churning. She goes to the cupboard for a handful of cookies, biting into one and swallowing without tasting it. Everett's not supposed to be nice to every Tom, Dick and Harry he comes across and especially not a thin woman named Fay. He's *her* husband. He's supposed to save his favors for her. If Everett has found someone else right when she has to confess her terrible truth, maybe she'll take all the pans and be done with it. She'll be the first to leave. Helen can tell him and to heck with it.

The phone rings and Rose picks up.

"Mom?" It's Valley's voice, but her tone is shrill, like the day Joanie fell out of the hayloft when her parents weren't home.

"Valley? Where are you? Are you okay?" The cord's coils grab at her fingers and pinch them into the grooves.

"I'm fine, Mom. It's Dad. We're at the hospital. He had some kind of attack."

"Is he okay? Which hospital?"

"Middleton. He fell down in the veterinary parking lot and couldn't get up. The ambulance came."

"A heart attack?"

"It's not his heart. It's something else. Dr. Burns is on his way. Dad wants you to come."

"He's conscious?"

"He says he's fine, but he can't walk. They want to keep him."

"Are you okay, Valley?"

"I'm just worried about Dad."

"I'll get there as soon as I can. Just stay with your dad, okay? Until I can get there?"

Rose hangs up and searches her pockets for her car keys. Whatever went on between Everett and Fay suddenly doesn't matter.

As Rose drives down Eden's main street, pausing but not stopping at corners, the words to the Hail Mary don't comfort her. "Father God, help Everett," she repeats instead, as if it takes a man to save a man. On her way out of town she sees no landmarks at all. She takes the curves in the road, barely slowing, and wonders after each curve that there's still more road ahead. Middleton has always seemed close. In her mind's eye Everett's ambulance is speeding ahead of her. Everett is on a gurney and Valley is holding his hand while EMTs check his blood pressure and start IVs. She feels the forced calm inside the ambulances she's seen on TV, each person doing his job efficiently and saying the right words, adrenaline pumping through the air. Or maybe that's in *her* body—the pumping adrenaline. She focuses on the white lines on the road, willing the car to keep to the right of them. Blip, blip, blip. If she passes one white line at a time, she'll get there.

The hospital corridor is beige. Rose's shoes tap on the tile flooring, tan with brown swirls, like the fellowship hall at Our Lady. The front-desk volunteer, an older woman with her glasses hanging around her neck, says Everett is in room 315. She pats Rose's hand and points to colored stripes on the floor. Rose follows a painted stripe—green to the elevators. Yellow goes to X-ray, red to admitting. If Everett and she survive, she'll make a quilt to commemorate it.

As the elevator ascends, Rose wonders what she'll see. For now, each step is a journey past the memory of herself off in the woods with Rob while Everett lay sprawled on hot tar. She might feel worse if she'd stood by laughing at the crucifixion.

When the elevator doors part, she steps across the threshold as through a proscenium—from her charade of good wife to a man she doesn't deserve into the unknown. The room numbers are mounted on the overwide doors. She begins walking, counting odd numbers to fifteen like landmarks on the road to reality. Outside the door to Everett's room she listens first, then rounds the corner. Valley is standing next to the window, her shirt covered in red-brown splotches. Blood. "Holy Mother, have mercy," Rose murmurs and backs out of the room. She props herself against the wall and slides to the floor to keep from keeling over.

"Mom!" she hears Valley holler right before her head drops between her legs.

A biting ammonia whiff jolts her back to the hospital corridor. A nurse kneels in front of her holding a white packet under her nose. Rose turns her head to get away from the smell. Valley is standing, hands on her knees, staring into her face. Her T-shirt is no longer bloody. "We're all okay, Mom," Valley says. "Dad is right there. I'm right here."

"I'm so sorry," Rose says, pressing her eyes closed, then opening them again. "You don't need me to take care of, too."

The nurse pats her hand, then feels her wrist and counts her pulse. "Your daughter forgot how she looked. That would throw any mother into a tizzy. I had her turn her shirt around."

"Who's been bleeding?"

"Kansas, Mom. She got hurt. We were at the vet's office when Dad fell."

"The dog?"

"We left her there. At the vet."

Rose sighs her relief, then sees Valley's furrowed forehead, remembers how happy she was romping around with the little thing. It's an awful lot of blood. She must be badly hurt. Hit by a car or something. Rose doesn't want to know until she's seen Everett. She struggles to her feet, the nurse at her side supporting her by the elbow and around the waist, and shuffles into the room to where Everett is resting, his head propped on two pillows. He looks thinner in the bed, the flesh of his chin spreading around his neck, his belly flattened by gravity. He wears a hospital gown, and his skin looks pale, Apart from that he looks normal.

"Can I pour you a glass of water?" Everett says. The only cup in sight is blue plastic with an elbow straw, next to a matching plastic pitcher.

Rose shakes her head. "Tell me what happened."

Valley follows the nurse to the door. "I was there, so I'll leave you to tell it, Dad. I've got to go call about Kansas."

Rose averts her eyes so she doesn't see the blood on the back of Valley's shirt.

"It was no big deal, really," Everett says when they're alone except for the long-faced man sleeping in the next bed. "I was in the parking lot at the vet's when I lost feeling in my leg and fell down. Next thing I know, an ambulance is there."

It's like Everett to minimize every detail. Nothing's a big deal ever. You'd think it was the ambulance's fault he ended up in the hospital, as if it happened along, saw him lying on the ground and mistook him for a casualty.

"You were walking to the car and suddenly you were on the ground?" Rose won't ask if he hurt himself. He wouldn't tell her anyway. "That's it?"

"There's more, actually. Dr. Burns told me last week, but with you off to your little room, I didn't want to make things worse."

Rose grips the bed rail between them. "I didn't know you went to the doctor."

"It's just this stupid leg. It keeps catching me up in weird places."

"What did Dr. Burns say? Tell me."

"He said it's very hard to diagnose. I fell off a ladder two weeks ago. I was running a wire and my leg suddenly went numb—like when somebody kicks your knee out from behind. Have you ever had that happen? You suddenly have no leg and you fall."

"When I was pregnant, Valley kicked a muscle in my leg here—" She indicates her groin. "My leg would buckle for no reason."

"I wish I was pregnant. But mine may be more serious than that. Dr. Burns thinks I probably have MS."

"MS?" Rose's mind races. She thinks of Vanna White turning M and S up on *Wheel of Fortune*. She thinks of Jerry Lewis and his telethons but can't remember what disease he's raising money for. She thinks of the kids in the March of Dimes pictures. She can't imagine Everett with braces on his legs.

"Multiple sclerosis."

"I know what it stands for." Those braces, she remembers, were for polio. For years before Salk and Sabin, her mother gave her change to drop in the plastic collection tubes. "But what does MS do?" She has trouble saying it, as if combining the letters might mean they have something to do with her.

"You know the rubber casing around a wire? Dr. Burns says it's like when that wears thin and a cord shorts out. Only in my body the casing is around a nerve bundle. It flakes off and the nerve messages can't pass along the nerve."

She watches her knuckles whiten on the bed rail. She can't bring herself to ask if he's going to die.

"The outcome is unpredictable," Everett says, as if reading her mind. "It can be severely debilitating and painful, but it isn't fatal. I may be fine for a long time yet, maybe even the rest of my life. It depends on how quickly the disease progresses."

Rose reaches out and passes the back of her fingers over his whiskers.

"I may be crippled, Rose, but I can take that part. It only affects me. But there's more and this part I haven't told Valley. I need you to help me."

Rose holds her breath again while Everett looks to the door, either to make sure Valley isn't standing there, or to keep from having to look at Rose when he says it. His eyes are fogging up, and he blinks. "You know—" his voice is strained "—I would never hurt her. Not if I could help it. I want her to have a wonderful life. Get married. Have kids. She shouldn't have to miss that. We've had our ups and downs, but you've got to believe me, Rose. It's been terrific. Really. Best thing that ever happened to me. I can't thank you enough." A tear breaks down his cheek and he raises his shoulder to rub it off.

She feels his anguish, as if it's rising in her. She turns his face to hers. "Everett. What's this about? Why would she have to miss it?"

He closes his eyes. He tries but can hardly speak. "They don't know for sure—" He stops. She waits, hanging right with him to help him get it out. He swallows. Then he blurts, "The disease may have a hereditary link." When he opens his eyes, she sees his fear. He gazes at her intently, as if waiting for the meaning to explode inside her.

"MS is hereditary?"

The pieces assemble in Rose's mind—a Morning Star emerging from the triangles of blue and gold when that nine-patch block is assembled. She is dumbstruck—stunned at the perfection, the design. God has answered her prayers. Redeemed her sin. Never did she imagine that something good could come of her conniving, that He could work around her sin and still make something beautiful. And the grace—the chance to deliver good news rather than bad. She can't imagine how it can be a gift to tell him Valley is someone else's daughter.

Rose searches on the bed bar for the buttons that lower it. When it's flush with the bed, she looks to the door to make sure no one is there. "I've got to tell you something, Everett." She crawls onto the bed. He scoots his hips over to make room. When she's lying beside him, she kisses the place where another tear has broken from the corner of his eye. The skin is extra soft there. It's her favorite spot on his whole face.

"Valley doesn't have MS," she whispers.

"I know you don't want her to, but wishing won't make it so. They want to start tests—as soon as my diagnosis is confirmed. I don't know how to tell her."

"We don't have to." Rose's arm rounds his ribs and belly, pulling herself in closer to him, though careful of his legs. "Remember how I couldn't wait to get married, Everett?"

He smiles faintly and his eyes soften with the memory. "I loved that about you." He kisses her forehead tenderly.

"There was a reason I couldn't wait." She pauses to breathe. "I was already pregnant."

The truth out there, Rose is falling through space. Everett says nothing, and the fall goes on and on, down and farther down.

"Who?" he says finally, the word barely audible. Then, louder, "No, don't tell me. I'd kill him."

She hits bottom. It's surprisingly soft. "Biology is overrated. You're Valley's father, Everett."

"Or Eden's biggest fool."

She hates his shame. Hates more that she brought it on. Except for the MS, she'd give anything for Valley to be his. "You're the one that loves her. It's never foolish to love someone."

"Am I the only one who doesn't know?"

"You're not the last, if that's what you mean. I tried to be honest, but he bolted when I told him I was pregnant. I didn't know what to do. Then there you were—on a white horse. Everett, I'll always be grateful, even if you don't want me anymore."

"Shit. All this time, I thought—"

"I didn't know how to tell you, and after a while there didn't seem to be any point. We were happy and he was gone."

"But what if he comes back? You know, to claim her."

"You're the father of record, on her birth certificate. She was so tiny she passed for a preemie. Even you were fooled."

Everett turns his face away. Rose waits. His chest rises and falls under her arm. High on the wall the clock stares down at them. The man sleeping in the next bed, slack-jawed with his hair standing up in tufts, looks strangely like a mule.

"Shit," Everett says. "Whoever dreamed you could appreciate a goddamn lie?" He lifts his head to look at her. "She's really not mine?"

She tucks her head under his chin and whispers, "I love *you*. *Only* you. The other was just a dream—a nightmare, really." When she hears herself say it, she knows it's true. The man beside her, every last ounce of him plus his incurable disease, is the man she loves.

Rose lies still so she won't miss Everett saying he loves her, too. The silence makes her weak. She untucks her head, so she can breathe.

Everett finally speaks. "I guess we could call it even."

"What?"

"It didn't mean anything," he says into her hair, pulling her tight to him. "Dr. Burns told me I probably had MS. I was hurting and wanted to tell somebody. She was a warm body."

The news shakes her. More as she lets it in.

"I couldn't tell you. I tried. Saturday morning. But you were in too big a hurry."

It happened Saturday. It must have been Fay. "*Did* you tell her?"

He looks down at her, his chin going double. "No. Whatever else I did, I didn't do that. I came home. I only wanted to tell you."

Rose lets out her breath. He hasn't betrayed their friendship. She's astonished at how that relieves her. Maybe she is right. Maybe biology is overrated. Still, she has to ask. "Everett, was she good?"

He holds her tightly to him. "I don't know," he says. "I wasn't paying attention."

CHAPTER 21

At nine-thirty that night—after a long meeting where Dr. Burns explained the possible but unpredictable outcomes of Everett's diagnosis, followed by the trip home where Rose wondered if she was dreaming and would waken to find her life restored to the status quo—she and Valley sit down to a supper of lime Jell-O salad, meat loaf and scalloped potatoes. Helen has left it for them—probably what she'd made for her own dinner—dropped by after Rosie called from the hospital with Everett's news. The aroma of warm meat loaf lies in a comfy blanket over the room. Rose hates to disrupt it, but she's got to say something before Valley hears it from Bethany.

When she's certain that Valley has eaten all she wants, Rose begins. Her tongue feels thick and her mouth tacky. "Valley, we need to talk. I've kept a very important secret from you." She tries to swallow but can't. "I told your dad today. I need to tell you, too."

The voice in her head—*You're going to blow it. This isn't the right time*—is so loud she's tempted to obey it, until she sees the darting dread in Valley's eyes and understands her daughter both wants to know and is afraid to know.

"*What*, Mom? You're scaring me. Spit it out."

Rose clears her throat. She wants to spit it out, except there's nothing but misery in it for Valley—no consolation prize as there was for Everett. "A long time ago, when I was in high school," she says, wishing it to sound soothing and not too real, like a bedtime story, "I went out with a boy I didn't know too well. I knew Everett at the time, but we weren't together yet." She stops.

"And?"

Rose is folding her paper napkin into smaller and smaller squares and creasing each fold carefully, not looking at Valley. "This other guy was a real charmer, a good athlete, very popular. I wasn't either popular or unpopular, just sort of acceptable—except to Everett, who had this huge crush on me, which I ignored. Anyway, I guess I was flattered."

"So you went out with him."

"I went out with him. And I did a very stupid thing."

"*What?* For god's sake, Ma, just *tell* me."

Rose frowns. There are no right words. "We went swimming and started kissing, and, well, we got carried away, until I let him...you know."

Valley looks shocked. "But you're always telling me not to."

Rose focuses on the fat congealing in the bottom of the glass meat loaf pan. "I know, lamb. I know. That's the reason. Why I'm always so worried. I should have told you before so you'd understand."

Valley holds her fork, tines down, in the scalloped-potato

pan and tugs on a slice, separating it from its layer. She removes another potato slice and adds it to the first. The onions get sorted into a separate pile. "So," she says finally. "That's it? That's the secret? That you did it before Dad?"

"That's half of it." Rose says. She's about to tell Valley to leave the potatoes alone, but stops herself. "I got caught."

"By whom?"

"No one. Everyone," Rose says, wadding the now-unfolded napkin up into a ball. Why is her daughter so simple? "I mean I got *pregnant,* goosie. Otherwise I'd have been fine." She takes up the spatula and serves the sorted potatoes onto Valley's plate. "There," she says. "Now leave the rest alone. We can eat them tomorrow."

Valley puts her fork down. "What happened to the baby? Where is it now?"

"Not it. *Her.*"

Valley sits up straight. "I have a *sister?* Where is she? Who has her? Or was it a secret adoption and you don't know?"

This is harder than Rose imagined. She speaks quietly but firmly, amazed that the thickness has left her tongue. "Valley, you don't have a sister."

"You had an *abortion?* Mom! How could you do that?"

Rose touches Valley's arm. Valley flinches. "Valley, listen to me. I didn't have an abortion. Or a miscarriage. And you don't have a sister. You're my one and only child."

Valley looks at her, stricken, as when she was six and Bambi's mother died.

"Then I'm…?"

Rose nods.

"Dad's not…?"

Rose shakes her head.

Valley shakes her head, too, her eyes glued to Rose's. She stands up. Her chair tips backward, teetering, before falling to the floor. Valley picks up dishes, stacking more than she can carry. The meat loaf pan slips from her fingers and thunks against the wood. Grease splatters.

Rose sops it up with Valley's place mat. "You take those," she says, nodding to the dishes Valley still holds. "I'll get the rest."

Rose listens as the faucet runs and the dishwasher door opens. Valley rinses and jams the plates into the rack. Maybe it's the best thing. To let her work it out, even if she breaks every dish.

Rose arrives at the sink with the glasses and the meat loaf pan.

"Dad didn't know till today?" Valley says over the running water.

Rose shakes her head and heads to the laundry, the dry placemat wrapped around the greasy one. When she returns her heart is racing. She needs to get this over with. All of it. "Do you want to know who your real father is?"

Valley busies herself wrapping the leftover meat loaf in foil, pouring the grease into a coffee can, and scrubbing the pan with a nylon brush as though she hasn't heard the question. Rose notes how deftly she does it. Valley is hiding her face behind lanky blond hair while she fills the detergent cup, closes the door and sets the dial. The dishwasher growls and the sound of whooshing water floods the room. "Dad is my real father," she says finally.

"I'm sorry, Valley. I wish it were different," Rose hollers over the din.

"Dad is my real father," she insists. She looks at Rose through the tears that have pooled on her lower lashes. "You've lied to me all these years. How am I supposed to trust you now? If I were Dad I'd be out of here so fast. I can't believe this."

Valley strides across to the counter where she picks up the car keys. Rose stands motionless. She hears the screen bang shut behind her daughter, its note of finality like a gun shot.

Rose runs after her. "Valley, no! You can't drive. You're too…" The car door slams on the word "upset."

Valley starts the engine, revs the accelerator, and shifts into Reverse. Rose follows alongside the moving car as she's backing up. "Stop and think, Valley. This is no time to drive. It's not safe," she pleads, bent over at the open window.

Valley barely stops before flipping the gearshift into Drive. "How safe am I with a woman who didn't want me?"

"What? Where'd you get that? Of course I wanted you."

The back tires spit stones at Rose as Valley takes off down the drive. She brakes before she turns into the road and calls back to where Rose stands by the kitchen door. "You got pregnant, goosie. Otherwise you'd have been fine."

Rose stands alone in the darkness, wishing for Everett. "Hail, Mary, full of Grace," she prays aloud, but the voice in her head is louder, repeating awful words, words spoken in the frustration of an awkward moment. She stares at the navy sky and goes over and over the telling. There it is, every time through, just as Valley heard it: *I got pregnant, goosie. Otherwise I'd have been fine.* Every time she cringes, but the voice won't stop, repeating, condemning. She can't bear it, Valley thinking she meant she didn't want her. How can she make a child understand? Of course she was terrified at the time, but it was entirely different the minute Everett married her. Valley's the best thing that has ever happened to Rose—a total joy. And Everett made it possible.

Valley will never believe that now. Not until she has children of her own, and maybe not then. Still, Rose has got to go after her. It would be unforgivable not to try. But Valley has taken her car. She hurries inside to the phone, dials Helen and listens to the phone ring on and on. Then she remembers. Helen's car is in the shop. Even if it weren't and Helen came immediately, Rose wouldn't know which way to turn. Valley could be headed anywhere. Dayton. Cincinnati.

She knows this: Valley is on the road, upset and driving like a maniac. The accidents Rose pictures are so real she can hear the crush of metal, the shattering of glass. Valley pulls out on Route 4 without looking, and *wham*, she's blindsided by a tractor-trailer. The gate splinters at the Church Street semaphore, and *thud*, the Galaxy is hit by a train. A drunk driver crosses the center line and Valley freezes, blinded by the car's headlights. *Crash*. Killed instantly. Reduced to a mass of blood and bone in a closed casket. At the funeral Our Lady is full of mourners, but Everett is in the hospital and Rob stands in his place at the graveyard out back.

Even with Valley buried, Rose can't stop the collisions. Valley dies over and over, and always with the thought she was unwanted. A tree the size of a sequoia comes out of nowhere. The car crashes through a guardrail beside a ravine and suspends in air before dropping Valley on the rocks below. Rose presses her hands into either side of her head. The headache is nearly intolerable, but she can't cry. There are no tears, no cleansing for what she's done. No. That well is completely dry.

Valley is sitting in the dark car, locked outside Middleton Hospital, when it hits her. Everett is no more or no less her father than any other man lying in that hospital. She isn't who she thought she was, but she doesn't know who she is instead. She's floating in space, completely ungrounded.

Over and over she replays her attempt to lift Everett in the veterinary parking lot—this man who is not her father—wishing herself stronger, able to help him, whoever he and she are. She remembers forgetting about the poor dog, laid out in that little cage, peeing onto a tray. Kansas will have to pull through on her own because Valley can't add how a dog must feel, shot in the hip and pregnant to boot, though she wonders who Kansas did it with and whether her pregnancy was intentional or accidental. She wonders why the rules are different for dogs.

* * *

After midnight Valley arranges herself on the bed, plumping her pillows, pulling the quilt out and wrapping it around her shoulders. It's a different quilt. Not her bear paw. Hers must be in the wash. This one is stiff and smells of moth-balls. She longs for the worn softness of her usual quilt. Her mother is always washing things that aren't dirty.

She's got to study. Maybe trig will help her forget.

But the problems on the page refuse to make sense. Sines and cosines. Tangents and circles. Instead her classmates' fathers sit at band concerts sleepy-eyed and bored on folding chairs in the gym. One of them might be her real father. She might have a half sister out there somewhere. Or a half brother. Some kid—some brass or percussion player, two years younger, who doesn't know she's related.

The first review problem is a graph. She is plotting a cosine function along the x-axis, but she sees a man lying on the pavement at the vet's office, unable to get up, though she is trying to help. His leg won't support him, and even after she moves the car up next to him, then insists he put an arm around her shoulder, she can't lift his deadweight and he can't get the leverage to help himself. She's desperate and now she's supposed to believe he's just some man out there. Unrelated. Not her father.

An unbearably heavy exhaustion settles over Valley. She can't sort the havoc. Maybe if she closes her eyes for a minute, she'll be able to concentrate on her math. It will only be a short nap. She opens one eye to glance at the clock. Twelve-sixteen. She will only let herself sleep for five minutes.

* * *

Valley tries to pull her father out of quicksand—it's sucking him down. She knows it's her father, only he's wearing a black hood like the one the hangman puts over the criminal's head. She isn't strong enough, and he's sinking deeper, so she frees one hand to crush a milkweed pod and pour its milk over his head. A strange nasal whining, like an oboe, keens through a hollow log. When the quicksand closes over the milky wisps of his hair, Valley wakens slumped down, the quilt yoked around her neck. The numbers on her digital clock refract weirdly through the glass of water by her bed, so she can't read the time. Her bed lamp casts a halo over the clock, her butterfly jar and her glass of water. The *lub-dub* of a heartbeat fills her left ear. Her body is rocking side to side. Her cheeks are wet and her mother's voice is softly crooning a hymn in her other ear.

"He sunk, Mom," Valley gasps, her voice breaking. "I couldn't save him. Take the hood off. I want to see him."

"Who, lamb?"

"My father. Who is he? I have to know."

Silence follows. Then Rose says, "His name is Rob Mac-Intyre."

The name is familiar, but Valley can't place it. She looks up, about to ask more, and sees that her mother's cheeks are wet, too. Valley tries to swallow and takes in her mother's face. Purple-and-yellow blotches darken the inside corners of her eyes. The full softness of her mouth, the tip of her tongue licking the salt from her lips and the fleshy lobes of her ears look vulnerable and blue. Her mother's clenched fingers curl like the feet of the mother cardinal that hit Half-Moon's window.

Valley takes the curled hand. It's too late to keep her from hitting the glass, but she won't stand by to watch her twitch and die. Valley takes the quilt from her shoulders and lays it over her mother. Then, imitating Half-Moon's slow, rhythmic movements, she removes the nylon stocking from the top of her butterfly jar and guides the twig that hosts the delicate pupa through its wide mouth. Her caterpillar, Gerald, has dissolved now, and his developing wings have not begun to show through the papery chrysalis. The lamplight shines through the liquid inside—the butterfly soup. Valley dips the branch into the glass beside her bed. Water droplets cling to the chrysalis, stem and leaves. She waves the twig over her mother's head. "I'm sorry too, Mom," she whispers as the water droplets trickle down her mother's face. "But I'll figure it out."

CHAPTER 22

Valley wakens at 5:00 a.m. with a new clarity. Math problems are much easier to figure out than everything else in her life. She crams for her final, showers, dresses and descends the stairs quietly, thanking God that her mother is still sleeping, not hanging around the kitchen to interrupt her focus with messy reminders. Valley takes a handful of Cheerios for the road, picks up her backpack and heads out the door.

As she walks down the driveway, trig feels clear and well-defined. It's actually possible to discover an answer she can verify in the back of the book. If she had to choose a profession today, she'd pick mathematician so she could pinpoint and graph the exact values for unknown Xs and Ys.

The morning air is heavy and close. Her wet hair feels good, dampening her neck and shoulders. The sun casts light through the trees in shafts she steps into, then beyond. If only it were as easy to walk through yesterday's news—back to ignorance. Her arms and legs feel rubbery and her shoulders ache, but she tells herself she can sleep later, when her test is over, when her father and Kansas are on the mend, when yesterday's news is as old and dog-eared as her math textbook.

Trig. Her last final. If she can focus on trig, she'll make it through the morning just fine.

At the corner where the sidewalk begins she sees a truck across the street with a man at the wheel. *Snake's truck.* Her first impulse is to turn around and run back home. But her father isn't there and her mother is asleep. Town is closer. People there will be up and about. Her pace quickens. She watches the truck, a green blur in her peripheral vision, pull away from the curb and roll slowly forward. She breaks into a trot. Her backpack bounces against her spine.

"Valley?" It's a man's voice, lower than Snake's, but maybe he can deepen his voice. She won't turn her head. She never wants to see that guy or that truck again.

The truck creeps along on the other side of the road, keeping pace with her trot. She mentally computes the distance and the time it would take Snake to reach her if he got out of the truck. The truck engine ticks and the sun glints off the hood. No matter how fast she runs, she knows it can keep up. The shades are drawn in the houses beside the road. Their doors will be locked. Still, if he gets out of the truck, she'll head for the nearest house, pound on the door and scream rape if she has to.

"Valley?" the voice repeats. It's definitely not Snake. She doesn't know who it is. She wonders why he's driving Snake's truck.

"Stop. I just want to talk to you. We met the other day."

She won't fall for that line. Kidnappers always claimed they knew you, that they just wanted to talk or give you candy, that your parents had sent them to pick you up—until you got close enough, that is, for them to grab you. Then they carried you off to do unspeakable acts before they black-mailed your parents and murdered you. Her mother said so.

"Come on. It won't hurt you to listen a minute, will it?"

She isn't stupid. Whoever he is, that truck is trouble. She won't be burned twice. She accelerates her pace, hugging the far edge of the sidewalk closest to the houses. Perspiration breaks out on her forehead.

"Valley?" The voice is closer now, too close. She can hear the engine tick. She glances quickly toward it, then turns her head forward again. The driver is wearing a baseball cap so she can't see his eyes. But he's pulled over the center line onto the wrong side of the road and is really close now, driving along the curb next to her. "I won't hurt you. I just want to talk to you. There's nothing to be afraid of."

Valley doesn't believe him. No guy had ever warned her to be afraid. Not Mark Thorburn. Not Snake. She breaks into a sprint, wishing more than anything her dad was sitting on the other side of Millie's screen door. Or Everett, rather—whoever he is to her now. She's still a block away from the donut shop. Whoever is there when she arrives will be better than no one. Millie will be there. Millie will help her. Valley will hide her behind the counter while Millie calls the police.

"I understand how you feel. Why you might not want to talk to me," the man says. "I just want to get to know you." The truck's gears grind into Park.

Valley pictures the screen door to Millie's. If she can just make it there, she'll be safe. She hears a *ker-clunk*, a sound she remembers vividly. The truck door opening. Her legs pump faster. Her lungs ache, like they'll burst through her chest. She slips her arms from the backpack and lets it fall. She hears footsteps behind her and wonders at which crack in the sidewalk he'll grab her. She reaches the next crack, then the next.

"Stop. Please," he begs. His hand pulls her T-shirt from her shorts. She flails her right arm back to free her shirt. He grabs her arm. "Goddammit, girl. Stop, I say."

Just when she turns to thrust a knee at his groin, a police siren yodels from a block back. The man's grip loosens and she twists free. She glances over her shoulder. Chief Dudley's cruiser pulls up to the curb, blue lights flashing. Valley leaps onto Millie's stoop, then stops with her hand on the door knob and turns to watch. She pants, her chest heaving. She still can't see the guy's face.

Chief Dudley gets out of his car, sunglasses on, though it's too early to need them. "Do you mind telling me what you're doing, driving on the wrong side of the street?" It's his booming police-chief voice.

"Just trying to get close enough to find an address, Ed. Can't read the house numbers so easily anymore."

Talk about lame. Valley pictures him squinting to make the lie more believable.

"Cut the crap, Rob," Chief Dudley says.

Rob? That's it. The voice from Millie's. He asked if she remembered Verna MacIntyre. The man is Rob MacIntyre. Her father. Even formulating the words, she can't get their meaning. It's too strange, too new. What's he doing in Snake's truck?

"You know where every house in this town is. I need to see your license and registration."

Rob gets back into the truck. Chief Dudley makes eye contact with Valley and shoos her toward school, flicking his hand to whisk her from sight. So, he saw what was happening. She turns and runs on, hoping he'll retrieve her backpack, though of all her stuff, only her trig book is left inside.

Rose is just out of bed, stumbling around the kitchen making the coffee, when the phone rings. She startles, thinking it might be the hospital, and collapses into a chair, suddenly a bit faint. No nurses with smelling salts hang around her kitchen.

"Rose, I think you'd better come down here," Ed Dudley's voice says in her ear.

"What's wrong, Ed? Is it Everett? Did the hospital call?"

"I haven't heard from Everett or the hospital. It's about Rob MacIntyre. He's been spouting nonsense at me. I need you to come down here to sort this out."

"I just woke up, Ed. I was up really late, what with Everett and all. It will take a few minutes."

"I'm at the station. I'll wait for you here."

Rose heaves a sigh as she puts the receiver back on the cradle. Her neck is stiff and a dull ache sits behind her right temple. She presses on the pain, but that only makes it worse. She should go back to bed and start over, but the thought of Rob down there spilling the beans is like an itch in the middle of her back where she can't reach. "Hail, Mary," she begins aloud, then tells herself to make the coffee. She needn't bother the Virgin when all she really needs is caffeine. A chocolate will tide her over until the pot perks.

"Go right in," Officer Mumford tells Rose when she enters the station for the second time that week. "Chief's expecting you." Rose searches his face for signs that he knows something, but he turns back to his logbook as if her visit is just one more entry in the day. If Rob spouted off, at least he did it somewhere else.

"Have a seat, Rose," Ed says when she appears in his doorway. She'd expected Rob, too, but he is nowhere in sight. Ed closes the door behind her. Rose takes in his facial expression and overall manner, her body tensed against more bad news. In his chair again, he pushes back from his desk and crosses his arms. "I've had my eye on Rob MacIntyre. I thought you'd like to know I picked him up this morning."

"What for?"

"Let's just say he crossed the line. The part that concerns you is that he was stalking Valley."

"Is she okay?"

"She's fine. She did the right thing—dropped her backpack and ran. I took it up to the school in case she needed it, but she was busy with a test, so I left it in the office."

"Thanks, Ed." Rose plays with her wedding ring, working it around her swollen fourth finger. When she asked Rob to leave her alone, surely he knew she meant Valley, too. But no. He did what he wanted. "What exactly did he do?"

"I was in my usual spot there, where the speed changes. I saw a green truck pull out and drive down the wrong side of the road. I thought DUI, you know, and pulled out to follow it. The truck stopped and Rob got out, apparently to harass Valley. When he grabbed her arm, I turned my siren on. MacIntyre claimed he wasn't stalking her. He's got some cockamamy story about being her father."

Rose looks up at Ed. He's watching her intently. She shrugs her shoulders. No words come. Ed rolls up to his desk and takes a piece of paper from his blotter. "Now, understand me. Before I could take any official action, I had to do some checking." He hands the paper to Rose. It's Valley's birth certificate. "As you can see, it's all nonsense. Everett is Valley's father. It's right there in black and white."

Rose looks at the typewritten words next to the space for father's name. Everett Lincoln Forrester. Then she raises her eyes to Ed's again. If he knows, if Helen told him, he's not showing it. His gaze is straightforward and steady.

"Thank you, Ed," she whispers. She doesn't say for what.

"That's why we have legal documents, Rose. Otherwise people can say anything they want to. Now, my next question is, do you want a restraining order? I saw him stalking her, so there's no problem getting one."

"What would it do?"

"Give us legal recourse. If he follows her again, she can file a complaint. It gives me the documentation I need to lock him back up."

"Does Valley need to be here? To do something like this?"

"She's underage. You and Everett are legal guardians. Since Everett's not here, it's up to you."

Rose clamps her matched-up palms between her thighs. It's all so complicated, so muddy all of a sudden. "Does Valley have to know?"

"She'd hardly feel safe if she didn't."

"Tell me exactly how it will keep her safe—so I can explain it to her, I mean."

"It will deny him access to your premises, for one thing. School's about out, so we don't have to worry about him showing up there, but you might want to let Valley drive herself anywhere she needs to go."

Rose nods.

"This way, if she has any trouble—him approaching her in public again—she'll be in the driver's seat." Ed smiles at his own pun. Then his face grows serious again. "Believe me, Rosie. If it were Bethany, I wouldn't hesitate for a minute. I'm telling you exactly what I'd tell Helen."

Rose nods. She trusts him. But this isn't Bethany. And Rob really is Valley's father, though clearly he doesn't have a clue if he doesn't know a young girl is terrified to be chased by a dog, let alone a man. A restraining order would give Valley power over Rob. If Rose had had that power at Valley's age, instead of vice versa, it would have saved lots of trouble.

But then Valley wouldn't be here, and she doesn't wish that. It's all so complicated.

"I need some time to think about it."

"You haven't got time. We need to protect Valley, especially with Everett hospitalized. What are you going to do if Rob comes to the house? With a restraining order in place, we know he won't because I can lock him up again."

Rose bows her head. Having Rob banned from their home might help Everett, too, especially since Rob plans to stick around Eden. But she'll wait to tell Everett until he's home and feeling better. He doesn't need to fret over their safety from a hospital bed. And he *would* worry. He loves Valley. She was too blind to see it before.

"Okay," she says. "Where do I sign?"

Rose drives from the police station to Shady Acres and finds Phil's trailer. She owes it to Rob to tell him what she's done so he's not surprised when Ed serves him the papers. Besides, the longer she thinks about it, the more she needs to tell him a few things. Is he that selfish, that heartless, to terrorize a child, let alone his own daughter? It's not what fathers do.

A green truck sits tailgate down in front of the construction office trailer. Rob lurches down its stairs with a heavy bag of Sakrete. Rose pulls up behind the pickup, opens her car door and stands inside its wing.

"What brings you here?" Rob says, limping toward his truck. He hefts the bag over the side. The truck bed drops under the weight.

"You know. Ed Dudley told me everything."

Rob rotates his shoulders gingerly and dusts his hands off, probably to buy time and plan his defense. "Ha," he sputters, wagging his head. It's a forced chuckle. "Dudley made a mountain out of a molehill. I just wanted to talk to her." Rob looks at Rose askance, as though he only has one good eye. "You really think I'd hurt my own daughter?"

"You already did. I asked you to wait until she wanted to see you. It was part of the deal."

He steps toward her car. "Sixteen years isn't long enough?"

Rose backs up behind the car door. She'll duck into the car if he comes too close. "What's wrong with you, Rob? For all the women you've known in your life, you don't know squat. How do you expect to be a father to Valley if you can't put your own needs aside for even one minute?"

Rob tucks his hands under opposite armpits. "I didn't mean to scare her."

"The things you don't mean are starting to add up. You didn't mean to conceive her either, but now you want her to thank you for it?"

"That's not what I meant. And you don't know what I want."

"I don't know what you want, Rob. But I can tell you this—I want you to leave my daughter alone. Until she wants to see you. You can't strut back into town and pretend you never left. I came to say I signed a restraining order to make sure you know I mean it."

Rob's jaw muscle begins to twitch. "You can't do that."

"Not if you'd left her alone, I couldn't. But you made it all very easy. Thank you very much, Rob. Goodbye."

Rose ducks into the car and backs away from the green truck. Rob's lips are moving, but her windows are up and she can't hear him. As she pulls around the truck, he is yammering something, shaking his fist at her. She accelerates and speeds out of the park. She's made the right move. Put Rob where she wants him. And Valley now has something Rose never had—the power to say no.

CHAPTER 23

Friday morning Valley drives into the vet's parking lot and stares at the spot where Everett fell—as she has every day this week—amazed the pavement isn't marked in some way. A week ago she was a different person. Before Joey. Before Snake. Before Kansas and the gun. Before MS. Before Rob MacIntyre. She feels older now by much more than seven days. And tired. Her head feels so heavy she can hardly hold it up.

She parks and sits still for a minute, longing for the luxury of normal, everyday boredom. She plans to cancel this week's flute lesson. Mr. Moore will have to understand that with Kansas and too many dads and finals, she couldn't maintain her practice schedule. Dr. Burns is pleased with Everett's recovery. That's the important thing. And Kansas has improved daily. Valley can practice all she wants when the two of them are back on their feet. She opens the car door.

Today she has an appointment with Dr. Weaver to learn how to care for Kansas at home. The receptionist directs her to room one, where she waits and studies diagrams on the wall: dog's intestines, enlargements of fleas with a pie chart showing the advancing stages of flea-bite dermatitis, a dog's heart infested with heartworm and photos of dog teeth, gums lined with tartar, advertising canine dentistry. She will keep an eye on Kansas's teeth. She certainly doesn't want them to fall out. Joanie said brewer's yeast sprinkled in with the dog food would keep the bugs off.

She scrutinizes the pictures carefully. She's learned more about bones and nerves in the past five days than she ever has at school. Anatomy had never particularly interested her before. *Myelin* was a word on a diagram of nerve bundles that she forgot as soon as she closed her textbook. Now Everett's health depends on it.

Dr. Weaver opens the door and leads Kansas in on a leash. Kansas hobbles, one back leg raised off the ground. Her tail wags when she sees Valley, and she has to lower her raised leg for balance.

"There you are, baby. Are you feeling better today?" Valley says, kneeling down to the dog's level. Kansas sits on the opposite hip and lifts her snout up under Valley's hand. She has a bandage on her hindquarters, newly wrapped gauze circling around her hip, under her leg and around her tail. "My goodness, Kansas. You look like you're wearing a diaper."

"I had to put that on because she was licking it," Dr. Weaver says. "She'll prevent it from healing if she keeps after it. We could use a lampshade, but the dogs hate it, so let's try this first. She doesn't want anyone besides herself to touch it, though. She growled at me this morning. I had to have Dana hold her muzzle while I dressed it."

Valley's never heard Kansas growl.

Dr. Weaver takes an X-ray from an envelope on the examining table, clips it up against a fluorescent window and flips the switch on. "Let me show you what we found." With a pencil she outlines the affected rear hipbone. "Fortunately, it wasn't a direct hit. Once we cleaned the blood up, we could tell by the sparse smattering of pellets. Some of the shot lodged in her flesh just below the surface. I popped a lot of it out, like you'd pop a pimple."

Valley grits her teeth. Her hand massages her own hip.

Dr. Weaver points to spots on the X-ray inside the ghostly shape of Kansas's hipbone. "You can see here the couple of places where shot penetrated the bone. But the bone is intact. It didn't shatter, so I want to leave them."

"Will that make a difference down the road?"

"She'll probably have some arthritis in that hip. Otherwise, she'll be good as new when it all heals up. Oh. The puppies are fine." Dr. Weaver bends over and waffles Kansas's ears. "You'll be a fine mother, little lady."

The vet turns to the examining table and shuffles papers in Kansas's record file. Valley thinks the appointment is over and gets up to leave when Dr. Weaver says, "Wait. There's something else we need to talk about. I can tell you're really attached to Kansas. I don't know quite how to say this, but— How did you say you got her?"

"My dad brought her home last Saturday morning." Her muscles tighten and her voice barely comes out, as though she's afraid that's the wrong answer. "I didn't ask him where he got her." She wonders what's happened. And what's so bad that Dr. Weaver can't just say it. Maybe Kansas has heartworm. Her eyes find the picture of the infested heart on the wall and she imagines Kansas's insides eaten away. She crosses her arms over her stomach.

"I need to show you something." From the bottom of the file folder Dr. Weaver pulls a Xeroxed flyer with a grainy black-and-white photo in the middle. "This came by fax yesterday."

The picture shows a young boy lifting a puppy to his round cheeks, their faces side by side, so Valley can see the dog's whole underside. No penis. The puppy is clearly female. Her ears look huge in the picture, drooping next to her tiny face, and her paws are enormous in proportion to the tiny body, but she has the same markings as Kansas, down to the white star on her breast. LOST DOG a child's wobbly printing says in capitals over the picture. There's a phone number underneath. Then an adult has written in cursive across the bottom: *Female beagle, one year, answers to the name Mandy.* The address is Union City.

Valley looks at the child's face. He's supposed to be looking at the camera, but his eyes don't wander from the floppy puppy. The puppy has a bow around her neck, and a basket sits in the little boy's lap, as though the pup arrived by stork as a birthday or Christmas present.

Valley looks from the photo to the vet. Dr. Weaver's brows knit up. She crosses her arms and leans against the examining table, waiting. Valley's mind is blank. Dr. Weaver is watching her, waiting for her response. "This isn't that simple," she says finally. "My dad's just found out he has MS. He's really fond of her. You've got to understand. I can't take her away from him now." It's not that she doesn't want the boy to have his dog. It's this larger question of who needs her more.

"It's up to you," the vet says quietly, holding the flyer out to her. "There's no way to positively identify a dog. No paw prints on file anywhere. But she is about a year old. And the markings are identical."

Valley takes the flyer and turns her back to the vet, squeezing her eyes shut so she won't cry. Why does everything have to turn out this way? Joanie's collie isn't owned by some other little kid. Mr. Cranford owns a gun, but he doesn't shoot their dog. He doesn't have some weird disease. And Joanie knows he's her father. These things only happen to *her*.

"I'll send you home with this ointment," Dr. Weaver says. "It's an antibiotic. If she'll leave it alone, you can leave the bandage off, but she may start to scratch it as it heals. I want her to take pills, too, to prevent infection. Do you know how to give a dog a pill?"

"My friend Joanie does," Valley says, though she knows it's irrelevant.

"You open her mouth, lift her chin and drop it on the back of her tongue. Then hold her mouth closed until she swallows it. Or you can stuff it in some mozzarella cheese."

The cheese method sounds better to Valley. She folds the flyer and stuffs it in her pocket, then takes the leash around Kansas's neck. "I'll bring the leash back when I get her to the car."

"Don't forget the ointment." Doctor Weaver drops it in the open purse Valley has slung over her shoulder.

"Thanks." Valley leads Kansas out the door. *Thanks, but no thanks* is more like it. It's not bad enough that Kansas nearly died on Monday. Now after all their efforts to save her, they're supposed to give her up. Yeah, right. Dr. Weaver can think again.

In the parking lot she boosts Kansas onto the Fairlane's front seat and gets in the driver's side. Kansas lies down with her chin on Valley's thigh. She can feel the artery pulsing in Kansas's throat. The poster is folded in her pocket where no one will see it. Only Dr. Weaver knows *she's* seen it. She'll change vets. There must be several in Middletown. "Hey, Mandy," she whispers tentatively, hoping for no response. Kansas lifts her head and looks at her directly, her tail thumping twice on the seat. Shit. Maybe it was her tone. She waits until the dog puts her head back down on her paws and says, "Hey, Kansas," in the same voice. The dog thumps her tail once but doesn't raise her head—as if she's tired of Valley bothering her for nothing. Double shit.

She turns the car from the vet's office back toward home. There's really no need to tell her dad. If he doesn't know, it can't hurt him.

As Valley passes the Safeway and turns down Main Street, she speaks aloud to the passing cars. "Little boys only think they want a dog. Their mothers do all the care. The mother has the child to love. The dog is extra work. One dog is as much work as the next. Any dog will do. We, on the other hand, need a house-trained dog. I'm at school nine months a year. Everett can't clean up after a puppy. Mom would hate it if a dog messed in the house."

Kansas looks around the front seat, as if she's expecting to find someone else in the car. When she sees no one, she looks up at Valley, then puts her head back down on her paws.

As Valley approaches Millie's, a crowd has formed outside the door, the men in suits, the women in dark dresses with stockings and heels. Mr. Flannigan's funeral Mass must be scheduled for today. It's the only reason so many people would dress up on a weekday morning. One couple in particular catches her eye, the man touching his wife's elbow, guiding her to their car. She watches them exchange smiles as though they're somehow enjoying the day together. They look familiar, but she can't get a good look at them without taking her eyes off the road. The man has his back to her now, straining his neck to button his top button and threading a tie under his collar. The woman is primping his suit jacket, smoothing the wrinkles. She picks at a thread and frowns. That's when Valley realizes. It's Mrs. Harper. She'd like to hurry on by before Mrs. Harper sees her, but the Cockburns step into the road and she has to stop the car and wait for them to cross the street. She flips her visor down, her skin suddenly prickly. Still, she can't help looking at the Harpers in her mirrors. Mrs. Harper hardly resembles the witch-woman in the window who wouldn't let Joey have his stuffed monkey. Valley hears Joey crying, his chubby hand reaching for that monkey, herself whispering aloud, "Give him the monkey. He wants the monkey." She shakes her head to shed her impression. Joey was okay, still feisty and able to scream. Her neglect hadn't hurt him.

When Mr. and Mrs. Cockburn finally clear the road, Valley hears Kansas lapping. The dog is coiled head to hip, licking her bandage. Her rear leg scratches at the air as though she can't decide whether she hurts or itches. The edge of the gauze is becoming ragged. Valley pulls Kansas's chin away from the wound, surprised at the resistance a dog so small can exert. "No, baby. You can't do that," she says kindly. Kansas jerks her mouth free and curls back around to the bandage. "No," Valley repeats sternly. The dog looks at her with soulful eyes, as though Valley has hit her for no reason. Dr. Weaver didn't say it would be this hard. Kansas needs a body cast to keep her from going after her hip. "You can't do that. I know it hurts, but you can't lick it," Valley says, grabbing Kansas's chin again and forcing her to make eye contact as she's seen Joanie do with her border collie. Kansas squirms and her eyes shift to avoid Valley's. "It's for your own good, whether you understand or not." She needs a monkey for Kansas.

Valley turns into the Feed and Seed and leaves the car running so Kansas will have the air-conditioning. "I'll be right back." She returns a few minutes later with a rawhide bone. Kansas is standing on the seat, watching for her out the windshield. "Here, baby," Valley says when she opens the car door. "Beef flavor." Kansas sniffs the bone, nostrils quivering, and takes it in her mouth. Then she settles herself down on the seat, bone propped between her front paws, and chews it with her head first to one side, then to the other, an ear hanging long on the downside with each switch. She looks so cute, Valley wants to cuddle her but hesitates to interrupt.

Why hadn't she been able to do this with Joey? To find a way to soothe him without losing her wits? A crying face rises up in her mind's eye, so real she can hear the bawling in her head. But it isn't Joey's face she sees. At the moment she can't even think what he looks like. It's the face of the little boy on the flyer. She pulls the poster from her pocket and looks long at the child's face. Then she memorizes the address, backs out of the Feed and Seed and heads to the highway. Her father is an adult, after all. He's old enough to understand.

CHAPTER 24

"No, bad dog!" Rose declares in a stern voice, pulling the nine-month-old puppy out from under her quilting frame. She fits her hand around his snout to give it a twist. Valley says that's what mother dogs do with their mouths, so it's the best way to discipline puppies. Nebraska yelps at the "snorking"—Rose's personal name for the snout twist. "I know you don't like it, but that's too bad." She carries the puppy to the kitchen pen. "If only Kansas were here to raise you," she sighs, locking the door. The puppy's feet are so big and her ears so long she looks hilariously out of proportion. Valley says that will change as she grows up, but Rose hates for that to happen. Nebraska's clumsy-puppy look is so appealing.

In the living room she gets down on her hands and knees to inspect the damage to her frame. Teeth marks pit the smooth urethaned wood of one leg, and her affection for the dog snaps briefly, as if she's pulled too hard on a knotted quilting thread and the knot has popped through all the layers of fabric. She should never have said yes to a puppy. Kansas was so well behaved. Why couldn't that family have let them keep her? Everett paid her vet bills—surely that was some claim.

It wouldn't be a problem if her frame was store-bought, but Everett was so proud when he had unveiled it at Christmas. He'd made it to fit—the perfect height for her when she's seated, so she won't strain her back. Thank goodness the puppy couldn't reach the fabric. Her Jacob's Ladder quilt is almost finished. She substituted red for the ladder. It looks quite striking against the background blue.

Rose hears male voices laughing outside the window and backs out from under the frame. It must be lunchtime. She'll have to show Everett what Nebraska did. Maybe he can sand it down. But there's no guarantee the dog won't do it again. Maybe Nebraska could chew all four legs. At least they would match.

"I'm home, Rosie," Everett hollers. "Ned's here, too."

"Hey, Ned," Rose calls out. She likes Ned. She's more confident with Everett going off on jobs now that Ned Draper's working with him. "Can you two come look at this? We've got to do something about this puppy's chewing."

Everett laughs. "What's she attacked this time?" He holds his right leg while he bends over to look at where Rose points. "Signed her name again, has she?"

"We won't have anything left at this rate," Rose says. "Last week it was the kitchen cupboard. Now this."

"You need some of that No Chew spray," Ned says, squatting down beside the frame. "I heard Lloyd Weeks say they used it when their basset chewed his grandmother's rocker. It makes the woodwork taste so bad, the dogs leave it alone. I'll pick you up some when I go to get those switch plates for the Currans' addition. Anything else we need?"

"How about a sandwich before you go?" Rose says. "It's noon. You have to eat."

"Thanks, but Millie's expecting me. I'll pick this stuff up and meet you back at the Currans' by two o'clock, Everett."

Everett settles into his recliner. "You don't need me to install fixtures. The pain's pretty bad today. I'm going to take a nap, then go do the estimate on that rewiring job at the theater."

"Do we want that job? That Dougherty kid is a pain. Why do you need that headache?"

"The kid's feisty, but so was his old man. If he's a pain in the ass, I'll bid high."

"Suit yourself," Ned says. "See you, Rosie." He lets himself out, closing the door behind him.

Rose smiles in the direction of the closed door. "Ned's real fond of you, Everett. I can tell."

"A little fussy maybe, but yeah." Everett lifts his legs with the lever.

"I'll bring your sandwich in here today," she says. But before washing her hands, she gets Nebraska from her pen and plops her onto Everett's lap.

"Come to Daddy, babycakes," Everett croons. He holds her up and she laps his face. Rose scrunches her nose. She only lets the puppy lick her hands. A twinge of jealousy pokes at her. Sometimes Rose thinks Nebraska has taken her place. She reminds herself that Nebraska's a dog, not a woman, so it's okay. Besides, he relaxes in the puppy's company. Relaxing lessens his pain.

Rose has just cut the ham sandwiches when Valley pops in. Rose does a double take every time her daughter walks through the door these days, though she tries to hide it. Everett's calm about the butch haircut and dye job Valley had Joanie do on her. He says they should be grateful she only hacked at her hair, considering how hard it is to be told your father is an ex-con. But he hasn't seen the tattoo on her belly. A viper with a flower growing from its coil.

"I didn't expect you, lamb," Rose says, searching for the Flemish Madonna she used to see in her daughter's face. Against Valley's fair skin the black hair is startling—like a witch on the cover of one of those Stephen King novels at the grocery checkout. "I thought you worked all day on Saturdays."

"Dr. Weaver is having me check the surgery animals tonight, so she sent me home. I'll need the car at nine tonight and again at three in the morning."

"You got some mail," Rose says, handing an envelope to her daughter. "From your dad."

She watches Valley take the letter, scan the sloppy cursive, and check the Cincinnati postmark. "He's not my dad," she says, dropping it unopened in the trashcan on her way by. "Unless you're not my mom. I suppose that's coming next."

The orange Rose ate midmorning suddenly feels stuck in her chest. Valley endlessly comes up with new ways to throw it in her face. When Rose is quilting, she listens to radio talk shows on handling teenagers, but no matter what she learns, she's still speechless when Valley lands a blow—not calm and rational, as they advise, thinking about Valley's feelings rather than her own. Helen, who managed to keep Rose's news a secret, says to ride the outbursts like a wave. She says Bethany is difficult, too, after she sees her dad. Helen is such a good friend.

Rose has never once regretted telling Rob no. A month after the restraining order, when he called to say he was leaving town—that he couldn't stand it with them right there in front of his face—she thanked him, for Valley's sake as well as her own. She doesn't blame him for trying to connect with Valley now. She is his daughter after all. Rose feels sorry for him. He skipped out and missed the boat. Even when parenting is hard, she would never give it up.

It would be much easier to destroy Rob's letters, not even show them to Valley, but if she did that, she might as well not have told her about Rob at all. Besides, she can't let Valley deny it the way she did. But every time a letter arrives, Valley gets funky and yells at her, then throws it away, unread.

Rose opens the silverware drawer and gets into the box of chocolates underneath the tray. She'll just have one, even though she started a diet that morning and has been good so far. A letter from Rob, read or unread, calls for a chocolate. She hears Valley tell Everett that Dr. Weaver has agreed to fit her work hours around her school schedule in the fall.

"That's good. Real good. I want you to have work you like," Everett says.

Rose forgets to enjoy the sensation of the chocolate melting on her tongue, knowing how bad Everett feels that Valley can only choose community college—after all the years he saved to send her to Ohio State. Rose shudders to remember the day he got his health insurance bill with the outrageous new premium. He'd muttered for a week that it would be better for them if he died outright.

Valley's been nothing but gracious about it, assuring him daily that Sinclair's a good school, oohing and aahing over this or that class she's found in the course listings.

So brave, they both are. Much braver than Rose has ever been.

Rose can't believe it's time for college already. It has all gone so fast. Even living at home, Valley will be gone most of the time next fall, between working and school. Thank God for the puppy. And Everett spends more time at home now. That's the only good thing about the MS. He comes in midday for lunch and spends a few hours.

Everett's sleeping in the recliner now, snoring softly, Nebraska coiled up in his lap with her eyes surveying the room. It's amazing how that dog thinks she owns him. Rose knows better than to go near them. Nebraska would raise her head and disturb Everett.

"Oh, I forgot to tell you," Valley says, the bathroom door bouncing off the tile wall. Everett wakens with a snort. "I scheduled my audition for the Bach Society in Dayton." Nebraska gets to her feet and stamps in Everett's lap, excited by Valley's voice. She picks the puppy up and waltzes her back and forth between the coffee table and the quilting frame.

Rose smiles at them. They make a darling duo, even if Valley's look is disturbing. She's a warped Madonna now.

"Put the dog outside if you're going to practice," Rose says. "Your dad wants to take a nap."

"Aw, puppy, they don't like our duets," Valley says. "*Ahh-oooooo,*" she howls, tipping her head back to imitate the dog. Nebraska cocks her head to one side with her tongue hanging out. She looks as if she's laughing.

The living room clock strikes the half hour. The day is getting away from her. Everett wants to nap, but what will she do if he sleeps too long? She's got to get him out of the house again. "Valley, you need to be back to work when?"

"Three."

"I need my car this afternoon," Rose says, "so Dad will have to drop you back at work when he goes to the theater. He can pick you up at five. Is that okay, Everett?"

"Sure. Fine. Anything," he says. "I can sleep fast."

Good. That's settled then. Rose smiles to herself. She doesn't really need the car. She needs to make sure Everett's gone when the new desk chair arrives. She can hardly wait to see how the leather looks with the blue corduroy slipcover and bolsters she made for Sister Mary Theresa's bed—to make it look like a couch. The new quilt will add the color the room needs.

It makes sense to fix that room up for Everett. The barn office is too hot in the summer, too cold in the winter, even

with the electric units he installed. She's already measured
to make sure his rolltop will fit through the door and has
arranged with the furniture men to move it when they come
with the new chair. Everett will never believe how soft
leather can be. And on the nights when the stairs are too
much, he can sleep in Sister Mary Theresa's bed. It has served
her well and she sees no reason why that should change.

* * * * *

Who knew Truth or Dare could have such unexpected consequences…

Suburban Secrets

by Donna Birdsell

Opting for the Dare, Grace, who has let her Day-Timer rule her life, suddenly finds herself on an undercover assignment cooking for a Russian mob boss. Suddenly, her old life as a suburban soccer mom looks like heaven!

There's got to be a mourning-after!

Saturday, September 22

1) Get a ~~dog~~ cat
2) Get a man
3) Get adventurous (go skinny-dipping)
4) Get a LIFE!

Jill Townsend is learning to step beyond the safe world she's always known to take the leap into Merry Widowhood.

The Merry Widow's Diary

by Susan Crosby

There's a first time for everything…

Aging rock-and-roller Zoe learned this
the hard way…at thirty-nine, she was pregnant!

Leaving behind the temptations of L.A.,
she returns home to Louisiana to live with
her sister. Despite their differences, they come
to terms with their shared past and find that
when the chips are down there is no better
person to lean on than your sister.

Leaving L.A.

by

Rexanne Becnel

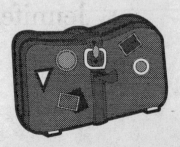

HARLEQUIN®
Next™

Stability is highly overrated....

Dana Logan's world had always revolved around her children. Now they're all grown up and don't seem to need anything she's able to give them. Struggling to find her new identity, Dana realizes that it's about time for her to get "off her rocker" and begin a new life!

Off Her Rocker

by Jennifer Archer

Available August 2006
TheNextNovel.com

HN53

We all need someone to tell our secrets to...

Butterfly Soup

by Nancy Pinard

Sometimes letting go of our secrets
helps us to spread our wings.

Life on Long Island can be murder!

Teddi Bayer's life hasn't been what you'd call easy lately. Last year she'd never seen a dead person up close, but this year she discovered one. And it's her first paying client.... But Teddi is about to learn that when life throws you a curveball, there's no better time to take control of your own destiny.

What Goes with Blood Red, Anyway?

by Stevi Mittman

HN54

Available August 2006
TheNextNovel.com

REQUEST YOUR FREE BOOKS!

2 FREE NOVELS TO INTRODUCE YOU TO OUR BRAND-NEW LINE!

There's the life you planned. And there's what comes next.

When life gets shaky... you've just gotta dance!

Learning to Hula

by Lisa Childs